TEMPEST ROAD

Justin A. Edison

To Misha + Family,
Enjoy!
-Goodly
Jun

ISBN: 1977910777

ISBN-13: 978-1977910776

This is a work of fiction. Names, characters, places and incidents are the product of the author's imagination or are used fictitiously. Any resemblance to similarly named places or to persons living or deceased is unintentional.

"The Call of Ktulu," inspired by H.P. Lovecraft's story "The Call of Cthulhu," is from Metallica's 1984 album *Ride the Lightning*.

Pink Floyd is the one-and-only Pink Floyd, whose 1979 album *The Wall* spoke to a generation (as well as multitudes of fans).

"Smooth," by Santana and Rob Thomas, is from Santana's 1999 album *Supernatural*.

Soundgarden is a grunge rock band from Seattle, Wash. Garbage is an alternative rock band from Madison, Wisc. Limp Bizkit is a rap rock band from Florida.

"Fat Bottomed Girls," by Queen, is from their 1978 album *Jazz*.

"Pour Some Sugar on Me," by Def Leppard, is from their 1987 album *Hysteria*.

George Orwell's dystopic *1984*, written from 1947-48 and published by Secker & Warburg (U.K.) in 1949, is often cited as the most influential book of all time.

"Alive" is a 1993 feature film based on the true events recounted in Piers Paul Read's 1974 book *Alive: The Story of the Andes Survivors*.

Stephen McGinty's *Fire in the Night: The Piper Alpha Disaster*, published by Pan Macmillan (U.K.), details the 1988 oil rig disaster.

M-19 was formerly an armed revolutionary guerilla in Colombia. It has since morphed into a political party under the title of AD/M-19.

F.A.R.C. (*Fuerzas Armadas Revolucionarias de Colombia*) was a guerrilla movement which began as a political protest in 1964. Over the next five decades, the group waged a virtual civil war with Colombian security and civilian populations (resulting in thousands of lives lost). As of 27 June, 2017, the group disarmed itself and has been renamed as the Common Alternative Revolutionary Force political party.

For my father, The Honorable Peter C. Edison,

who taught me that everything in life is a game.

You just have to know how to play.

Chapter 1

There's an empty, smelly steel tank and someone's inside it. He's hitting the wall with a sledgehammer as hard as he can, desperate to get out. Metal-on-metal. Hurt. Another swing. Metal-on-metal. I want to cry out. Throbbing. The giant overlord has gotten the point. Metal-on-metal. Teeth-cracking pain. Blood slaps my ears. Won't the man stop?!

A hand grips my jersey by the front. It's the sweeper. He won't let me past.

Quick step with my left, bring my right arm up. He's jerking my shirt by the collar. My arm bashes into his forearm. Hair bounces. Sweat flies in my periphery. Push off with my right foot—free—cutting inside of him.

My heart's rattling against my chest wall. I'm a machine, built to do exactly this.

Jackson knows me, my intentions. Twelve yards away, the orange-clad keeper pivots in my direction, silver jai alai baskets for hands. The ball comes to my feet. There's a yellow-green blur from the left. Tap the ball with my left, launch with my right. Up, forward, over the sliding man.

The hammer strikes metal. Gritty, smelly air pulsates. Ringing. Ahh!

The keeper—all silver-orange and grimacing, crooked jaw—is coming out to end this. Elated faces rise behind him. Horrified faces cringe behind him. Someone else shifts into the goal.

The grab of my cleat nubs in the turf. Righty step-over. Jackson is walled off, no good. The keeper is almost on me, arms and legs wide like an octopus. If I can just tap the ball up over his arms—

Free! In space. Past the keeper!

"They might have something here. MacLeod's streaking!"

The ball is mine. All will and control. Made for this. Another jersey-pull, which doesn't matter. This shot is mine. Done it a thousand times. The ref can't call it now! The defender has slid over too far, covering right in front of me but not the left side. An arm swings through my view, fingers clawing at air.

The bright lights seem hot. The stands are tilting, listing. Tap with my off foot, my right—

"MacLeod's loose. Bearing down on the keeper like a jaguar! MacLeod!!!!!"

Hammer head into iron. Sparks and dust. Ahh!

Crescendo of roaring noise. Rapid tsunamis of blood—my blood.

A hand on my shirt again, jerking me. How can it grab? My shirt is soaked, skin-tight.

What?!

Am I reliving it?

Colors whirl. Take the shot! Don't worry about spin. Don't worry about pretty.

The man desperately swings his hammer into the steel wall again. It hurts! His face—he's been beaten, bloodied.

Wait. Am I the man?

Two billion people on their feet.

2

The sweeper didn't jerk me, really. He didn't have time—

"Wake up!"

The hand yanks his shirt, fingernails digging in, chest hair pulling away.

What the—

The hand grips him again. Side-to-side jerking.

The hammer head strikes the wall. Ahh! It's my skull. He's smashing my brain!

MacLeod holds his breath, shaking all over. Anything to stop the pain.

There's something in his mouth.

What?!

He can't see.

What's in his mouth? Why can't he see? His vision isn't just dim, it's *blocked*.

No, what is this?!

Metal-on-metal, banging the wall of my skull.

He catches his breath, trying not to throw up.

Stop the banging! Please!

He exhales steadily—that will make it stop. And again. His lip quivers against resistance.

Feeling returns to other parts of his body.

3

Wait, my hands!

They can't move. His hands are stuck, bound.

His legs, too.

As the feline goddess of sleep is dismissed, MacLeod is sure the hand that was jerking him almost pulled him over. He can't steady himself. He's seated in a chair, and he can't move.

Oh my God, where am I?!

My head—the banging!

"I can't believe we got this done, man!" A man's voice—right in front of him.

MacLeod pushes back against the chair. He can't go anywhere. The voice is inches from his face, and he can't do a thing.

The speaker said this to someone else in the room. He has a distinctly European accent.

What in Hades? Got 'what' done? No no no.

He bites on the thing in his mouth—a gag. It makes his lips hurt, digging into the soft skin.

The speaker cackles. He leans close to MacLeod, reeking of vodka and grit, grabs him about the head and kisses him on the temple. MacLeod flinches and the strange man hops off, humming.

What is this? He needs to get away from me.

Footfalls across a wood floor, echoing.

Where am I? I have to get out of here!

4

MacLeod turns his head this way and that, trying to imagine what his eyes can't see. A world forms. He's inside someplace—the outdoors would be louder, feel different.

"Can you believe he's here? It's crazy," the man continues. It's a peculiar accent, neither French nor German.

MacLeod leans forward a little. He can't hear a response. A car honks in the distance. Is he in a city?

Why did they blindfold me?

And he's fuzzy. He didn't even have that many drinks. What happened the night before? *Was* it the night before?

Come on, man. Tell that guy to put down the sledgehammer. Think!

He suddenly recalls the club, the girl. He'd flown in, like the rest. He was at a nightclub with a third of the U.S. Men's National Team in Ciudad Panama. Coach Higgs would be peeved if he knew they were going to a club, but they went anyway. It was after the team dinner at the hotel. There was dancing, decent music, a few American songs thrown in. Drinks. Lots of girls. *The* girl. Chatting and dancing.

Pretty. Beautiful, even. Green eyes and long red hair. She had a French accent, but he wondered if she was a fellow Scot, anyway. The red hair—another *ginger*.

His hand on her hip, drinking, her leaning into him. He needed to blow off a little steam. Did they go somewhere? They must've. No, he wouldn't have been that stupid.

This is all wrong. It's not right. There was something else…

Fuzzy. He tries to shake it off. These guys drugged him. She was working for them—that's the only thing that computes.

5

They were in Panama for World Cup qualifying, opening game. Is he still in Panama now?

He swallows, fighting back a stinging sensation in his eyes. He tries his hands again. They're bound pretty tight behind a hard, flat surface—like the back of a folding chair. They're tough, whatever these guys used. Not handcuffs. Not metal. The material is warm, biting into his skin. He pulls harder, until it hurts. Plenty strong, all that training. No good.

What did I do?

MacLeod shakes his head again, trying to clear it. Scents of metal and popcorn in the cool air. Around him, the shuffling of material moves back and forth. When he tries to pry his legs apart, all he gets is creaking from the chair. His pants feel rough and stiff—not the slacks he was wearing.

A door opens and closes behind him. Footsteps, boots on wood approach.

He startles when fingers play over his hair. Is it a woman? That's perfume, a familiar scent.

"Hello, gorgeous man," she says. The way her boots clomp, he believes she has turned toward him.

That voice. The lady from the club?

The boots clomp away to the left. She's going to someone.

"The streets are clear," she says. "So is the radio."

French accent, same as last night. It's her.

When she walks into another room, a chill runs over MacLeod. He bites down on the gag.

I think I'm pretty fucked, here.

6

A sinking feeling takes over—the one any man might get when the bridge of reality dissolves and he finds himself dropping into a surreal unknown.

Banging and shuffling and zipping come from another room. Her boots click-clack around among others'. Packing bags, he surmises. An electronic beep comes from there. The activity pauses, then it starts again. Boots clomp out.

"Van's ready," she says to whoever is at the window.

The boots approach, that flowery perfume. A breeze from her passing cools MacLeod's forehead. He must be sweating like a dog.

The door closes quietly to his right.

I don't like the sound of this. Might be a great time to get loose.

He jerks on the binds for his hands. Nothing at all. Herdoñez has had him doing tons of push-ups, one-ninety on the butterfly.

Why can't I break free?!

Someone comes over. Is it the lunatic who kissed him?

"You trying to leave us?" He slaps MacLeod in the chest. "You can't quit this party. We're not even started, yet."

Look up at him. Face your enemy.

"Oh, you poor man," he says. "You can't even see. Don't be frightened. We're not here to hurt you."

A man by the window laughs. It's a snigger.

The weirdo goes off to the left. After a moment, he comes back, carrying things. There's a shift in the air as he walks right by and out the door.

Blood slaps in MacLeod's ears. The gag tastes like a kitchen towel. He can't bite through it. Things are still swimming. The man in the tank's reaching for the hammer, to start banging again.

Why is this happening to me?

New footfalls announce the man from the window. He stops in front of MacLeod. "Do you understand that we mean business?"

MacLeod looks in his direction and nods.

"That's good." He has a soft voice, Latin accent.

Boots. The girl has returned. She comes up to them. She and the new man may be embracing, kissing. Something hard and heavy taps his knee—right about the sweet spot, the lavender-hued ridge left over from surgery. He flinches.

"It's time," she says to this man, the one in charge.

MacLeod would like to kick them. At least it would be a feeble attempt at *something*. They'd probably laugh. The alarms in his head are ringing too loudly to focus on anything else. The man with the sledgehammer, banging out his message.

Perfume. She's leaning close to him.

"Are you ready, Hero MacLeod?"

Deep, ragged breath. Things shattering, a gunshot to crystal.

Oh no. They mean Mitch.

Chapter 2

'Hero MacLeod?' That says it all. The Man Who Pulled It Off.

Traveling, in a van. They took him outside for a second. They forced him on his side and pushed him back, bound and gagged. And they shoved heavy stuff close to him. Now he's speeding along in the back of a van, surrounded by tools and oiled equipment and vicious thugs.

But who are they? Who does this?

Lying on his side, bouncing along in darkness. The sledgehammer man took a break as the previous night's actions started to shift into place and solidify. There was a sequence to the events.

He'd taken the flight to Panama, the day's work done. Then arriving at the hotel, checking in to his upscale bay-view room. Then the nightclub, celebration and drinks all around. Seven players from the team, there. They were all in the famous *blacks*—black tees with a hand-sized American flag over a skeletal soccer ball on the chest. They had MacLeod put one on. He didn't want to go bare-chested in the middle of a nightclub, so he wore it over the gray tee he'd donned post-meeting. Photos. Team. Part of the team. The celebration was a taste of things to come. The *blacks* were the same shirts they sported after winning it all three years ago.

It was so stunning—all of it. A late sub-in and a quick assist to beat the Netherlands in the World Cup quarterfinals. Then, in the semi against Brazil, two goals, the game-winner coming in the ninety-third minute. In the final, another last-minute goal to beat Italy and win the whole enchilada. No side in the history of soccer had ever been so preposterously lucky, people said. It was decades' worth of do-gooder, positive karma delivered in frantic moments, the stars-aligned heroics of eleven men and their cohorts. Every major newspaper across the globe ran with a cover photo of players in gaudy red-on-blue and trumpeted headlines of 'Miraculous' or 'Stunning' or 'Impossible.' The *Yankees* were world champions, thanks largely to MacLeod.

Along with the famous *blacks*, seven or eight celebratory shirt lines sold like crazy. People who'd never heard of MacLeod's up-and-coming Premier League team, Culverhouse Crossing, donned their jersey—orange with black crosses down the sides. Everyone was a Sentries fan, everyone was a *Yankees* fan. Millions flocked to Chicago for a victory parade that supposedly had New Yorkers feeling left out, for once. Charities were funded, youth soccer league rosters swelled, the cash flowed in virtual rivers. In Cleveland, MacLeod's mother and siblings were deluged with interviews. His Uncle Mortimer in Glasgow groused about the sudden fame and TV appearances (which he secretly loved) and all of Scotland celebrated as if one of their own had just brought the trophy home. Most everyone danced at the party.

Thirty-two months later, the champion *Yankees* squad marched through a cheering phalanx of supporters and saluting soldiers to board a plane in Dallas. The U.S. would begin its next World Cup qualifying round in Panama. Half the cameras were focused on the thirty-year-old hero from the last campaign, MacLeod.

Hero? You better toe the line, man, or you won't get out of this alive.

Someone is sitting close to him, talking. Is it the lunatic? What's his accent? He sounds like Holoçec, the Culverhouse keeper. Always shouting commands, his face extra red against his powder-blue shirt.

That guy's from Prague, isn't he? Or Pilsn?

"Hey, are you comfortable, Yankee?"

The bound man grunts a response—he's not used to wearing a gag.

There's laughter. A fourth person has joined them, MacLeod is sure. A man. Maybe back here with him and the lunatic.

"That happens, man. The gag," the fourth adds. "You ask them something and they forget they can't really talk, but they try anyway. It gets me every time."

Latin accent. He makes a grumbling sound that mimics a dog talking, and both of them laugh.

So one of them is experienced at this sort of thing. Bloody brilliant.

They've been going for many hours. Tied up in the dark, with the constant vibrations of a moving vehicle, it's hard to tell. Where are they taking him? And why?

Possibilities have been running through MacLeod's head—gnarled dripping things on a nightmare factory's conveyor belt. His shorts are already damp, due in part to the close-quarter heat.

The van bumps and rocks. Something metal slides against the back of his head. It feels heavy. His fingers grope for anything sharp. The binds must be those plastic zip ties he's seen the police use when they detain someone, hands tight against the back.

And what would you do, then? There's four of them.

He tries and fails to catch his breath, as if his ribs are compressing his diaphragm.

Just relax. People have noticed you've gone missing.

11

MacLeod wills his brain to un-fog, fingers pushing to clear stiff mud from the surface of truth—the effects of whatever drug they put in his drink.

The girl must've done it.

He was at the club, celebrating with the team. A few well-deserved spirits with jokes and stories, followed by dancing. The redhead girl dancing with him—she *and* that towering brunette in a Brazilian jersey. Dancing together, too, and laughing. At some point, the Brazil fan jumped on another player, another guy from the team. Had one of the girls handed him a drink?

Hammer-head to metal wall, sparks and dust.

They flash back—snapshots of going down the dark hall to the restroom. Urinating, washing up, his disheveled reflection a little fuzzy in the stylish oval mirror. Then, when he came out, it happened.

He'd turned back toward the roving light beams and artificial fog, and then it was gone. He couldn't see—he only felt rough movement.

This is all just a spot of holiday, right? Just roving through Panama, motoring to the coast to watch the pretty boats come out the Canal. Grab a picnic basket and a ukulele, you'll have a fine time.

Against the gag, his lip trembles. The WD-40 smell takes him back to the steel tank, where the man can't get out.

In the darkness, a mind occupied with thoughts of escape. Of *not* toeing the line, *not* getting out.

***

A Friday afternoon in May. Spent but satisfied with his five-mile effort, MacLeod grabbed his sweatshirt and water and took the back route toward his locker. His high school was a ghost town populated only by the sweet smells of freshly cut grass and approaching storms. He was meeting Madison at the movies at seven. His brother took the beat-up Honda to a party, so MacLeod would have to hoof it the two miles to the cinema. He might impress this girl with his casual cool. It seemed to open the doors for others.

Voices ahead, an argument. "Come on, give me my shit!"

MacLeod paused at the corner of the equipment shed, out of sight. It was Riley Cooke—that pain-in-the-ass.

"Come get it."

That sounded like Mel Schenker. Decent guy, big football star.

MacLeod heard scuffling feet, a grunt.

"Yup. There we go."

That sounds like Coleman? What are these two doing hanging out with Riley? Schenk hates Riley—always fucking around in Trigonometry, driving Ms. Perez crazy.

MacLeod's new casual cool urged him to take a step forward, to carry on with his business. But a curious sound or tinge in the air halted him on the balls of his Adidas-clad feet. Among the scuffing of sneakers was an odd sound—a contact, an expulsion of air. Somebody had been struck.

MacLeod heard Coleman grunt, as if in approval. Then panting.

What is this?

"Come on. Keep trying," Schenk taunted.

13

"Fuck you. Give it back."

Something flying and caught—a backpack.

"What's in that drum, Dave? You think that's where Ole Jimmy keeps his oil?"

"No!"

"Lemme look."

Another lunge and a hit. Coughing.

"Give it back. Fucking kike."

Coleman said, "Oh no, he didn't."

"I think he did."

"You did *not* say that, Riley."

Coughing. "Give it back you—"

It was cut off by a tackling sound. Just like when Darcy plowed into Mills after that slide tackle, MacLeod recalled.

Riley cried out desperately. Contact, a grunt. Again.

Words punctuated by hits. "The world—is sick—of—your shit! You—faggot waste of—space! Stupid shit. Here's—a sayonara—from the class—of ten!"

It paused. The violent *whump* that followed had to be a boot going into Riley's body. Followed by a yelp.

"And to think you were trying to get in Annie Murrow's panties. What a—" *whump* "—fucking joke!"

Another yelp.

It ended. MacLeod suppressed a breath, listening to Riley's desperate intake of air amid sobs. He sounded like a dog that had been run over.

"We, uh, we better get out of here," David Coleman said quietly.

"Yeah." A sniff. "Guess I got a little carried away. Time to split."

What happens if they come back this way and find me? What would Schenk say? We've never been tight, but...

MacLeod took a step back, ready to retreat around the corner, to stay hidden. Schenker and Coleman took off in the other direction, the frequency of footsteps increasing. Soon, the only sounds in the world were Riley's weeping with the ripping of undeniable thunder.

MacLeod crept back the way he'd come, feeling in his bones that Riley had probably deserved it.

***

The van stops for a second time. Maybe they'll let him out to take a leak.

"The farmer finally moved his truck," the girl says.

They turn onto a rutted path. The van bounces back and forth on gravel. Someone flips a magazine page.

"Hmm, look at this chica," the girl says. "She's sexy."

A man grunts in reply.

"Look at her ass, though. It's a couch cushion. I think the women down here all wear thongs." Another page flips.

15

"Would you like that, Mon Amour? If I got collagen injections in my ass so I could strut around the flat and open your beer with my cheeks?"

The driver laughs. Not much of a talker.

"Are you comfortable back there, Darling?" the girl asks MacLeod.

Let me out of here. I'll show you comfortable!

Rocking back and forth. More stuff knocks into his feet. Is anything heavy or sharp going to fall on him? He's trying to shove out that scene from that Stephen King movie, where the guy's tied up in bed and the lady takes a sledgehammer to his feet.

Jesus, this could be worse. I can't do anything about it.

After a curve, the van comes to a sliding halt. "Mérde," the girl says. "It must've been the fucking storm."

"What's up?" the fourth guy asks.

"Ah, the bridge." That was the lunatic. "Is it too deep to cross?"

"Probably."

They sit idling for a minute.

"How far is it?" the girl asks.

"From here? About eight kilometers. I had to walk it once."

After another pause, the girl says, "There. We can ditch it there."

"Sí."

16

The van backs up, tires spinning underneath the floor. Then a sharp turn followed by rough ground underneath. Stuff shifts, pinning MacLeod's legs. This gets more uncomfortable as the van bounces around, then finally stops.

Fuck, now what?

The world gets brighter when doors creak open. Grunts signal the moving of heavy items. Things are pulled off his legs, the daylight becoming threatening.

"Get the tools," someone says.

Hands lock on MacLeod's ankles and pull, and he is roughly dragged across the vehicle's floor.

"Hey you, Yankee. Are you going to behave for us?"

He nods obediently, the warm, moist air under his chin exchanged for coolness. He must be soaked.

Hands pull him to sit upright.

"Are you? If not—" There's a click and a loud hiss nearby, above him.

Someone laughs. The awful hissing approaches, coupled with a strange, foul brightness.

What in Hades is that?!

"Acetylene," a man says, intuiting his thoughts. "You know what that is? It takes the number off the engine block. It can do other things, too."

MacLeod shakes his head. The noise and light seem far too close.

No no no no no!

After a second, the alien threat retreats. Another creak— a door being opened. The engine hood, he guesses. Work begins.

17

"That's good. Be smart. You're a long way from home."

He is hauled to his feet, to stand in thick grass or weeds. Metal clinks sound right near him. Maybe a screwdriver. Someone helps steady him.

The drugs have mostly worn off, he realizes. Before, he wouldn't have been able to stand upright.

"Got to piss?" the girl asks.

She takes MacLeod's arm and walks him over a few steps—away from the crackle of the torch on the engine, or whatever they're doing.

"Let's have a peek," she says, unzipping his fly. He winces when her cold fingers find his penis.

Oh, I don't like this.

"Feet apart. You don't want to try anything funny right now," she adds.

He tries to relax, fighting fear and nerves. After several deep breaths, steadying himself, he douses the ground.

God, the relief!

Droplets spatter his leg where the sock has slipped. He's not wearing his Ecco loafers, he realizes.

"You done? Should I put it away, or do you want to walk around the jungle with your dick hanging out?"

He makes a noise, trying for compliance.

"Hey, are you done playing with the prisoner?"

Her response to this is a move with her arm. The air change is probably her giving someone the finger, MacLeod surmises.

"I think she likes him," the lunatic says, working.

"Bah, chinga tu madre," someone replies.

Laughter, then.

Excellent, they're all friends. College fraternity stunt.

The girl puts his penis away and zips him back up, careful not to snag his soft flesh with the metal teeth. He exhales a sigh of relief.

The crackling and hiss stop. She leads MacLeod back over to the group. A metal clinking sound has ceased. They stand for a few moments while someone closes a van door.

At least one thing is familiar.

Someone grunts and strikes something hard. This is followed by an odd hiss, and the action is repeated. The van shifts. He believes they're popping the tires. That would keep someone from running off with the vehicle, for one.

"Incendiary?"

"Yes, yes."

Incendiary? Doesn't that mean…

"Throw the hoodie on him," someone says. The older-sounding guy, the leader.

They yank off MacLeod's blindfold. He shuts his eyes against stinging brightness, the hammering man at it again. Each strike—a more insistent alarm.

This can't be good.

Chapter 3

Blinking rapidly to adjust, MacLeod finds a world of green and brown under a gray sky. The jungle.

Jesus, what am I doing here? Why are they letting me see their faces?

Before him, the girl stands in cargo pants and a dark windbreaker. A black shirt hugs her chest. Her red hair is gone, replaced by short brown. Her eyes and face are the same he remembers, though.

Beside her, a stern-looking Latino man is shouldering two bags. He's clean-shaven and built thick. He's young, too. Holding a hoodie.

At the back of the beat-up van is a man with long brown hair. Caucasian. Ripped cargo pants. Dirty hands working on something.

The lunatic, most likely.

Another Latin man approaches. He seems to be about MacLeod's age, thirtyish, but they might as well be from different planets. He sports a black goatee and a cold glower. The obvious leader, older than the rest. A dark object protrudes from the bag over his shoulder. MacLeod recognizes the metal tube with the small fin on the end: An AK-47.

He can't take his eyes off the gun, which is getting closer—a shark in the water.

"We say, you do. Comprendes?"

"Comprendo," MacLeod returns calmly, trying to control his breathing.

The leader notes this quick moment of linguistic recognition with a narrowed eye.

MacLeod looks down to find he's wearing jeans and hiking boots. They're all in boots.

A cord goes around his neck. It feels like plastic rather than wire. Smiling, the girl pulls the knot around to the back of his neck.

"What about his hands?"

"It doesn't matter. He won't need them, now," she says.

The younger Latin man brings the blue sweatshirt and throws it over MacLeod's head. After some tugging, they have it down over him, doubly trapping his hands. The feeling of powerlessness is cranked up a notch.

Why bother?

"Lift a foot," the younger man says. MacLeod complies, and the man fits something around his leg. "Other," he says, tapping the left foot. MacLeod does so again, and a tight thing is slid up his legs, to above his knees.

He would know the item even without its red, high-friction appearance: One of the large rubber bands trainers use for physical therapy. They allow movement, but not much.

Someone—the girl—makes a motion and the cord tightens around his neck, pulling him backward.

Oh, not good!

"We could drag you by your neck or feet, but I don't think that would be too pleasant, do you?"

MacLeod shakes his head.

"And you will not try to run," the young man says. "Do you need convincing? Josh has his tools."

At the back of the van, the lunatic pauses his work and displays a pair of pliers. He clicks them twice.

Pliers! Convincing?

"No running away from us, Darling," the girl says in MacLeod's ear.

He shakes his head until she steps around so he can see her.

"Good boy. Remember," she adds, her evil smile enough to finish the thought.

The one called Josh is holding a device. Yellow and red wires run out of it, on into the van. A bomb. He points to the older one, who promptly shuts the passenger door.

"Good, good. Doors? Excelente."

Josh gently sets the device in the middle of the van's floor. He has a guitarist's spider-veined hands. The older man backs up, a backpack and duffel bag waiting in the grass. Josh pushes something on the device and carefully lifts his fingers from it. He withdraws like a mime in show.

A bomb! Is it going to go off? Why would he do that?

MacLeod takes an awkward step back, against the leash. When Josh closes the door, he does it cautiously, as if listening for an animal to react. The wire isn't visible outside the door—something to do with the bomb. He carefully clicks the door in place, then turns to the rest.

"Perfecto. You see? When somebody opens the door, poof! Lee-tul surprise. The fire takes care of everything. No evidence."

22

"Bueno," one man says.

"El auto es en fuego," Josh sings. "El casa es en fuego."

He's crackers.

The group leader hefts his backpack and duffel bag, coming to MacLeod. "We walk now," he says.

Of course we do.

***

The green animal has devoured them. Trees with leaves the size of kindergarteners. Vines suspended from a labyrinth of branches and green. Purple flowers dotting the undergrowth, beckoning: *Follow this muddy path right down my gullet. It won't hurt.*

This world was the real thing, not the facsimile of a jungle you find in zoos or theme restaurants. Beautiful, preferably from a distance. The hoodie offered false protection. If an animal jumped at them from the side, he wouldn't see it in time. Was that a benefit? Would he want to know beforehand if a massive snake or dinner-plate spider or crocodile was on him? This was the real jungle.

The hoodie was not for his benefit, for comfort in the lukewarm rain. Satellites and planes looking for him couldn't see him. They could only spot five people walking in the woods. Chances are, they wouldn't pick out the cord leash, running the back of the sweatshirt. The girl has been holding it. Josh, the lunatic, stayed behind him, though MacLeod would definitely rather keep that guy in sight.

The two Latin men are up front. The way they've been acting and muttering in Spanish speaks of brotherhood or

23

lifelong friendship. The younger one has a handgun, MacLeod's noticed, while the older one with the goatee—their leader—is relaxed about the AK-47's handle sticking out of his bag. He could grab it and shoot in a hurry.

They've crossed a number of streams. The first one, with warm water up to his knees, showed the remains of the aforementioned wooden bridge downstream. Falling rain seemed to be dampening all sound, lending the impression of a less bug- and bird-ridden world than a white city boy from Cleveland would've thought. Greenery arched and climbed in tangles all around them. In scattered clearings, the enormous leaves seemed to hail from the Jurassic period.

It isn't hotter here, yet. Maybe seventy degrees. I think I'm lucky they're doing this in February. July must be brutal.

What's going on back in Panama? Have they learned I'm gone?

His mind conjures images of shut-down highways and an airport frozen by men in uniform, though the likelihood of these actions taking place is dubious.

He wonders if someone noticed him being taken out the back of the club. At the very least, guys would report on her— this witch behind him—and maybe noticed their simultaneous disappearing act.

"I have to admit, man," Josh says, coming up next to him. "You against Man City. Whew! That was just insanity, you know? Crazy shit."

What?

Oh, Manchester City, he realizes, versed in the lingo. Culverhouse Crossing played them on Saturday, right before MacLeod hopped a plane to join the U.S. side. Fun game. MacLeod had both goals, and the one in the 67th minute went off

Hickock and Noe and Jaeger before it came back to MacLeod for a heel-in. How could a flying heel work in the Premier League?

"Beautiful, beautiful," Josh continues. "I'm a big fan. I mean, I'd probably ask for your autograph, if we weren't marching you through a jungle to certain doom, you know?"

He laughs—a cackle which seems over-the-looney-tunes-moon crazy.

'Certain doom?' Can someone fake this? He's a theater guy and he's just acting, right? Just trying to get under my skin?

The elastic band on his legs provides odd resistance through his jeans, above the knees. It's awkward, so he keeps his steps small. They must not be in a terrible hurry, as nobody's shoved him in the back, yet. His best bet is to play it cool, and escape notice when he can. Beside him, a shotgun's handle is inches from his elbow, sticking out of Josh's duffle bag.

Just swinging along innocently.

"Oh this?" Josh says, following MacLeod's fixed eyes. "This is my little Babushka." He casually gets the weapon out and displays it—thirty inches of dark menace. "See? Shells go in the slide, here. Pump once, it ejects the spent shell out the side. Pretty fast, by the way, if you ever want to play a joke on your friends." He points it. "This one has a safety switch, very important. You don't want to blow someone in half by accident. And, eh, you aim and get a wide stance and shoot."

MacLeod has been staring against his will. It's broken when one of the men ahead says, "Josh." Maybe an admonishment.

Josh ignores him. "I cannot demonstrate right now, as we're trying to be quiet as rabbits. But, you must be careful how you hold it when you fire. The recoil is strong enough to snap your wrist." He makes a bone-snapping noise and casually puts the weapon away.

Great. Learn something every day.

Josh drops back, probably to talk with the girl. The rain lets up as they come to a creek. MacLeod takes his time navigating the rocks. Turned sideways for a moment, he glances back at the girl. Sharp burgundy lips, feline eyes and collar-length dark-brown hair. Behind her French accent, she may have Scottish or Irish roots. With those hips and the snug tank top peeking out of her rain jacket, she can do *alluring*. Something out of a magazine. Throw on a bandolier of bullets and call it 'Jungle Revolutionary' by Calvin Klein.

What is she doing here with these psychos? She seems to be enjoying this.

And this Josh dude. Is that his real name, for a Czech or Slavic? I don't recall a Josh in the Bible—though that doesn't mean a rip out here.

When do I get to wake up and go home to Emma?

The two guys ahead, MacLeod's decided, must be brothers. Same jaw and curvature above the nose. The older one's all business. It would be no shock to learn this is regular weekend fun for them both.

The sun comes out when their curving path starts climbing. Under the damp hoodie, his body temperature increases by ticks. Extra weight on a stair-stepper in a hot room—like one of Herdoñez's insane training exercises. He closes his eyes and steadies his breaths to fight off a sudden nausea.

It's just nerves. You're okay.

Almost immediately, the sunlight's brought out the zoo aviary smell of his surroundings. It's never been his favorite scent—that blend of moist soil and bird droppings and half-eaten fruit. Here and there, he picks up an acrid stink and pungent flowers. Since childhood, he's imagined it was the sunlight that brings out the smell—molecules moving about faster, microbes doing the cha-cha.

Habeus corpus stinkus, Your Honor.

The sound of a helicopter interrupts his musing. The leader lifts his hand to call for a halt. They're under thick, pale-bark trees, with only bits of blue sky visible. MacLeod can't find the passing chopper—which means they won't be seen.

"Could that be for us?" Josh asks, the tone more curious than concerned.

"No," the girl answers.

"It's three-twenty," the leader says, scanning the canopy. "Barely eight hours. No chance they're looking for us."

"You're not that lucky," the younger brother says to MacLeod. A nudge of the arm with his rifle, like this has been a moment of camaraderie for them.

Oh, your mother must be so proud.

They continue as the helicopter's chopping moves off to the left. Their being spotted wouldn't have done much good, anyway, MacLeod reasons. These guys seem smart enough. By eight hours, the leader must be referring to the team breakfast at the hotel. It was scheduled as a big to-do with a U.S. senator and local politicians and all. 'Bienvenido a Panama, Gentlemen! After your magnífico game, any chance I can interest you in vacation homes? Or in buying stock in one of our fine local companies?' That's how these things worked.

Security would be tight there, too. Ironically.

MacLeod doesn't know that he could *ever* get used to the security. Guys playing for Culverhouse had to take up residence in gated mansions or secure condo buildings. Life in the Premier League. Safety is a component of *the life*, as routine as putting on the boots. Majerus, the Manchester United phenom,

27

is surrounded by three bodyguards at all times. Rumor has it, the guy doesn't 'pop in' anywhere—except into the latest willing lovely.

Stateside, MacLeod remembers, the time after the World Cup victory was absolutely nuts. The Men's Team headquarters got bomb-threat calls and faxed missives for months. The gals in reception had learned to laugh it off. Coaches got death threats, too. At the massive victory parade in Chicago, there had been four SWAT teams of snipers to watch over everything from rooftops.

All about a soccer game. How did any of it make sense?

Chapter 4

Mosquitoes disperse when MacLeod shakes his head. The hoodie helps—if it doesn't just trap the little bastards close to his skin. He can't honestly do a damned thing about malaria and dengue fever, now. "It's not the time to worry about them," Emma would say. He should focus on the things he *can* control.

At the moment, that isn't a whole hell-of-a-lot.

He nearly bumps into the younger brother, who has stopped. Ahead of them, the leader has raised a fist and is still as a statue. After a moment, he points to the left, tapping his ear. The girl and Josh swiftly move MacLeod under a large tropical bush. They sit him down and crouch beside him, followed by the brothers. At a different time, he'd worry about what's moving on the jungle floor. Now it's deathly quiet, save for the slight metal squeak of their leader affixing a silencer to his pistol. Eyes up, his hand twists it on with oiled ease.

What's happening? Someone's here?

The younger brother gives the rest of them a warning look, and they wait in silence. Soon, there's a faint jingle of metal and boots. It gets closer, someone on the path. The leader slowly extends his gun. MacLeod can only see bits of the track through the big leaves. What is he about to witness?

He should close his eyes, but he can't. Somebody's about to be executed. The jingling gets closer and closer.

Boots appear. They pause. The leader's about to shoot.

Keep walking, you fool. Move on or you'll be killed.

The stranger wears green cargo pants with equipment and a net. When he turns, MacLeod can make out a huge holstered knife strapped to his leg. Above that is a black case

29

with the outlines of tubes. He appears to carry something over his shoulder.

The man is thirteen feet away. Any second now, there could be the air-gun sound of shots fired through a silencer. Then, MacLeod imagines, the screams or grunts and the crumpling of a man shot dead. Like in the movies.

"Serpiente?" he calls. "Serpiente?"

Moments pass without a shot. The traveler mumbles something and moves on, clomping down the path. The leader removes his silencer.

"Game hunter," the girl mutters. "Trying to find a big snake for the zoos."

"Sí," the younger brother says.

MacLeod breathes. The man is gone. Will he sleep well tonight, or will his dreams be populated by a shadowy menace hiding under bushes? He *doesn't* go missing, and nobody wonders why Uncle Bernie isn't home for dinner. And nobody ventures out into the jungle looking for him, MacLeod surmises.

Who lives here, anyway? Where the hell are we?

From previous cursory glances at maps, the Panamanian isthmus didn't even look wide enough for this adventure. How could they have come this far without hitting another village or a real road or the ocean? How far did the girl say it was?

At a fork ahead, the path to the left climbs sharply. Friends have told him about this—hiking trails in Colorado that shoot up and have you sweating like pigs to reach a viewpoint. With a break in the canopy above, he can see a great green bulge before them—a real mountain.

Are there mountains in Panama?

They take the steep route and MacLeod's restricted strides shorten. With the gag, it's like trying to breathe through sludge.

"Hold on," the girl pants.

They stop. She reaches under his sweatshirt, up to his neck, and works the knot in the cord around to the front. Her warm fingertips on his Adam's apple give him a weird jolt— something he wants, someone he doesn't. Now the cord is dangling out the front of his sweatshirt.

"Enrique," she says, handing the cord to the younger brother. The leader watches, one eye on the sky.

"I'm not dragging him along," the one called Enrique returns.

"If I slip and pull him down, then we're all in trouble. Got it?"

Enrique rolls his eyes. He takes the cord and wraps it around his hand.

"You, MacLeod," the girl says, nudging him. "Do you want to be garroted slowly, or are you going to walk? Time to show off your *physique*," she adds in her near-comical French accent.

They climb. A waterfall soon appears, down on the right. It empties into a blue-black pool surrounded by mossy boulders.

It is travel-brochure lovely, MacLeod decides, but much too far to jump. With his hands bound back, a trip down the slope probably means a broken neck. Even so, would that be better than facing *whatever* is waiting for him at the destination?

At the next glimpse, the waterfall is already thirty yards below them. Soon, the trees drop and a view opens to the right. Sweating madly and breathing through his gag, MacLeod tries to tally the money in various bank accounts. For someone who

31

grew up without much spending cash, there seemed to be strangely little time for worrying about such things back home.

Should I offer to bribe these guys? Is that part of the plan, to get me sweating and talking about money? How much money could I even offer? There are companies that have insurance for this kind of thing, but am I in that position?

One small detail would make a world of difference.

On the difficult ascent, he nearly loses his footing. Enrique pulls on the cord to help him. Thorny shrubs bracket the narrow path, which is becoming just a strip of rust-colored earth against the side of a mountain.

MacLeod winces against a cool breeze, the inability to wipe drops of perspiration from his nose and jaw. To the right, an amazing view has opened. Clouds make splotchy shadows on the jungle floor, sliding among other green peaks. They've probably climbed a thousand feet in twenty minutes. His friend Whisenhunt would have a fit up here, right now. On planes, he has to escape with closed eyes and Ambien, plugged into Turkish dance music.

Ahead, the tight path hooks a sharp left around the mountain. It's a runway illusion. With enough speed, one could simply zoom up the ramp and right off into the puffy clouds. It is narrow, too, down to eighteen inches. What happens, he wonders, when a mustachioed Colombian farmer appears with his burro and sacks of coffee beans? Somebody will have to step aside.

'Never mind us, Señor. Nothing to see here.'

Climbing steadily, he wonders why he's imagining a coffee farmer from another era—a relic from YouTube.

When they turn the corner and the path levels out, his breath leaves him.

Jesus Christ, not a chance!

In the distance, a thin path snakes around a sheer, gray wall. Vines cling to its vertical face, and little solid rock seems to hold the path up. MacLeod's pulse goes to throbbing when his eyes travel the flimsy road closer and closer, up to the leader's feet. Wind hits his face from *below*. Beyond the toes of his boots, the path simply drops away.

In the reverential pause, there's near-silence. Breathing and the shifting of packs. Unheard, a small white plane crawls by, miles and miles distant.

MacLeod foolishly looks down. A fall would mean a plummet of untold seconds.

Their leader has started. MacLeod's cord yanks.

"Hey," Enrique says. "Want to die, here? Just use your head. Don't look down. Walk!"

Where is the safety chain on the wall? What lunatics would use this path?

He takes a deep breath. With small steps, and someone's hand gripping his left shoulder, he makes his way around the cliff. Dizziness and vertigo and self-preservation vie for supremacy.

This is the momentary lapse of reason Pink Floyd should've been singing about. I'm fucked I'm fucked I'm fucked.

Relax, man. Just a slow-motion attack up the baseline. Keep the ball straight. Walk the tightrope up until your mate's made his run. All there is to it.

Tears well up. Sweat drips down his chest.

Don't look down. Okay, focus on your feet. Don't ask why the path hasn't eroded away.

Inch by inch.

One step at a time. Toe the line. You'll get through this.

Finally, after several minutes of edging along and vines passing at a glacial pace, it's done. He glances back, hardly believing he's navigated *that*.

Never again. As long as I live.

A hand pushes him forward. Back into the safety of jungle.

Chapter 5

"Look at this," the girl says, holding up a faded rag from next to an upright board. She's standing fifteen feet off the trail. The older brother casually pokes around, too. A blue plastic cup rolls aside. The other fellow, Josh, is pissing somewhere behind MacLeod.

"'M'-something. Could it be M-nineteen?" She looks closely at it.

"Who?" the younger brother asks.

"Communists," the older brother reports.

"Ah, those fools," Josh says, jumping in. "All that rah-rah people-power bullshit never got them anywhere, did it?"

"Except dead." The leader nudges something with his boot. "Mira."

"No shit?" The younger brother drags MacLeod forward so he can see. "After all this time?"

"Bugs haven't left much," Josh says.

A body? Here, five yards off a jungle trail. Seriously?

The leader glances at him. "We're wasting time," he says. "Vamanos!"

The girl smiles as if nothing weird just happened, and she steps over to take his leash.

MacLeod runs his tongue over the gag, comparing it to the kitchen towels Emma prefers—a little coarse to scrape oil from fingers. Not gentle on the cheeks, though.

His being gagged—silenced and robbed of power—is but one of the tactics at play here, he realizes. Whoever these people are, and whatever their purpose is, they've been paid quite a lot. Somebody with real power and *cajónes* is paying, he imagines. Somebody who doesn't fear (or can avoid) the reprisal from abducting an American of his status. They all have crossed a point of no return.

With each new footstep on foreign earth, the suspicions plaguing his frontal lobe take on a degree of boisterous solidity. He *has* done something wrong. It has opened a fissure in the reactor, and no amount of adhesive or welding repair will draw the loosed noxious gas back inside. 'The writ is filed,' as the expression goes. He can't undo what's been done.

Neither can his captors. But that isn't the only mistake playing out beneath a tropical canopy.

***

"You're in luck, MacLeod," the one called Enrique tells him. They have descended quickly, the path diving into afternoon shadows. "We're there," he continues. "And no mudslides to contend with."

Through the trees, the path forks at a pond. Hanging vines, mossy boulders, ferns and little purple flowers. And a cabin. MacLeod's face pinches up, his brain sorting and sifting permutations of the word 'there.'

Something moves in the water, too small to be a crocodile. It is the small white structure that has everyone's full attention, though. A tree stretches over it and vines hang down on one side. The one-story abode has screen doors by a stoneware cooking area, and an outhouse beyond.

Stretching from the near tree is a laundry line—with clothes on it.

In a flash, their leader hands the AK-47 to his brother. Enrique sets down his bag and takes the weapon smoothly. No words between them, eyes fixed on the cabin.

Behind MacLeod, a bag drops. The girl's hands are under his hoodie, taking hold of his cord. The appearance of a long object to his right is Josh readying his shotgun. The leader puts a finger up to his lips and directs Josh to the right.

Oh shit oh shit oh shit! What is this?

He leans over to see bright colors on the laundry line, a tie-dyed T-shirt among them.

The brothers creep forward, with the leader in front, handgun aimed at the cabin. Josh is hurrying off to the right.

"Don't move," the girl whispers, leading MacLeod to the nearest tree. Will they wait it out here? Is it to prevent his being seen? Or to keep from being hit by gunfire?

Is this really happening?

He stands among ferns and forces himself to study vines on the tree trunk. A beetle, a tiny red spider. The girl watches the cabin with keen interest—eyes narrowed, a hint of smile on her lips.

The image of a little boy appears in his head. He's weeping quietly, afraid his father *is* going to pull the trigger and shoot the helpless doe.

Yelling. Many voices. One of them is a woman.

MacLeod faces the ground and squeezes his eyelids tight, mouth closed against ragged breathing.

Whatever happens…don't watch. It's all just a nightmare.

The yelling is muffled, he realizes, when one of the yellers comes outside. The voices get clearer, back-and-forth in Spanish. The woman is definitely pleading. She keeps repeating something interspersed with many "por favor"s. Her voice takes on the pitch of panic. The speech is too rapid for translation. MacLeod wishes he could cover his ears.

Let them go! They haven't seen anything. Just let them flee with their lives!

Among them is a faint, high-pitched voice.

Jesus, a child. There's a kid in there!

Please let me be swallowed up by quicksand so I don't have to hear this!

He sucks in a breath, his face gnarled with tension.

Crack-crack-crack! Crack-crack!

The rifle shots are head-splitting loud.

A scream. The woman's screaming.

"Por favor—*por favor!*"

Crack-crack!

MacLeod hears himself grunting through the gag. There are tears at the corners of his eyes and his upper lip is wet. When he looks, the girl smirks back at him, shaking her head.

Bang! Footsteps on wood. *Bang!*

There's movement. It sounds like something scraping against the floor.

Crack-crack-crack-crack-crack!

"Niño?"

Crack-crack-crack!

The girl has the shoulder of MacLeod's hoodie. She's pulling him forward, toward the house. He doesn't want to go. He doesn't want to see.

"It's over," she says.

MacLeod tastes vomit, slippery bits of onion.

As they approach the house, a sharp fireworks smell fills the air. The brothers come out to meet them. Both of them are pissed, Enrique bouncing and raring to go. Smoke trails from the end of his rifle.

Josh runs up to them. "What happened?" he asks, excitedly. As if anything about what just happened *isn't* obvious.

"The boy got away! Should I go after him?" Enrique asks his brother. "I might've hit him."

MacLeod's heart jumps.

The leader scowls at his brother.

"I'll go and—"

"Leave it," the girl says, possessing some authority. "It's fifteen kilometers to the nearest village from here. He has to cross two rivers. The jungle will take him."

Oh no.

"How did you miss him?" Josh asks, practically gushing.

"Cállete!"

Enrique is about to charge off—after a child—when his brother stops him with a hand. He mutters something in Spanish. Enrique rolls his eyes and swears under his breath.

Suddenly, his focus turns to MacLeod.

"You!"

He grips the front of MacLeod's sweatshirt and pulls.

Me?

Enrique practically drags him to the back of the cabin. MacLeod's eyes follow the smoking rifle, swinging about wildly. It almost tags him in the ribs.

Keep that away from me.

"You, MacLeod! Take a look at this. Eh?! Take a good look!"

He has pulled MacLeod to the house, up to the back screen doors.

Oh, Jesus!

A man's body is lying face-down. Latin complexion, white T-shirt and red shorts. Half the T-shirt is crimson from two bullet holes. His left arm is open at the back. What must have been his triceps muscle lies flopped aside, still attached at one end. He's wearing a gold necklace. Part of his head is gone. Flaps of scalp have black hair and pink material, sitting in a lagoon of blood.

The world swims. MacLeod has to lean on something. The smell floods his nostrils, pouring in. Raw lamb which Emma cubes for stew, and a foul odor coming from the dead man's stained shorts.

MacLeod realizes he's standing on a chunk of squishy pink material.

Vomit comes up, spills out. Enrique holds him in place.

"You see this?" He grabs MacLeod about the head, forcing him to look. "We left a note to warn people. Did they

40

listen? No, they didn't. Look what happens! *This* is what happens when you fuck with the wrong people!"

Nine feet away, a bare leg is lying on the floor. The woman.

MacLeod collapses against a wall. Blurry vision, the distant awareness of thick spittle over his cheeks and neck.

Facedown, the woman is wearing sandals. Her leg is hooked around the unpainted doorway to the next room. It's how she fell when she was shot. MacLeod can see bare thigh up to purple-and-white panties.

Josh nudges him aside, so he almost falls in the expanding dark puddle. Exuberant, he hops over the dead man and stands over the woman's corpse.

Is he going to shoot her again? He couldn't squeeze off a shot outside, so now he's got to get one in? Oh, God.

"How could you do this, Man? Aw, and she's so lovely, too. Caliente!"

He leans over her. There's a soft sadness in his eyes, gazing at her, brushing her hair aside.

Now he's setting his shotgun down on the floor. He mutters something and licks his lips. Then he disappears into the next room.

"Still warm," he mutters.

She's moving, retreating. He's dragging her away.

What. Is. He. Doing?

The female captor is next to MacLeod. He believes somebody called her Cora.

Ripping. The jingle of a belt. Grunts, animal grunts, coming from the next room. Rhythmic movement and moans.

He can't be...

The girl, Cora, snickers and shakes her head. "Josh. That is in such poor taste," she mutters.

Enrique is behind them now, pacing.

The grunts become louder and slower, and then die out with a flourish. This is followed by the sound of something heavy falling on the floor. Then the rustle of clothing, and a zipper going.

"Ah, bonita," Josh says from the next room.

He just...

Dragging sounds follow.

MacLeod finds his way outside, staggered steps further from the carnage. Vomit comes up again. As he falls over, he's vaguely aware that his gag and hoodie are now all a spewed-on mess. He crashes into a pile of something and drops on the ground. Chunks of it tumble onto him. A mesquite smell. A wood piece hits his ear. Abstractly, he wonders if the hoodie softened the blow.

His hands and arm hurt, pinned beneath him. His left ear, too, and his ass. He landed on a pointy thing.

A curious kind of yell compels him to roll and look up.

The leader has thrown Josh against the wall of the cabin and is holding him there. His contorted face is five inches from Josh's maniacal, toothy grin.

"No mas! Never again, Muchacho!" he commands through clenched teeth.

MacLeod can feel the leader's rage, Mount Tambora behind sepia skin and a tarantula goatee.

He releases Josh and goes over to his brother, who is watching. He orders Enrique something with two words. Enrique shakes his head when he walks by Josh, who is smiling like a fool and adjusting the crotch of his pants.

Breathing hard, the leader comes to stand over MacLeod. Cora joins him, chewing on a fingernail.

"Did you enjoy the show?"

Chapter 6

"Don't cut him. That would make me weep," Enrique says.

The leader, cutting MacLeod's gag, sneers back and sends his brother an air kiss.

The smell of vomit is like a drain, sucking out all energy. Cool freedom bursts across MacLeod's face. He watches the leader toss the gag outside, where it lands with a 'splat.'

This is insanity.

He spends a few moments just sitting still, opening and closing his sore mouth. Trapped, dirty, an exhausted witness.

Un cautivo.

"Besides," the leader says, "our guest will be un buen muchacho. Es verdad?" He slaps MacLeod on the side of the head.

The cleanup happened without his assistance. They didn't force him to stand there and watch, either, as Enrique dug holes to bury the bodies. Josh mopped up the blood and remains with pond-water rags. Cora had inspected the cabin for missing items and found syringes, spoons and heroin in the small bedroom.

MacLeod wonders about the foul luck that lured two druggies and their kid—or someone's kid—to this place out in the jungle. The whole thing was almost too bizarre to believe, but it had happened. Now the squatters were dead. It was real.

He'd been dropped into a netherworld, a strange reality far from clean lines and expensive footwear and bills. A place where *this stuff* happens. Who could throw an escape rope down? When would someone blow a whistle?

And the kid. Does he have a chance out here? Where will he run to?

Probably a cute little four-year-old with a mop of dark-chocolate hair and a too-big goldenrod T-shirt. Of course, the kid never saw anything that could help. MacLeod's not sure what he would've understood, except that bad people came into the house and committed horrible violence. And that he had to run. He could be of no help.

MacLeod's face heats up with shame and regret.

What's wrong with me? Some poor boy is running for his life through the jungle, and I'm worried about my own mollycoddled neck!

An encyclopedia entry passes through: Snakes and bugs and crocodiles and jaguars. Cora had practically smiled when she said it was fifteen kilometers' distance to the nearest village.

She's taking off his hoodie, now. Seated on a bench, he feels ten pounds lighter when she pulls it over his head.

"Well, do you have anything to say?" she asks, tossing it aside. "Like 'Thank you?' Or are you just going to try to spit in my face?"

MacLeod takes a deep breath and clears his throat. Bits of pepper and corn dislodge. His hands are still bound behind him. Whatever he needs, he realizes, only *they* can give it. What's the point of being hostile now?

"Thank you," he tells her. "Water. Do you have any water?"

Impressed, she gets up. When she returns with two bottles, she opens one and sits next to MacLeod. For a moment, she watches him and drinks her own. Then, in an act of charity, she raises the other to his cracked lips and he drinks half the bottle.

In doing so, he's suddenly conscious of his neck being exposed to her. The vicious dinosaurs from *Jurassic Park* come to mind.

"We have to use bottled water down here," she explains, setting his on the floor. "Even Enrique and Arturo. The parasites would turn your insides to jelly."

Arturo. Our leader is Arturo.

"Merci," he tells her, finding an instant of distraction in the curves of her chest and not-too-thin arms.

"Oh, that's good. Charming. I would like it if you tried to charm your way out of here." She has something in her hand, now. The pair of scissors.

He tries to not wince. "No, it was never my forte."

"Well, the unrealistic American being realistic. Sublime."

His fashionable seersucker oxford is either still back at the club—or someone else has taken it, for keeps or for evidence. He's wearing the *black* over a tight gray T-shirt, and he should not protest about their imminent ruin. Cora gives him an appraising look. With care, she pulls his shirts at the back collar and begins cutting. He leans forward, like it's merely a quick haircut. The metal is icy when it touches his spine. Cool air spreads across his back. Down one arm, then the other.

"Was this shirt expensive?" she asks, referring to the *black*. "It's famous. A favorite of yours?"

In front, fingertips brushing his throat, she cuts down. She avoids the loop of cord around his neck and stands up to finish. On the last snip, splitting his T-shirts at the bottom, the scissors swoop close to his crotch. He flinches, his breath caught.

Jesus.

"Oh, that would've been bad," she oozes. "I could've kissed it to make it better."

The clothes fall away in pieces, black and gray and colors. He feels weirdly undressed in front of her.

"Bien. You *are* an Adonis. All those hours in the weight room," she muses. "Flex for me? Arturo tells me he can lift a hundred twenty kilos on the bench press," she says, cleaning his chin and the scissors with his wasted shirts. "What about...?"

She doesn't finish the question, her eyes caught on something. They are wider, MacLeod notices. She tilts her head and shifts closer, examining something on his left side.

What? What does she see? Is it a big spider?

He looks down, heart thumping in his ears. He sees nothing wrong except his own Celtic-stock flesh. Nothing on him.

Oh, but that's the point, isn't it?

Josh is still drying the 'kitchen' floor with a ratty towel. He leans over from his work and smiles at MacLeod. "Okay, can we flog him now? I bet he's the sporting type."

Sporting?

Cora's mouth is open a bit. She laughs nervously—and it *sounds* forced. "If you really want to. But I didn't bring my flogging whip. Did you?"

"There must be some reeds in the forest we can use."

Quickly, she moves to find something. "Yeah, uh, go ahead," she replies, rifling through one of the duffel bags. "The, uh, crocodiles won't mind if you borrow their cover."

"Munchy munchy," Josh says, working.

47

The leader—Arturo—watches from the back porch area. He's talking into a satellite phone, long antennae. His speech is too quiet and rapid to understand.

Dark cloth moves into his face, blocking his vision.

What is she doing?

Cora's breast is pressed against MacLeod's face. The material is soft cotton on his nose, a sweetness combined with body odor. She's standing over his knee, close enough that a strip-tease would be considered excessive contact, in breach of company policy.

Is this a show?

Her hands work something. She starts stuffing it over his head. Another hoodie, he realizes.

"What, are we teasing the tiger now?" Josh asks.

"Better for him," Cora mutters, finishing the job.

What happens now? What has to happen?

He rolls his shoulders to stretch against the new hoodie. It feels like a medium.

"Good, make it tighter," Enrique says. He comes to MacLeod and gives the sweatshirt an extra downward tug.

"Happy, now?" Cora asks. "I don't think Arturo cared."

"Well, good for him! I prefer it *this* way," he grumbles.

"Christ, man, relax!" Josh says, his work complete. "So stressed. It's not good for you."

Enrique glares at him. "Don't start with me."

His accent, his pronunciation and everything. He could be from Miami for all I know.

"Tell me you weren't jealous," Cora says, amused.

"Jealous? Of *this twig?* No no no."

"Enrique," she says, "don't be. He plays in the goddamned Premier League! They all look like him."

MacLeod decides to stay quiet, not wanting to piss off Enrique. The guy has plenty to be enraged about, now.

"Well, not Chuga," Josh says. "That guy's muy grande!" He flexes to make his point.

MacLeod watches, unable to place the name.

"What do you say to that?" Enrique asks. "You wish you were as big as Chuga, or Xavientar?" He sneers. "Then maybe you could break those binds and make trouble for us?"

The absurdity of it all nudges MacLeod. "But I can't," he says, before he can stop himself. "I can't do any–"

Something hits him with amazing speed. His left cheek stings as he reels.

Enrique gets level with MacLeod. "I don't think I would talk, if I were you." He says this slowly. "Your clock is ticking, MacLeod. If you want lots of pain before the end, I can help you with that. Comprendes, Amigo?"

A little nod. What else can he do? Enrique stands up, leering at him, and joins his brother outside.

MacLeod's left eye itches. He hopes it's sweat or blood rather than a tear. It isn't the first time he's been struck in the face (soccer players sometimes being what they are).

"Don't take it personally," Cora says, with a hand on his shoulder. "He's just stressed. We'll all get through this okay, right? Well, everyone except you," she clarifies, and walks out.

49

"Okay, okay," Josh says.

Now what, Psycho?

"Right. Maybe we have a Parcheesi board, huh?"

MacLeod looks from him to where Cora disappeared, a single word lingering on the tip of his brain.

Why?

The word summons two faces: One he knows as well as his own, and one he barely knows at all.

Chapter 7

"You shouldn't wear such a low-cut dress to work. Your udders are practically popping out!"

"Thanks, Mom. Really supportive."

It was late, past bedtime, and MacLeod was supposed to be asleep. Instead, as if on the watch for change that signaled trouble, he'd crept into the hallway and now stood in shadow, wondering why Grandma had said "udders." Maybe they were talking about a farm book Janice liked. Grandma had read to them again at bedtime, as Mom hadn't gotten home.

"I'm just saying," Grandma said, working on something quietly.

"I know what you're saying. I'm not daft." A sigh. "Look, Martin likes it when I show off a little. He says it puts his clients in a good mood."

"I'll say. They probably have trouble standing up after you leave the room."

"Thanks. I think," she added, rustling something out of a paper bag. "Peanut butter. Two for one."

MacLeod, all of seven-and-a-half, had heard 'two for one' before. Maybe his father used to say it a lot, before he split. *We are two and now you are one? Is that how it goes?*

"Did you eat?"

"Yeah. Lucia brought me a plate of lasagna. That little office is a disaster. Have you ever tried eating in a phone booth?"

What's a phone booth? MacLeod wondered.

"What about the green dress? I always thought that was so pretty."

"It's falling apart. It's got to be ten years old. My sewing skills were never comparable to yours. You want to take a crack at it?"

"Sure. Saturday, before the game. During cartoons. Do you want me to take it in a little?"

"Maybe. Don't start again, okay? It's not my fault I have to compete with twenty-year-olds who can't find their ass with two hands. I need this job."

"Is that jackal ever going to pay you for working the conference last month?"

"He said he would. He better. The kids need new jeans, growing out of their cousins' old stuff. Maybe Clyde will let me slide a month if I show him a little. I haven't missed in two years, you know."

Grandma sighed. "We'll make do."

"Yeah, of course. Spaghetti dinners and hand-me-downs and bargain bin movies. Fuck. Some life. Kelsey at the office keeps asking me why don't I get a cell phone. As if I need one more mouth to feed." Another rustling noise. "Nobody to call, anyway."

MacLeod sat chewing over that remark. He was so distracted, picking at a loose chip of paint on the wall, he didn't look up until his mother was standing over him.

"Hey Soccer Star," she said quietly, giving him a hug. "What are you doing up? You should be asleep."

He couldn't see her well in the sad under-the-cabinet light from the kitchen, but he could feel that she was still plenty strong. Grandma was behind her, silent.

"I couldn't sleep," he said.

"Okay, okay," his mother whispered. "Let's get back to bed, so you can grow that brain of yours and be successful."

"What-what's *successful* mean?"

She stifled a laugh, moving him down the hallway. "I'll teach you tomorrow."

Over the following days and weeks and years, she did teach him about success. What once was equated with 'hard work' and 'using your brain' became 'picking something you love' and 'travel funds' and 'money for college.' At some point, the switch was flipped. *Make enough that I can get Mom and Grandma out of that depressing rental on Dobbs Street.*

Success, however, relies on more than nose-to-the-grindstone work, he understands now. It's a funny thing. If one takes into account all the dedicated effort, injuries and insults

52

incurred in the chase, the pedigree *and* the timing, Lady Lucinda is still shooting in the dark. For a thoroughly secular *heathen* like him, there isn't a prayer on or above earth to direct that magical, glowing bullet your way.

Schenk, for one, got it. All the way to the NFL.

The sunsetting of high-school days was never a period MacLeod figured he'd look back on with lead-heavy questions and a tinge of sadness. He was out of there, happily on his way to Notre Dame on scholarship. A boat was in the water, pointed and waiting (and, unlike the one for others, his didn't have *U.S.S.* painted on the hull).

After the beat-down, Riley was absent that following Monday and Tuesday. When he came in on Wednesday, he was silent and subdued. His face was *tired*, but showed no sign of a beating. Recounting the events he'd heard—with his mind filling in visual gaps—MacLeod took it in silent shock. (Years later, in a workshop on domestic violence, the intentional avoidance of facial injuries clicked, regrettably.) In fact, it seems like Riley didn't say another word the rest of the year. In Trigonometry, Ms. Perez kept glancing his direction, expecting a snarky comment. Nothing came. Once, MacLeod almost walked up to Riley's locker, manufacturing a reason for the out-of-place checkup. He lost his nerve and continued on to Madison's locker, thoughts turned to date material. The ever-confident Schenk seemed to be playing things rather low-key, too.

At graduation, held on a hot night at an amphitheater, the Honor Roll grads were lined up first. While Werst gave her valedictorian speech, MacLeod looked back from his salutatorian spot, past Mitch at fifth, to Schenk at eighth. Three spots behind him, before Madison, was Riley at eleventh. Others looked proud or nervous or relieved under the stage lights. Riley looked broken, the smile wan.

***

"Congratulations," Arturo says flatly to MacLeod, calmly lowering his satellite phone. "You are now the target of a worldwide manhunt."

MacLeod stifles a sigh and studies his dinner: A protein bar of peanut-butter clay. It's the same for all of them. Though there is canned food in the cabin, Arturo doesn't want to risk a grill fire being seen or picked up. They're still close to the 'action.' Between intentionally small bites, MacLeod ponders the thermal-imaging capabilities of American satellites—and if any of it truly applies to this situation.

Otherwise, he figures, the manhunt should be a kind of positive. All those people care—fellow Americans (hoping and praying), the almighty government launching a search, and so on. Arturo's face, however, offers a reality check: Neither he nor the rest seemed worried in the slightest.

Their plan, or someone's plan, has already beaten the offside trap. They've got the ball and are running free in enemy territory.

It's getting dim, approaching his first real night in captivity, another *never-before* to ponder. He savors the last bite of bar, pretending he can channel the salmon-and-quinoa that Emma prefers. Having a little mobility now helps. He's capable of feeding himself this scrumptious meal.

His additional freedom—limited in scope—is thanks to the day's other highlight he'd like to forget. He'd had to go Number Two. The urge came on like a rushing bull, a latent effect of the drugs. Arturo cut his binds so he could attend to his own business in the makeshift outhouse—with the door open and Josh's shotgun pressed against his jaw.

During the process, MacLeod looked down to find a small white scorpion sitting on the bench, a soccer ball's width

54

from his bare thigh. Josh calmly reached over with his left foot and crushed it.

"Could be a bad one. You never know," he explained. The weapon stayed in place, its metal tube end chilly against his whiskers and bone.

MacLeod had tried not to tremble, thoughts on accidental discharge (which he'd never realistically know about). Afterward, Josh bound his hands in front with another plastic tie, and let him rinse them in the pond. "Don't fall in," Josh warned, holding a handful of his sweatshirt and leash. "There's probably piranha!"

Of course, Arturo and his gun had watched over the entire process.

This was followed by the captors showing off a little ingenuity, MacLeod had to admit. They put the noose and cord back around his neck, with the hoodie over it. They trailed the cord down the back, over his ass, between his legs and up the front to his hands. With a carabiner, they attached it to the hand tie. So, if he jerked his hands up, in an act of stupidity or defense, he'd nut himself *or* strangle himself, or both. Cora tested its effectiveness—Hell's pulley system and was pleased. Even slight movement caused his testicles to wring hands in alarmed protest. The only reason he can lift his hands enough to feed himself now is because he's sitting crouched over.

Cora, seated next to him, cocks her head at his profile. "So, where's the best place you've traveled, other than this? And I do not mean love tunnels."

Love tunnels? Oh, women.

MacLeod glances about, wondering what he should answer. The list of places he'd *like* to visit is long.

If they think....

55

"The, uh, the Amalfi Coast was nice."

Josh slaps a mosquito on his neck. The raw-lamb odor still hangs in the air, stubbornly hanging around when the sharp gunfire smell left. He wrinkles his nose.

Cora smirks. "That *is* a pretty place. What about Angkor Wat? Didn't you like the temples?"

Enrique and Josh are listening. MacLeod's history—his travels—are known. *Why* doesn't matter. Only that they are. And she seems privy to a secret that, apparently, she must conceal with a façade.

Otherwise...

"Uh, yes," MacLeod answers. "Quite beautiful."

Arturo returns to the cabin, having strolled down to the road. It appears that he's been conferring with his cell phone again. MacLeod wishes he could get a read on the guy, other than *all business*.

"Bueno, Mister MacLeod. News has spread and they're turning Panama upside down. Everything is closed. The FBI and DEA have come, and Special Forces are en route. All, of course, with the Panamanian government's *approval*." He adds a sneer to this last word. "Naturally, the governments of Brazil, Nicaragua, Costa Rica and Ecuador have pledged support—whatever that is worth. People are setting up vigils throughout your great country, and your President is an inch away from condemning this as an act of terrorism. You are now the most sought-after man since Osama bin Laden."

"Oh, okay," MacLeod says. "That's...something."

He glances around at the others, who are all relaxed in the twilight. Enrique has put a cigarette in his lips, but it is unlit. MacLeod wonders if it's a measure of self-discipline for him, or if Arturo has forbidden smoking. There are stories of smoke being detected miles away by dogs. Could any of that be true?

"So, uh, what's happening tomorrow?"

"We move on," Arturo says.

"Right. Where are we going? Are you guys taking me to the coast to put me on a boat?"

"No."

"So…are we going to the Canal? On foot?"

"Canal?" Arturo asks. "Not a chance."

"Look around you, man." Enrique spreads his arms. "We're in the jungle."

Thank you, Captain Obvious.

"Yeah, I-I got that. It's, uh, pretty. Scenic."

"Scenic," Josh sniggers. "Nice. The Alps. The Great Wall of China. The South American jungle. We could be like Indiana Jones, wandering around looking for treasure. Gold and temples," he adds with a dreamy expression.

"You didn't think we'd be that stupid, did you? To stay close to the *crime scene?*" Enrique clarifies.

"Well," MacLeod starts, clearing his throat. "You, uh, seem to have things kinda figured out, getting us here and all." He glances around. "I mean, I don't know where *here* is. We've been traveling all day. I, uh, guess I didn't realize Panama was so big."

"Panama!" Enrique is laughing. "The canal, right. That explains it. No-no-no, Amigo. We're in Colombia now."

Oh no. We're what?

57

MacLeod grunts. The bar he's finished feels like a lump of creek bottom, driving point-first through his gut.

Josh says, "Land of coffee and jungles and cocaine."

"Help is *not* right around the corner. Comprendes?" Enrique asks.

"Don't sweat it, Darling," Cora says. "We came for the *scenery*."

"Maybe we'll run into Escobar's ghost out here, man," Josh says. "That would be fun! I heard he used to flee the police in his underwear."

"What?" Enrique asks, cracking a smile. "That's not true. That can't be true."

"Sure it could," Josh says. "Haven't you ever heard the stories? The police are closing in on his mountaintop party house. He says 'Goodnight, Sweetheart' and bounds off into the jungle wearing only his tighty-whities. Imagine that. Do you think he was fat? It would be even funnier if he was a poochy motherfucker."

"That would be pretty hilarious," Cora admits.

Birds call. Crickets have started up, or MacLeod's just now noticing them. There were crickets by the drainage creek near his house growing up. He's heard they are food in China and Indonesia. There must be crickets all over the world.

Something large moves behind them, closer to the pond. Arturo glances in that direction with idle curiosity. In the dark, he seems to crack a smile. A man in charge.

Macleod glances about, at their surroundings. Nothing here—not the normalcy of crickets nor the quiet of un-toxic air—can give him comfort.

From boring Cleveland to wild, chaotic Colombia.

Next door, Brazil is a crumbling democracy, but it's got to be better than this.

Chapter 8

"And here it is, Ladies and Gentlemen. Down to a penalty kick. If Gandolfini puts it past Carpenter, the World Cup goes to Italy. There won't be but a minute left in stoppage time for the Americans to attempt some heroics.

"Gandolfini's focusing all his attention on the ball. The American keeper looks lightning-rod tense. Here it is.

"For the win. Gandolfiniiiii—NO! The keeper blocks it! Unbelievable! Ball comes out to Spazzio on the right. A try—and it's blocked! Carpenter got it again! Sensational! Ball's out to Ferguson. And he's seen something 'cause he launches it. He's got a man downfield. It's MacLeod..."

MacLeod opens his eyes and squelches a cough.

It's morning. Foreign sounds and a lightening world herald a new day. Plants outside give off a yellowish, warm light. These, as a captive sees it, are all deceptions.

Looks like it's going to be hot as hell today. My feet will roast.

They're still encased in the hiking boots, per Cora's command disguised as advice. She likened it to the desert. You don't want to give the local wildlife a warm, dark, moist tunnel to get cozy in.

The prickly, cramped, sore-back world of his reality settles into place. He's in a kennel—a jumbo-sized plastic dog kennel with a metal door and latches. He knew better than to complain about the accommodations. Obviously, a crate that's large enough for a St. Bernard can hold a six-foot-one man, insult and ridicule filed away for another time. After another stop at the loo, he had to crawl in the kennel with baby movements, restricted by his leash and binds. In another act of pseudo-charity, Cora let him get moderately comfortable, in a fetal position, before she closed the cage door and slipped a padlock through it. This damning security had one benefit in preventing additional surliness, he reasoned. Enrique, for one, would've known where to exact payback for having to watch a captive in shifts. MacLeod didn't need any more retribution coming his way.

As it is, he's got Enrique and the maniac right here. Josh is asleep on his side, with his back pressed up against the kennel door. Even if MacLeod had a knife—and the nerve to target soft flesh—he couldn't have done much to help himself. Both parties, it reasoned, understood there wasn't going to be any Hollywood-type escape during the night. Rather than dwell on the nature of his confinement, he turned to memories of soccer and feminine sweetness to block out the assumed presence of ants and spiders. A snake coming through the place, he told himself, would have no interest in something his size.

Logic has come to dominate his life, lately. It just happened while he got older—a principle to regret but beyond his power to change. The passing of years, the passing of hours at school desks, the predictable ebb and flow of moving triangles. If ever there was a time to wish for childhood again, this is it. First learning about soccer from Missy Carpenter down the street—the laughter, the encouragement and patience. Her, two years older and developing breasts already, kissing him (eleven and terrified) in the drizzle.

Or that time in the park, finding Lady Lucinda. MacLeod reached for the beer bottle (recycling machines paid quarters) and found a treasure underneath. Cradled in the long grass was a nudey card. He snatched it up before the other boys, who quickly gathered around as if he'd found gold. There, in his hand, the image of a blue-eyed, smiling vixen in black Western wear. A bulbous ass barely concealed. Tassels hanging from her top (the most enormous chest he'd ever seen). Six-shooters in her hands. The white cowboy hat looked alluringly soft. All of her did. *This* gift, titled Lady Lucinda, sat protected in MacLeod's hand. His heart was racing, he was sweating. Silence reigned until Ramirez broke it idiotically with, "Is she a hooker?"

She, Lady Lucinda, belongs to that other world—the one he lived in until logic took over.

Now there will be no more surprises, no first erection, no first car or first kiss. Mark Twain wrote of his training as a riverboat captain. In having to learn all of the Mighty Mississippi's ways, she lost her magic and mystery. It seemed a tragedy.

Arturo is up. He crosses the floor in beige socks and steps outside to stretch. He and Cora had the back room to themselves. If they were shagging, they did it like thieves in a museum.

Arturo leans on the patio railing, head down, listening or thinking. The weight of stress shows in his posture. MacLeod, always a student of situations, wonders what it is that makes a man like him take on this job. He's clean-cut, fit, and has probably put in long hours doing tasks he didn't choose. The more he spoke, the less un-American his accent became. And he didn't *feel* like a terrorist, certainly not a random thug. He is more level-headed than Enrique, and he lacks the zeal or craziness of Josh. Could this be one more rueful task at someone else's request?

But who would do this? To me?

MacLeod's whole head sizzles, though, whenever he starts re-targeting the 'Why.' With little else to ponder, *that's* becoming increasingly clear.

***

They're on the move in a world of green and shadows.

For a pleasant flash, it was reminiscent of a college roadtrip. A power bar for breakfast (coconut-flavored), the gathering of stuff into bags, a trip to the outhouse (ignore the scorpion guts), no tree-branch quickie for Arturo and Cora (a pity) and they were off.

Enrique was happy to gag him again. Then he pulled the hood up to hide MacLeod from aerial and satellite surveillance. It felt unnecessary.

If anyone is looking for me. Doesn't this shit happen all the time? Even to Americans?

Ten yards to the left, the trees thin out and the land opens to a dry, brown hillside. Occasional palms dot the slope. Arturo wisely keeps them under the canopy. Though the scrubby hill—*Colombia?*—would make for easier travel, there's no reason to take risks. There could be more helicopters today.

Occasional thoughts of prayer have been dismissed sardonically. Though his mother and grandmother tried, none of the MacLeod kids took to religion. The world was full of worthwhile distractions, and—for a kid unusually versed in history—there were too many on-stage tragedies to believe a play director held sway. (The most he would acknowledge was an audience member throwing peanuts or Molotov cocktails.)

By the time he entered high school, MacLeod probably couldn't have been converted at all. Tabloid tales of Ye Old Virgin appearing in a block of Havarti and a man hearing celestial horns from a bagpipe-shaped cloud added a comical tinge to any such thoughts on faith.

Not much room for it in Emma's life, either. She might be praying for me, though.

Should a mighty deity be willing to show up and get him out of this mess, he'd consider renouncing atheism. Foolishness could be debated in degrees of severity. For now, he's got an endless trek among earthy smells.

He rolls his head around until little joints crack. The normalcy of it feels good. As if on cue, Josh comes up next to him. "Hey," he says, "that quad step-over against Calcavechia last week. You're a freak of nature. Godlike skills."

MacLeod's gag is still in—Josh isn't going to disobey Arturo again—so he chooses to accept a one-sided conversation. He gives Josh a nod of gratitude. The others aren't paying attention.

"So tell us about the money, man. I want to hear the juicy stuff. This year, you're making, what, *seven* million or something?"

Must be right. Dollars or pounds?

He thinks about it, then nods.

"So, you have a contract, but do you ever go out there and say to yourself, 'If I put it in the goal this game, that's an extra two hundred thousand!'? Is that right?"

He's on a roll, and he's obviously done the math. The captive needs to keep it friendly, so he nods and shrugs.

"Don't you have nineteen goals this season?"

MacLeod jerks his head up to increase. This is a number he knows with certainty.

"Twenty goals! Twenty-one? That's crazy, man. Ripping! I wonder what the record is."

Big head-jigs this time, even though it must look ridiculous. He glances up to see if Cora's laughing.

"Thirty?" Josh asks. "Thirty-five?"

Jamieson Dobbs finished last season with thirty-two—an absolutely stunning campaign with Man City. MacLeod had to just wave in his rearview mirror—even with a four-goal performance at Newcastle. Still, everyone was rooting for Dobbs by the end of the season, and the lucky bounces kept coming his way. Relegation-bait Crystal Palace and Stoke didn't even have that many as *teams* last year.

"That game at Everton, where you had a hat trick? You must've seen something, because you scored on them in the second minute."

MacLeod doesn't recall in particular. Probably the one in December, in weather—his first hat trick since coming back from injury. It must've been pretty sweet—maybe the Everton defender was favoring a foot—though it's no surprise he can't remember the exact particulars. There were other things in his life, too.

Josh is elated now, carrying on. "Scoring goals, getting girls, smiling for the camera. Oh, what about the endorsements? I got to hear this," he says.

How long do I have to keep it up for this psycho?

MacLeod nods and shrugs. The endorsements *are* astounding. Half a million to stand around a bathroom set and repeat 'Rich, delectable lather,' until the voice and words were just right. Never a great voice, never an actor. They had a girl show him the proper way to spread gel on his face (twenty minutes for that, alone) so half the women in Surrey would buy it for their husbands. "Do your gig, sign your papers, take it to the bank," they'd said.

At least, he knows, a bunch of that money went to charitable causes.

"Get paid to look good. Get paid to tie your own boots. Ah, nice!" Josh spreads his arms wide, as if he's been hearing his own conversation on the subject. "And now, think of the endorsement money, man! Out here with us on this adventure! 'This is the brand shirt I was wearing when those guys kidnapped me! Eddie Bauer jeans, they'll take you on an adventure!' 'They'll take you places!' You could be the biggest star the world's ever seen. Hollywood movies, the whole thing!"

Career advice from a man who got down and dirty with a corpse, yesterday. This couldn't be stranger.

Enrique gives them a look like he's tired of hearing them "talk."

Josh sees it too, because he drops back to be with Cora. They start chatting quietly in French. MacLeod doesn't know a single word of French beyond 'merci' and 'croissant.' He tunes them out for a while.

Without the ability to scream out loud—and knowing how absurdly ineffective it would be—he returns to the parade of what-ifs marching through his mind.

What if...what if...what if...

As complicated as it all was, there was also rebar-rigid certainty in his past. He'd toed the line all his life, hadn't he?

Chapter 9

After a brief leg atop a ridge crest—views of the snow-capped Andes to one side, a green land of stark contours and Mayan ruins to the other—the forest path levels out ahead of them. MacLeod, thoroughly sick of the gag and the restrictive band on his legs, has been allowed to suffer these in silence. The others have been chatting, tales of college antics and thievery in Antwerp and 'Chess-key Something-or-other.'

Suddenly Arturo stops, his fist raised. Everyone freezes. Enrique glowers back to the rest, calling for silence. MacLeod has an itch in his throat—a rogue glob of phlegm that won't cooperate. He tries to clear it quietly, which is nearly impossible with the gag. A coughing fit will probably bring Enrique's swinging fists.

This time, there's no signal to depart the path. Arturo creeps forward without his gun or bag. He comes to something close to the ground, at a spot between two trees. The item must be tiny. Whatever he's looking at, MacLeod's twenty-ten vision can't pick it up.

What, does the guy have jungle eyes?

Arturo peers at it from several angles, his feet planted wide. He is definitely steering clear of something.

Oh God, is it a mine?

Arturo's investigation continues, slowly scanning up and down.

"It's a tripwire," Enrique whispers, as Josh and Cora have crept up.

"For a mine?" Josh asks, excited.

Mines: Devices set in the ground or by a tree, designed specifically to blow off a leg or fill the victim with shrapnel. Mines: Boom...instant pain...agony...realization of blood-loss and loss of mobility...victim screwed...death not coming quickly. Mines: Cambodia, "Platoon," "Bat-21." Get me the fuck out of here!

"No, I think it's a sensor."

"For who?" MacLeod asks through the gag. It doesn't come out as much. Enrique looks at him, as if surprised he's piped up.

"Rebels, most likely."

Rebels?

"Rebels," Cora repeats. "Fuck. They must've expanded."

Josh says, "Or we're on the fringe and they just want to know what's creeping about."

"That's probably all it is," Enrique says.

All the way out here?

"How?"

"It's battery-operated. You trip the wire, it sends a signal like a text message. Don't you know anything, MacLeod?"

Well, no. In my part of the world, we settle territory disputes with things called pens and lawyers and free kicks.

"How far away could they be?" Cora asks.

"These days, you can probably pick up a signal within a hundred kilometers."

"Oh, that's good," Josh says. "Do you think the rebels are, you know, fifty kilometers away?"

Enrique gives him a sneer, like he's the most naïve fellow in town. "No, Amigo. More like five."

***

Why not kill me in Panama, if that's what they wanted? Easier than marching me up this god-awful road.

The vision again—the man trapped in the smelly steel tank. He's banging his sledgehammer against the wall. He wants out, he wants answers. What *really* doesn't add up?

All things considered, this scenic march takes a thousand times' the effort of a couple bullets. Whoever he's meeting at the end must be quite important—as *he* is clearly that important to this mystery person.

Too late to hope this is all an elaborate practical joke, like that movie-in-a-movie in Vietnam.

They made it past the tripwire—Arturo didn't tamper with it—and haven't seen another one since. The reasoning was sound, Enrique explained. Many such devices send a signal with the loss of power. So if their leader *had* popped the batteries out of the sensor box, it would've been the same as activating the tripwire. The rebels would know.

Rebels. You've got to be kidding me. These idiots didn't know we're trying to sneak through rebel territory? Even more brilliant, Arturo!

They've stopped again, within sight of a rope bridge over a river. Before them, the ribbon is black in shadowy sunlight. MacLeod steps to the right, and mentally marks it off as thirty-two feet of bridge, twenty-four over water. He knows this distance well. Skid marks in the Carlson wreck measured exactly

69

thirty-two feet—one foot for each day that poor Lucille clung to life via a ventilator, before succumbing, in the aftermath.

Thoughts of escape disappear as burst bubbles. The water's too still. It isn't muddy and swift, with boulders he could cling to and evade gunfire. Bullets pinging, freedom purchased by wet exhaustion—the way it happens in the movies. Clearly, that's not happening today.

Arturo is getting bundled rope out of his bag, his gaze fixed on the other shore. The rope bridge itself is two parallel lines with a third one below. The one they're going to traverse is knotted and tied to the support lines here and there.

Looks like the Boy Scouts of Latin America put this baby together. Your Honor, may we have a sanity test on this one? Tomorrow works better.

Without breaking his focus, Arturo unknots a length of red climbing rope and hands it to Cora. Following his look, MacLeod can't see anything in the weeds beneath the bridge's other side.

"Crocodiles," Enrique tells them. "Two of them, sleeping."

Crocodiles? Don't make me do this.

Arturo has tied the climbing rope around his brother's waist. Cora adjusts the slack and turns MacLeod around. Tightening up the gap, she ties the rope around him. Another adjustment, and he and Enrique are so close they are practically spooning.

"You and me, Bro," he sneers in MacLeod's ear. His foul breath and body odor are powerful. "Step carefully."

Arturo has shouldered both bags, now, to be the first to cross. He glances at MacLeod, displaying his gun. The silencer's hole looks too small for a bullet to exit.

"No fucking around," he says, firing a round into the bush. The rapid dart-gun sound makes MacLeod flinch.

Arturo holds the barrel up close to MacLeod's right eye. "Comprendes, Señor?"

The heat is comfortably close. MacLeod nods quickly, certain his eye could be burned out or melted for disagreement. He'd do anything to avoid that.

Arturo steps onto the rope bridge. Gun in his right hand, left on the rope. He steps slowly, his feet perpendicular to the rope. To MacLeod, the world feels deceptively quiet. A distant bird, the rubbing of the rope against the anchoring tree trunk from Arturo's movement. It has worn the grayish bark thin, though the trunk itself is eighteen inches thick.

"Our turn," Enrique says.

Arturo is off the bridge by the time MacLeod and Enrique, as a pair, edge their way up to it. It reminds MacLeod of the fourth-grade lunch line, when the jerk behind him was so close it made sense to turn and throw a fist. Except, this time, it's life and death. He ducks under the near rope, focused on the mossy boulder underfoot. Enrique is clenching a handful of his hoodie at the left shoulder, his body right behind.

With his tied hands confined under the sweatshirt, MacLeod can't grab anything. Mimicking Arturo, he sets his feet across the walking rope. Leaning forward against the line is a leap of faith. Enrique presses against him and grabs the support rope with his hand. His knuckles go white.

Fuck, I'm Bambi on ice. This is ludicrous.

Breathing and concentration are difficult. With a nudge, he starts sliding his feet left, one at a time, to make his way across. On the far side, Arturo pushes in against the near rope. The effect is that MacLeod is sidling with his body at a 45-degree angle, knots and imperfections drawing across his chest.

"Steady," Enrique says. "You don't want to go in that water."

Comprendo, Bro. I'd fucking drown.

His thoughts run to how a man could possibly tread water with his hands down by his crotch. It simply can't be done for long. But his captors have chosen security over pragmatism. He knows both buckets. Still, he's never imagined weighing such choices while navigating a rope bridge in Colombia.

Over the water, now. Slide…breathe…slide…breathe.

Why doesn't Arturo just shoot those lizards, and we wouldn't have to worry about them anymore? He's got a silencer on that thing!

"Keep moving."

Then again, MacLeod wonders if it wouldn't be better if they all get across without disturbing the crocodiles. Still no sign of them.

Slide…breathe…slide…breathe.

At his shoulder, Enrique grunts with effort. It probably takes a lot of strength to do what he's doing—holding a man steady and upright while crossing a handhold bridge.

"Stay focused," Enrique hisses.

MacLeod concentrates on progress, tales of others' corporate-retreat obstacle courses in mind. Those would have laughter and beverages. Finally, Arturo grips the front of his hoodie. MacLeod edges his way off the line and down onto the black soil. Relief washes over him. Enrique takes his leash, panting.

"Bueno, Señor," he whispers. "You live another day."

He rotates his arm, looking tired. No sympathy for him, though. No admiration.

Cora is across, stepping like a cat. It's likely that she's been trained, like the brothers. Josh too, MacLeod figures, watching the fifth member of the party begin across.

It'd be a shame if some crocodile leapt up and snapped his leg off, wouldn't it?

This doesn't happen. Cora has started untying the rope around Enrique, leash tucked under arm. It wouldn't matter if she did MacLeod's part, first. He has no power to run, at the moment. He *wouldn't* run.

The day after his father left—his mother had found the note that afternoon, then flopped over the Formica counter and wailed—MacLeod saw a punishment being exacted at school. A fifth grader had stepped out of line, apparently. From the hall, he could feel Mr. Belmont's anger. He had the boy by the ear, dragging him across the top of a desk and out to the hall. "Had enough of your bullshit, Durandel!" The *unnatural* sound of a desk scraping the floor was surrounded by awed silence and Durandel's grunts. MacLeod turned and speed-walked back to his kindergarten class. A paddle was coming out and he didn't want to be around to hear it.

MacLeod returns to the present, the jungle. Arturo is alarmed—fixed stare, gun moving robotically forward. It must be the menace by the water, though MacLeod still can't see them.

Josh is halfway across. He's not going to be eaten today. Cora calmly tucks the climbing rope back into one of the bags. She whispers into Arturo's ear with a smile.

Suddenly, he shifts his aim at a spot near the water.

Josh has frozen, staring. Cora pulls MacLeod away as Enrique reaches for his own weapon.

Phew-phew-phew! Phew-phew! Phew-phew-phew!

MacLeod flinches at the noise—destruction so incredibly close to his own body. Arturo steps forward, firing again.

Phew-phew!

He edges forward, with Enrique behind him and ready to spray the place. Arturo's hand pushes aside his brother's AK-47.

"Muerto," Josh gushes, hurrying over.

"Fuck," Arturo bursts. He bangs his gun against a tree.

Josh looks on, enthralled.

"They must've woken up," Cora says. "Come."

She guides MacLeod forward, around a tree. The roots are thick, making for awkward steps with the band.

She wants me to see this. Another lovely display, my fault.

On a muddy bank shrouded by reeds, two eight-foot crocodiles lie still with tails in the water. The near one looks intact, save for three holes in its head and a dark pool beneath. The other, from the 'arms' forward, is a mess of brown flesh, blood splatter and raspberry-colored body parts. It is how MacLeod has imagined an animal, or person, would look after facing a machine gun. Imagination meets reality: Muscle, bone and fat are nothing compared to the rage of mile-a-second metal cones. He knows *that* much about firearms.

The first time he saw a live demonstration, his Uncle Mortimer had blown a bottle to pieces in Scotland. It simply disappeared. Nothing was left on the log, green shards in the weeds.

"Can we skin them? That's worth a lot," Josh says.

74

Arturo still has his gun drawn, pointed upriver. "No."

"Too bad. That's a minor travesty, man."

"Maybe you'd like to deflower one, this time," Enrique says.

There's laughter, everyone but Arturo. MacLeod hides a smile.

Josh spreads his hands. "I don't even know where the hole is. Somewhere in the rear, I guess," he cackles.

"Should we bury them," Cora asks.

Arturo looks back at her. "Too much time. We're exposed, here. Enrique," he says, gesturing.

Enrique follows his brother's look. Quickly, he fetches a fallen tree branch. He and Josh use it to push the first corpse into the river. Judging by their grunts, it weighs a lot.

"Come on. Rápido!"

The first one slides under the black water. They work on the second.

"A fun little encounter with the local wildlife," Cora remarks, amused.

MacLeod wonders if she and Josh met in a horror movie special-effects class.

"There could be more," Arturo says, checking his clip and reloading, like a professional.

The second croc goes in. Left behind is a dark-stained patch of mud, which Enrique tamps down with his boot.

Is that good enough? If someone was tracking us, would they notice this concealed patch of violence?

75

But who in the hell would be tracking you, Hero?

"Let's move!"

MacLeod sets his jaw, his thoughts now on a trail of carnage in their wake.

Chapter 10

At the hospital's physical therapy wing, MacLeod hobbled in on crutches and paused to take in the training room. His first day. A number of weight blocks and resistance machines hummed with malice. The ones for legwork were closer, chanting. He chewed his cheek in anticipation. But if not for this, he might not walk right again—to say nothing about kicking a soccer ball.

The motivational posters on the walls—beauties and Atlases and athletes grimacing with effort—could do little to distract from the cold white and chrome metal of the machines. MacLeod looked down at his right knee encased in a black neoprene sleeve. They were in this together, him and his knee.

"Good morning," came a cheerful, energetic voice.

He found a dark-haired woman coming over with a clipboard. Pretty eyes, inviting lips, also six-foot-one.

"Arhea," she said, extending a hand. "I'll be your physical therapist for the next six weeks."

He shook her hand. Strong grip. "I'm—"

"MacLeod, yes, I know," she explained with a smile. "Pleasure to meet you. Now," she started, her makeup-brush eyebrows lowering, "this is going to be tough. It isn't for pussies. I will push you. I will make you sweat and cry and shout obscenities like an animal. I will make you *hate* me," she added, with an expression that said she'd like nothing better than to hump his face or hump his jock. "But we'll get through this together. You toe the line, bam, you walk out of here like the six-million-dollar man in forty-two days. I do my job, you do what I say, and you get to go back to doing what it is you do best. Sound good?"

"Okay, Arhea. Am I saying that right?"

"Yup. It's like a pirate stammering. Arr—hey—uh, but all run together. Right?" She slapped the seat of a leg-lift machine. "Come on, game time."

He gave her a look. The souped-up machine had air hoses and thick cushions. The eyes in his repaired knee, however, bellowed that it was still a torture device in disguise. A last whimper. He started hobbling over.

"You can do it," she said, as if to a child. "Tell ya a secret about me. I was playing keeper once, college intramurals game. I dove to block a shot, and mistimed it big-time, 'cause I blocked it with my schnoz. See?" She pointed to a crook in her nose. "Talk about humiliating. I was prettier before that shot."

He paused, nervous. "I-I think you're plenty beautiful, now."

Arhea grinned and adjusted her stance. "Sweet. Flattery's nice, but it won't get you out of this. Come on."

Things were still busted. Only he, with Arhea's help, could repair them. He lowered himself into the seat, wishing he'd brought a towel to bite into. Leg into position. Deep breath.

The exercise was the voluntary grinding of biological stones in his leg. Enough willpower to finish, not enough to keep from crying in front of a total stranger. First step on a long road.

***

Hours from the bridge, MacLeod can still smell the sharp metallic scent of Arturo's weapon. It's a singular detail enhanced by the monotony. They're simply traveling, one foot in front of the other over reddish earth in a green world. Miles of it.

78

At some point, they passed within sight of a helicopter's carcass—vines hanging from rotor blades, part of the hull turned mossy, being reclaimed by the jungle. Nobody paused to gloat or proselytize or mourn. Another dead piece of the world in their wake.

Soon, they're crossing an open, brownish valley between walls of *verde*. Palm trees sway on the hillsides. To MacLeod, the place suddenly seems as wide-open as the Atacama Desert in that IMAX film. It's impossible, isn't it? Seven billion souls on the planet—untold millions relatively nearby to the south—and nobody else is *here*. No cars, no planes, no glass towers of office denizens ready to proclaim they love their work, their company, their fine country.

Here, there is only quiet, dry solitude licked by breeze. It feels bizarrely normal—the shrubs and rocks untroubled by malice, clothing decisions, spent cartridges. A party of misfits gets easy passage to the music of remoteness. Even their pace is killing him—no hurry, no concern, taking their sweet time. Five people walking the earth, that's all.

MacLeod swallows against the warm air. He could use more water—his saliva long gone thanks to the once-floppy chew toy. When he wriggles his mandible, pain explains the severity of chafing on his lips. This moment, like every other for the past sixty hours, is an instance he can't have imagined happening in his life, to him.

Yes, one day, you will wake up a hostage to others' whims and menace, and strangers will take you on a hellacious journey.

There's no lifeline, no one to call. One thing he has come to understand, after a cynical schooling in economics and political willpower: Nobody's coming to save him. He sighs into the breeze.

No way out.

Fear gives way to fantasy. A great storm crashing down to carry it all off—these thugs, the lying politicians, the Columbus teenage driver who wiped out a family because she was too busy Snapchatting her boyfriend, the hard hats and excavators and dump trucks and flag men from that traffic-snarling project on Giles St. (the one that seemed to exist only to prevent him from getting home after a thirteen-hour day to reach Emma's pure grace and bizarrely-*knowing* Korean eyes). All of it could go, should go. A twisting, churning correction on the life he had—a wiping of the slate.

Cora's sharp eyes are looking back at him in amusement. She and Arturo are in the lead, his hand cupping her posterior.

A pleasant, friendly couple—not a damned care in the world.

She faces forward and there's quiet laughter, a lover's joke. The storm disappears from thought. Palm fronds are rattling uphill. Puffs of cottony cloud laze in slow transit. Great emerald stalks of bamboo approach, beckoning with shady whispers.

MacLeod takes in all the calm incorrectness of this world. Deep within him, his sigh seems to rattle skeleton bones in a chilly cave.

Can't some horrible tempest come along and free me?

Chapter 11

"So what happened with that Chilean keeper you were romancing? Renata."

It takes MacLeod a second to return to the tedious if lush world of his present state. Josh and Enrique have been carrying on for what feels like hours. He's been relatively happy to be left out of the conversation, so his sudden inclusion by a madman catches him off-guard. When the name rises to the surface—with it, a pretty face—it is paired with insult.

How does he know so much?

Playing it cool, he shrugs and nods.

"The sports rag said she was tall. Six-three, right," Josh asks. "What was that like? Was she on top all the time?"

This time, he offers an exuberant nod.

"I've never had Latina snatch before. I bet it's spicy—all those fire peppers, m-hm. Hey Rique, what's Chilean pussy like?"

From behind, Cora snickers.

Enrique says, "You couldn't handle it. Eat you up, East Bloc."

The two men cackle.

As MacLeod turns to glance back at the female representative, a whistle draws his attention forwards.

"Wow, look at that! A palace."

"That's the spot, man."

MacLeod follows Josh's gaze to a stunningly white structure. They are skirting a lake on the right. Across an arm of water, about a quarter-mile away, sits a grand vacation house. It has gutters, windows with glass and a deck with railings.

Whose house is this? Someone else who's about to die?

"Do you think there's piranhas in there, Enrique? Maybe we go for a swim, eh? Cool off a little?"

Enrique smiles back, having located his sense of humor after yesterday's growling. It could've been the stress, MacLeod figures. His sister doesn't travel well, all anxiety and anger. On road trips as a kid, it would be hours before she ditched her crabbiness and became human.

They pass under a fat snake crossing a high branch. It's no stretch for a captive to imagine the beast dropping on Cora— a well-deserved moment of entertainment. Would he have the stones to shout, "You scream like a girl!?" Cora might just *eat* the thing.

Arturo has them wait off-trail while he checks out the house. It isn't long before he's back and pulling a key ring from his duffel bag. MacLeod ponders this detail while they approach. Keys mean more than permission, in his book.

The house has two floors, a deck that overlooks the lake, and lights. A mesh metal gate separates the house from the path and shore—to keep out the local wildlife.

"Very nice," Josh says. For once, MacLeod agrees with him.

Still, it seems a bit foolish to have a place all the way out here, alone, with no real road access. The building materials and furniture would've been boated in. There are no other structures visible, no other sign of any village or town nearby. The heat and the scent of sunlight on painted wood takes MacLeod back to the real world. This *is* a palace compared to the first place, he would

82

agree, and it makes even less sense than their first accommodations.

Cora plops down on a bench and tilts her face toward the late-afternoon sun.

'Quite a bit o' eye candy,' MacLeod's teammate Ryan would say.

How does a woman like that *get mixed up in a bad job like this? How did she* become *Cora?*

"No lights," Arturo reports, disappearing inside.

"We don't need to use the generator and attract attention," Enrique explains.

Josh lifts an open hand in confusion, looking about. There's nothing else man-made within sight. He chooses not to point out their obvious isolation, though.

"Fine," Cora says, eyes closed and face placid.

Josh shrugs and leads MacLeod inside through the deck's sliding glass doors. The house's modern amenities don't disappoint—a real kitchen, a den with a TV and couches, and pottery on the walls. To the right is a kind of picnic table with an orange tablecloth. Sensing a spot of freedom, MacLeod takes a seat in the cooler shadow.

The men have dropped their bags on the tile floor, and the heavy, dark shapes of their weapons call to him. Ideas come to mind, though they are absurd ones. Even if he could get his hands free, what then? Grab a gun and hide by the fireplace, or under the end table with the ridiculous white elephant lamp? What he 'learned' from Uncle Mortimer all those years ago— essentially squat—covers what he knows about using firearms. He's never *wanted* to know. No, MacLeod will *not* be *going all S.A.S.* on anybody today.

This place's vacation-home normalcy is too surreal to allow proper focus, anyway. Decorations on the fireplace, books on the den shelves. It's as if someone helicoptered in their Lake Eerie guesthouse and dropped it randomly on a map.

"Need to hit the loo?" Josh asks him.

A real toilet.

MacLeod shakes his head. Josh nods and attaches the leash to a wrought-iron coat rack behind MacLeod. Arturo has left the room, but Enrique stands guard in the doorway.

When Josh returns, he rifles through one of the kitchen drawers and finds something he likes.

"Now, while we're here in this nice house, I must remind you that we're a long way from help, right? A long way. Still, no screaming. No shouting into a radio or anything, right?"

MacLeod nods. He watches Josh lift the item from the kitchen drawer. It's a meat hammer.

"I want to believe you. You seem like such an honest fellow. All those interviews. However, precautions are good. So, if you do call out, maybe I just—whap!—smash one finger for you. Just a little tap. Quite painful."

He makes a quick motion with the hammer. MacLeod flinches against his will.

"I saw it in one of your American spy films. So bad. The hero was screaming. Very bad. But I really don't want to do that because you are beautiful and it would be a shame to hurt you. So, no screamy, no whappy, okay?"

MacLeod nods furiously, certain this lunatic needs little incentive to carry out a trial run.

"Excellent. I'm happy we understand one another. We've made progress," he adds, spreading his hands and bringing them together like a priest. He replaces the meat hammer and departs.

Enrique peruses the books and magazines. Arturo steps outside and gets on the satellite phone. MacLeod watches him pace by Cora, wondering who he's talking to and why this apparent boss has risked so much to pull all this together. Even for a low-tech operation like this, the cost-benefit ratio feels like it must be unpalatable.

Then a sneaky feeling creeps to the fore again—the one saying this hasn't got a thing to do with money.

"Enrique," Josh calls from outside.

"Qué?"

"Fútbol! Bring the superhero!"

Superhero. Me?

Enrique is suddenly giddy, unhooking MacLeod's leash from the coat rack. "Vámanos," he says, pulling him up. MacLeod's neck aches, rubbed raw in places.

"What, a live demonstration?" Cora says, watching them emerge from the house.

Arturo mutters something and pulls the phone away from his ear. "Wait wait wait," he says. He soon clomps after them—Cora does, too—out to a little clearing on the far side of the house.

Showtime!

Josh is checking for snakes in the grass. An acid green soccer ball sits nearby, still shiny-new from the factory. Arturo goes to the far end and assumes a post with his gun. This, as MacLeod sees it, is unnecessary. Any inclination to attempt escape is squelched, flattened, diced. Like any sensible captive, he supposes, the idea of running is locked firmly in 'preposterous.' How far could he realistically get, anyway?

"Hold still," Josh says, sliding a warm item up between MacLeod's cheek and the gag. With a slight pull, the gag falls away from his face, severed by a butterfly knife. Josh puts the gag and knife with his jacket in the grass. He and Enrique are down to T-shirts.

"Charity," Enrique observes. "Okay, okay."

MacLeod's mouth is free, cool and dry by comparison. He looks around their small pitch, all in shade. In the hoodie, he knows from experience, he'll get hot quickly.

Although it could provide a decent excuse if I don't perform well.

No, he'd rather have the freedom. It's time to play a card.

"Cora, do you mind, please? I'll burn up in this thing."

She gives him a look, a slight twitch in her smile. "I do *not* mind," she answers, setting her handgun down in the grass. "A pity I didn't bring my Ben Wa balls on this trip." She pulls his sweatshirt off and unclips the leash cord. Next, the PT band comes off. She whistles at him, collecting her weapon.

"Christ, again with the shirtless," Enrique complains. "Does he have to?"

"Don't be challenged by his manliness, Rique," Cora says. "He gets paid to run fifty miles a week."

Enrique mumbles something. In the distance, his brother smirks.

MacLeod rubs his knees and takes slow lateral strides, afloat with this shining moment of kindness.

"For safekeeping," Cora remarks, throwing the band around his neck.

He nods, ready to accept the sweaty-rubber smell for eternity if it means he can remain in this state.

Is this what Stockholm Syndrome feels like? A bunch of humans mutually trapped in a regrettable situation giving up their roles and reverting to being humans again?

Doubt it. Josh isn't human. I don't know what Cora is— her own species, temptress insanus. *Arturo's just anger incarnated.*

Josh sends the ball. Enrique works it between his feet. "So, you think you can play this game, huh?"

Todos los días, Motherfucker.

MacLeod picks it up casually, juggles it on alternating feet and then his thighs. It feels natural, like *home*.

"Is that all you can do?" Enrique asks. "Where's the seal, the nose?"

MacLeod bounces it on his forehead a few times and over to him. "I was never much good at party tricks. Leave that to the show-boaters."

"That right?" Enrique challenges. He heels it to Josh, who does better juggling than one would predict from his long-haired rattiness.

Crazy Camp has skills.

Josh lofts it back so MacLeod can cradle it in mid-air, switch feet, up to his chest, and juggle it on his thighs. He sends it back to Enrique, glad he hasn't messed up, yet. One coach joked that the pros could do this kind of stuff in their sleep. Like it demonstrates real mastery over the ball, over the physics of the game.

No, party tricks don't. Mastery comes when you can work the ball like your foot is a spatula, turning and pushing at will until you put the ball in exactly the right spot at your teammate's feet.

They start. MacLeod runs them ragged as they try to steal the ball away. Josh laughs and swears like mad. "Jesus." "Fucker!" "Your mother teach you this in the womb?" "Aye-aye-aye! Had you, you *kretén!*"

Enrique likes it, too, but says nothing. He's persistent, he's got zeal. The way he bounces left and right, trying to get the ball without stomping on MacLeod's ankle—which he could do, no yellow card. He's got to win it the honest way, MacLeod believes.

"Goddammit," he swears when MacLeod heels it to himself between his legs and spins around, the fifth time this session.

"Vanquished," Josh announces finally, flopping in the grass.

They're all sweaty, satisfied with a warm-up sheen.

Mental note to coaches: The tied-hands stuff is great for training. You can't use your arms for leverage (or balance).

In the E.P.L., he knows, a lot of yellow cards are shown for grabby hands.

Immediately, Cora comes to put the restrictive band back on MacLeod's legs, above the knees. He hides disappointment, stretching. When he finishes, he finds Arturo standing right before him. Arms crossed, gun in hand.

Do I say something now? Would it set him off? Or would it give me a better chance of getting out of here?

"Bueno, MacLeod. I suppose I should say, 'Thank you for exercising the men.' Or 'You have amazing skills. We are

88

fortunate to be among your *magnificence.*' Something along those lines?"

"No, sir."

Do it. Try!

"'Sir'?" Arturo's eyes are wide in surprise, flashing threat. "Why do you use 'Sir'? Why would you call me that? Out of sarcasm?" A smile has crept into his lips.

He's smiling. Things are going south. Do something.

"I-I'm used to doing it. As a sign of respect. Arturo, please, I'm not who you think I am."

"You are MacLeod."

"No, I'm—"

He's cut off by the leash choking his neck. He coughs, turning to find Cora, who wears a wicked smirk. "Sorry, Darling," she says. "We don't want you to enjoy too much freedom. And we all have reasons for being here."

MacLeod opens his mouth when the hoodie goes over his head again. He's a man returned to his prison. Pressure makes him look up. Arturo is resting his gun arm on MacLeod's collar. The muzzle taps against the lower corner of his skull.

"Would you repeat that? Something about a mistake? Mm? You think I make mistakes. Is that right?"

His insane eyes seem to beg for a fight. Clarity comes to MacLeod, sharp and cruel as a man banging his hammer on a steel wall.

If I tell him, and he believes me, he'll just blow my head off right here. They'll bury me out here just like they buried those druggies. Nobody will ever know what's happened to me. Emma will never know...

No, I can't do that. I'll toe the line. I'll play the game, become one with the lie.

A drop of sweat crawling down MacLeod's nose prompts him to clear his throat. "I'm sorry, I was mistaken. It won't happen again."

"Bueno," Arturo whispers. "Bueno."

At last, he withdraws.

MacLeod narrows his eyes, prepared to feel the metal chunk bang into the side of his head. It doesn't come. When he turns, trembling, Enrique has his leash.

Is there a choice, here?

Chapter 12

After dinner—more bars—Arturo changed his mind and cranked up the generator. There's canned soup and chili in the kitchen cupboards, and a microwave. Not for them, though. The leader has his reasons. After this afternoon, MacLeod is more willing to accept this behavior as immutable. They let him have two bars, as if in gratitude for the workout.

Enrique has turned on the flat-screen TV and is flipping around. MacLeod watches from the picnic table, drawn to evidence that there is, indeed, a world out there, again. Latin soccer…soaps…mop commercial…news.

Arturo looks at his watch. "Diez," he mutters.

Enrique nods, clicking. "Donde…qué número…?"

Beside him on the couch, Cora is reading under a lamp. Her book has a scholarly cover.

"Mitch MacLeod," an abbreviated voice announces in English. MacLeod looks up. The channel is CNN. The footage cuts to a sky-blue and white airplane, with numerous soldiers standing in formation at the foot of the stairs. President Palmer, in cargo pants and a blue sweatshirt, descends toward them, looking stern.

"President Palmer wasted no time in canceling his appearance at the Southland Economic Summit so he could travel to Panama. Air Force One touched down less than thirty minutes ago, carrying a U.S. President who admits to being quote-unquote 'deeply concerned.' He is currently in talks with the Panamanian leadership about what has been called both a security fiasco and an international embarrassment."

Enrique chuckles. "They're talking about you, Amigo."

The coverage switches back to the studio, where a gorgeous Indian gal in magenta addresses the camera. "Once again, just to update those of you who, uh, have not heard the latest: U.S. Men's team star Mitch MacLeod has gone missing from his hotel in Panama. There are reports that he was at Sol de los Trópico dance club the night before he disappeared, near the Panama City hotel where the men's team was staying. The team was competing in a World Cup qualifier against the Panama National Team. Local authorities have locked down the city in their efforts. Sources tell us there *may* be a link between this, uh, event and an apartment fire which ripped through a building in Caucasia, Colombia this morning, killing three people. Once again, that is only speculation, at this point. For more, let's turn to our law enforcement correspondent in studio, Kellen Mercer. Kellen, can you shed some light on all the speculation?"

The camera pans to a tall African-American man in a beige suit. Standing before a wall of image panels, he resembles a law professor.

"Yes, Isha, I can. Of course, there is much speculation at this point, so early in the, uh, the case or the disappearance, rather. But a Pentagon source has reported that SEAL Team Six departed from an undisclosed location this morning. One can only assume that they have already landed on the Central American isthmus, presumably in Panama.

"We also know that General Manuel Herrera, the chief of national security for Panama, telephoned both Senator Murray, who was already on-site, and the White House, pledging utmost support and cooperation with the investigation. We also know MacLeod's tw—"

The screen flicks off. Cora sets down the remote, glancing at MacLeod. Enrique leans back, idly working on something in his teeth.

"That news lady was hot," Josh remarks. "Isha. Reminds me of a woman in the Czech Chamber. Vice Minister of the Interior, something like that. The smile, curly red hair. She liked to wear these navy-blue dresses, they were a little snug on her *prdel*. Beautiful!"

"She's your lady, huh?" Enrique asks.

"You got it, Bro. As soon as we're done with this business, I've got a date with her. Candlelit Italian dinner by the clock with the cellos going. Perfecto," he adds, kissing his fingers.

You're crackers, MacLeod thinks, hiding a smirk.

"Does she know you're coming?" Cora asks, still looking at her book.

"Oh," Josh says, puffing his chest out, "her kitchen door is *never* locked to me!"

The three of them laugh.

The lights go out. No one reacts. Somewhere in the house, a humming noise has ceased. MacLeod didn't realize it was there until it stopped. His eyes adjust to the dimness, assigning colors to muted tones. Outside, the sky is a medium-tone blue. Arturo comes in the patio doors, pulls down a mosquito net and zips it. With a last searching sweep of the darkness, he closes the door and locks it.

Cora drops onto the bench next to MacLeod, setting her book on the table.

So much for a game of chess.

He stifles a sigh and glances at her book. "What's that you're reading?"

"Tirole, the economist. You know economics?"

"Not a thing." It's a half-lie.

93

"Market shifts, the minimum wage, the rise of women in the marketplace."

"Oh, okay."

"Much of it is pure shit, of course. Half the time, I say, 'What does this guy really know?' It's all speculation, anyway. The gap between theory and reality is the width of the Atlantic."

An odd bird sound comes from outside. Josh has gotten up to busy himself. MacLeod hopes Enrique follows suit.

"What about you? You went to university, right?" Cora asks.

"Yes, I did."

"And what did you study, there? Aside from football. They wouldn't give that to you as a degree, I hope."

In the expanding darkness, her expression carries a warning.

This isn't the time.

"No, no," he tells her. "I studied physics."

"Physics? Why physics?"

The actor falls in line, stage lights ready.

"I just thought it was cool stuff. Sound and gravity and lasers. I remember how I got started. You'd laugh."

"I am a captive audience," she announces with a flourish. "Please tell the amazing story."

"Okay. So, one morning I was on the Presque Isle beach in Erie. You wouldn't know where it is. It's kind of gray and hazy, the sun is a bright dot above, the way I picture it is in Paris. Quiet and peaceful, seagulls flapping about. So I'm walking along and I feel a presence. I turn to look. Nobody behind me, to

94

the east, but overhead, like it's creeping up on me, is this *huge* jet. It was starting to bank, to turn. It made *no* sound until it was right over me. None.

"Then the wall of sound hit. It was like a roller coaster in a tunnel, it was so loud. The plane heads northwest, back out over the lake, maybe going to Chicago. And I wondered how it could be possible. *How* could that thing make no sound...or how could I *not* hear it?" He shrugs. "True story. I was hooked."

This much was all correct, if second-hand.

"Hmm, there's more to you than I would have believed. A bright-eyed boy looking up at the mysteries of the sky..."

Keep selling it.

"I don't know *what* I would've done with acoustics and lasers," he admits. "College. That seems like such a long time ago. Nine years."

"Since then, you've traveled the world, played in all kinds of games. Given your sausage to a lot of girls, I imagine?"

"A few," he tells her.

"No special lady?" Cora asks.

Faces flash before his eyes. Emma. Shruti, Michelle, Gretch Timms. Renata, with the perfectly formed mouth and playful eyes and luscious hair—the one who got away. The heartbreaker.

"No, not yet." He adjusts his seat, spinning the story. "I've been warned. You know, told not to get serious about anyone, until after."

"After what? Your playing days? Why?"

"Well, a lot can happen to a footballer in a career. What if I get transferred to Roma or Paris Saint-Germain? That mid,

95

Rohrer. The guy's in a different country every season. What if my leg goes to shit and I can't play as well, and I get relegated. Or they ship me to the States?"

Cora laughs. "There's a lot of women who would put up with that lifestyle."

"Yeah, but you make them sound like, what's the term, *gold-diggers.* I'd like a *real* woman."

"Someone who'd care about more than your glamor and her allowance?"

He looks at her, wondering what game she's playing.

Keep it up. It's the only thing keeping you alive.

"Yeah. Something like that. I mean, suppose there's a woman who's truly in love with me. She'd be going nuts right now."

Poor Emma. She must be pacing those steps up the street. Her man takes an unscheduled holiday in Latin America. She's gotta do something physical about it, up and down, up and down, sweat eclipses anxiety.

The image of her, though, sweaty and red-eyed. Like, on some level, this hasn't been real without imagining the consequences.

Like this was something I asked for!

"Truly in love," Cora snorts. "What is that?"

MacLeod shrugs with practiced nonchalance.

"My father is one of the twenty wealthiest men in France. Maybe top ten. Does it matter?" She looks distant, gazing at the wall but not seeing anything there. "You are a curious man, I can tell. You've probably been wondering what happened to my mother. Allow me to tell you a story. One

Sunday, about three years ago, my father returned early from a business trip to Tallinn. He's used to sneaking around so he doesn't wake the rabbits. He loves his rabbits. Now, what an amazing sight to walk into the study and find his wife, my mother, and his C-F-O being amorous on the couch. I suppose 'amorous' is the correct word for it. She's got his cock in her mouth.

"Now, I will admit that she was certainly a lonely woman, married to that man. My father has always had three girlfriends at once. Maybe she and Ralph Martin had a special relationship, even. I don't know. Could be this was her way of getting back at him, or it was a sunny day and she really felt like giving someone a blowjob. Who knows? I suppose it doesn't matter all that much. My father grabs her head and splits her skull against the end table. The great Antoine Fournier has a private jet and girlfriends to suck him off anytime he wants, but he sees fit to do this. To leave his wife's—*my mother's*—teeth impressions on the Roubichet table when he kills her."

Cora runs her tongue over her own front teeth, remembering. "Did my mother know what was happening? Did she think of my little brother, Robert, who passed away from spinal meningitis, as her brains were…And then," she says, perking up. "What my father does then is unbelievable. Poor Ralph is sitting there on the couch with a limp dick and her blood in his sideburns. And my father tells him: 'This is our little secret, understand? Because if you mention a word of this, I will have your wife and your three daughters boiled alive and fed to the guard dogs in Toulouse.' You Americans always like to ponder, 'Where do the monsters come from? Where are they?'" She snickers. "They've always been at home."

MacLeod swallows and forces himself to take in fresh air.

"So," Cora continues, "my mother officially dies in a dreadful SCUBA accident in the Seychelles. These things happen. C'est la vie. And poor Ralph Martin lives in thrall for three years, unable to leave, unable to say a word, knowing that four lives—those he cares about more than anything in the world—hang in the balance. At Christmas, he died of a heart attack. Good. The curse is lifted. Antoine Fournier goes on business trips with stork-legged Danielle, to the chateau in Nice, life goes on. All is good."

MacLeod glances at the couch end table with the silly elephant sculpture. "Do you mind if I ask, where were you when this...how do you know about it?"

She laughs. "I'd set up cameras for a class project. I was going to shoot my father playing with his rabbits, slowed down and set to Mozart. Imagine."

You watched the whole thing?

"I'm...s-sorry."

She makes a noise of assent. "Something else the phenomenal Mitch MacLeod could not picture happening. Not with his fame and his charities."

Images come to mind. The foster kids he's seen on a friend's laptop, the soup lines down on Taylor, refugees from Syria. "You can do good things with charities," he counters.

"Mm, I've read. You are like Midas."

He gives her a look. *Flattery from a sad psychopath.*

"Does it take effort, to step down and walk among the commoners?" she asks. "Would you ever go for a midnight stroll through a rough part of Cleveland? The real world?"

He winces at this, at being challenged by *her*.

"Sure. How could it be worse than what you're doing now?"

98

"Good," she says, smiling. "Bravery in context. Did you not anticipate this price you would pay?"

"*This?*" He glances about, at his hands in binds. "No. Did you wake up one day and decide to become a revolutionary?" When her only response is baring a few teeth, he presses. "How much are you getting paid? To get back at the world of men...or whatever?"

"Bien," she whispers. "The star shows his stripes, now. I knew they were there, underneath."

"That's right. How about a real answer, for once?"

Cora leers at him perniciously. "I get what *I* want. These men get what *they* want," she adds quietly.

"Payment," he says, trying not to choke.

"*You*. The one-and-only Mitch MacLeod."

Chapter 13

"Gandolfini's focusing all his attention on the ball. The American keeper looks lightning-rod tense. And here it is.

"For the win. Gandolfiniiiii—NO! The keeper blocks it! Unbelievable! Ball comes out to Spazzio on the right. A try—and it's blocked! Carpenter got it again! Sensational! Ball's out to Ferguson. And he's seen something 'cause he launches it. He's got a man downfield. It's MacLeod. Could this be another miracle..."

MacLeod wakes to the view of thin metal bars. Another kennel.

Can this get any worse?

Yes, of course it can. Shut the hell up.

An itch tickles his throat. He does his best to squelch it, to stay silent.

Why?

Because noise and drawing attention won't help.

***

"Betas, get in here," Missavit commanded, storming past the row of tidy desks. One of MacLeod's papers fluttered. He quickly grabbed the appropriate binder and hopped up to get in the partner's wake. At the neighboring desk, Milly Bettancourt swore and got off the line to follow. Harris and Duggan as well.

100

For six years he'd been doing this. The once-gleaming hope of environmental law had morphed into a broken-off ledge. It was somewhere behind him, high above this lava pit. The hard numbers were against him: Four hundred applicants with lengthier CVs had gone after the lone environmental opening in the area. He hadn't slogged through enough regulatory kaka to stand out, and the horizon bringing the end of his loan grace period got closer every day. Enviro was now a pipe dream. Besides, hadn't that shooting star already picked up a MacLeod for a ride?

Missavit veered into a conference room and stood by the door, so everyone had to pass his volcanic vents. The Number Three man at Cleveland's Number Two firm was such a miserable gargoyle that people cut him a wide path. 'Charming Chernobyl' usually handled the Alpha team. He got kicks (one could presume, lacking an evidentiary smile) out of intimidating the Alphas and reminding the Betas of their lesser status.

Though he had no desire to see more of this golem—the short-cropped hair and perpetual scowl—MacLeod assumed promotion to the Alphas would happen soon. He'd done everything anyone had ever asked. *Somebody* had to face "relegation."

Chair wheels squeaked under body weight and the door slammed. "Somebody better explain what the fuck happened with Harrison. Jobst doesn't like the 'C' plan. Why didn't we go with Section Six?"

Even in his magazine-ready mug shots, the man's smile and intentions seemed devious. Charming Chernobyl certainly knew that.

After a vacuous moment, Bettancourt took a deep breath. "We went with 'C' because—"

"Because you wanted to know if that landmine was still active? Guess what? Wrong call, Bettancourt." He looked around. "Who was on comps?"

101

MacLeod raised a feeble hand, fingers anticipating a spinning blade. "Harris and I, sir."

"What did the comps tell you? To support a 'C'?"

"No, sir," MacLeod muttered. His quick words felt like an indictment against Milly, the only woman in the room.

"You had the lead, right?" Missavit said, jabbing a claw at Bettancourt. She nodded. "So you decided to go rogue on this one? Got a little gambler, a little cowgirl in your blood?"

"Sir, I—"

"Shut it!" He turned to MacLeod and pointed. "You and Harris, resubmit with Section Six and *profuse* apologies. I don't care if the building catches fire—do not leave your desks until that's done. Now!"

MacLeod got up, hearing Harris' chair wheels protest behind him.

Before he was out the door, Missavit's berating of Bettancourt continued. "Mary, if you step outta line one more time on my watch, you'll be down at Legal Aid!"

MacLeod blocked it out. At his desk, he opened the binder with trembling fingers.

What I have to do to get out of this shit ...

***

The bright sun beckons him outside. *It looks warm and happy out there. In Culverhouse Crossing, it's probably pissing and five degrees.* He calculates that to be forty-one in Fahrenheit. The same for Seattle. Cleveland is probably twenty degrees colder with a crust of snow on the ground. They'll belong to winter for another two months. He would not have stayed so long by choice.

Busyness in a distant treetop. Creatures out there are free to be themselves, while he's trapped in a kennel in a bizarre house. For the first time in years, he realizes, he's off-schedule, too. Nothing is required of his brain. Nothing is required of him as a person, except that he be here (for whatever damning reason).

There's a lake outside, he remembers. Is someone going in it today? Are they, as a group, staying awhile—*a spot of holiday in the bush?* Maybe things will liven up after breakfast—another bar. He'd kill for a pillow-sized Denver omelet right now. He'd probably kill for a lot of things—Freedom, Emma—but he'd start with that. A little butter and protein and roughage to feel human. He'd like reassurance that he isn't wasting away.

Those climbing stories where the climbers get above a certain altitude and the body starts consuming itself, eating its own muscle.

He shuts his eyes against the hunger. He can deal with it. Those guys in "Alive" dealt with it for weeks because they didn't have a choice. The snow, the mountain, the cold. Theirs was a world without choices. MacLeod can be tough. He can deal.

"You're a Scot. There's nothing for it," Uncle Mortimer would remind him (though that surly bear of a man clearly hadn't missed too many meals in his lifetime).

A phone rings. The ringtone sounds like "Smooth" by Santana. Arturo pads by the kennel, unzips the patio netting and steps outside, answering.

"Smooth?" Really? That's a laugh.

103

He wonders how a Latino man feels about the great Santana's most popular song being sung by somebody else—a white Aussie, to boot. Music has always been the best vehicle for irony. He knows players who have to train all-out to Limp Bizkit, "Fat Bottomed Girls" and "Pour Some Sugar on Me."

Imagine getting that song stuck in your head, humming it on a plane. Coaches can be such cheeky wankers.

Arturo paces the deck outside, eyes on the lake. It's the first time someone has called, so there must be a reason they'd risk it. Cell phones and satellite phones can be tracked.

Does this mean Americans are closing in?

He shouldn't think about that. It's not *healthy*. Reality check: He's lying on the floor of a metal dog kennel, hands bound, surrounded by four armed thugs. And so far from civilization he might as well be on Neptune. A party of five gone off the deep end, their world ruled by a dark sun.

Chapter 14

Through an act of sheer charity, MacLeod is seated at the picnic table and reading a *National Geographic* issue. Amazing pictures accompany a fascinating story on quetzal-worshipping tribes from the Brazilian rainforests. Dances for 'weddings' and trials for misdeeds. His thoughts run to the ruins they saw the other day, then dissolve in the black cloud of yesterday afternoon's workout session. Fifty-one times since then, he's asked himself what would've happened if somebody noticed a thing missing from his shirtless form. Someone other than Cora.

Does she know? Is that what I saw that first day? It feels like a game we're playing—except this one's going to end up with someone angry and someone dead.

She is outside, sunbathing in a green tank top and shorts. Beside her, Josh is whittling something. Twice already, he's asked what dangers might be in the lake. Idly, MacLeod has pondered what would happen if the Darwin-Award candidate went in and got eaten. They need his gun and brains for a reason.

Enrique is playing solitaire at the kitchen's breakfast nook. MacLeod keeps his eyes on the magazine pages when he senses Josh coming inside. He doesn't want to give either man an outlet for their boredom.

After a toilet flush, Josh comes to stand over him.

"So how did you get started in this, man?"

Ever the fan, this guy, MacLeod thinks.

It isn't too difficult, going back over nineteen years of tight turns and coaches' lectures and shots caroming off the cross-bar. Fifth grade is when it *really* began.

"Well, I guess it took off when I met Misty Isaksen. She was seventh grade, a couple years older than me. She said American football was for nitwits, that I should learn an intelligent man's game."

"Was she cute?"

"Yeah. Dark eyes and freckles. I wanted to impress her, I worked at it. She coached me a bit over the years. She convinced me to enter a charity tournament when I was seventeen. I played well. And a rep from Notre Dame was there and offered me a scholarship, so I went there. And Uncle Mortimer, too. That was big."

"He's in Scotland, right?"

"Yes, Glasgow. Hard-core training with him."

This was all true—the MacLeods went when Uncle Mortimer heard about their 'penchant for footy' and insist they 'swing by,' on his dime. The training itself was twice-a-day sessions with older boys on a field in Dunbarton. The choppy Clyde coursed right by the pitch, making for a rainy and bitterly cold gauntlet. No gloves, no whining. "You're Scots, for God's sake, not Nancies!"

Feeling Josh is waiting for more, MacLeod continues the story. "Things went, you know, pretty well at Notre Dame. We won some trophies."

"U.S. champions in university, right?"

"That's right. My junior year. Mom insisted I finish my education. Pro teams wanted me for striker, but I listened to her and stayed. Physics."

"And your dad? What did your dad say?"

"Oh he ditched us when we—when I was six," MacLeod corrects himself, sensing the echoes of anger and regret. "He wimped out. Too tough with three kids and a...you know. It's kind of ironic. He's a huge football fan. *American* football. Season-ticket holder for the Browns, and his son never likes the game and goes on to be a soccer star. How does that work?"

Josh shrugs. "The universe is a fucked place, that's how."

Right. I guess so.

"So, uh, after college, the New England Revolution called and I got a tryout. They had me spend a year in development in Canada, playing in Montreal. Misty's aunt was a pro trainer. They both flew up and helped me work out a couple kinks. Pretty soon, I was ready for the big-time."

"As a starter in Major League Soccer, nice. Though it isn't shit compared to La Liga or the E.P.L."

"Then what happened," Enrique asks, coming over.

Where was I?

"Right. Playing for the Revolution, three-and-a-half years. Then Culverhouse called."

"Ah, the Sentries," Josh says. "You had this finesse play against Liverpool one time. Your man sent a long ball deep up the middle to you. Chartrand was coming in from the right. And it was like you trapped it and scooted it to him behind you in one motion, and he scored. How did you do that?"

MacLeod remembers the play—the *trapdoor*—as it was on enough highlight reels. A top play on ESPN's *SportsCenter*, since an American did it.

"Lots of practice. Those long-ball traps are an art form. I think Mateo showed me that one. He was from here, Cali."

"No shit? That's funny. Ah, I just remembered that. You're free kick against Newcastle, upper-right corner. It probably helps being a lefty, right?"

107

MacLeod nods. The act continues.

"Was it a hard decision? Leaving the country to play in England?"

"Not really. I've got a friend who was just up the road at Hull. He said you get used to it pretty fast. Paying in pounds, driving on the left side. Weather's nicer than Boston for most of the year. 'The women and food in England have gotten a lot better,' he said."

"The food?"

"Yeah, I guess it used to be crap. I mean, we pretty much eat what the team chef gives us. Lean, healthy stuff. I miss a good Philly, though."

"Isn't that a fat black hooker?" Enrique asks.

Bigoted jerk-off.

"Naw, come on. A Philadelphia steak sandwich? Thin-sliced beef, grilled onions and peppers, mozzarella, mayonnaise—amazing! It's like a heart-attack in a foot-long bun. I haven't had one of those in years. Chef would have me drawn-and-quartered if I ate one of those. Our trainer, too." *What's his name?* "Dinnoch, a fellow Scot, yells at us all the time. 'If ye put crap into your bodies, then all you'll get is crap on the pitch! Ya hear me?'"

Enrique is looking MacLeod over again, *assessing* him. "I gotta know," he says. "Italy. Three years ago. *How* did you catch that ball?"

He's talking about the World Cup final. The big play. Ferguson finding MacLeod, him taking off like his life depended on it.

Like my life depended on it...

108

Cora grunts from the patio. "Ugh, if we talk about football anymore, I'm going to cut out his tongue."

"What," Josh complains, heading outside. "It's the big game. It made our hero famous!"

"No more," she says, standing up.

"It's the big play," Enrique protests. "You gotta let us…" He's heading outside, too.

Arturo walks into the den, oblivious to his party's arguing, perusing a laminated map.

"No more," Cora says, grabbing the knife from Josh. It's a huge blade. "No more football! I have dreams about it. We're stuck out here in this fucking jungle. I can't take any more from *you* or *you,* or *him,*" she says, pointing the knife at the men in turn, and then MacLeod.

She's sneering—not good.

She starts walking towards him with the long serrated knife in her hand. She passes through the seam in the mosquito net.

What is she going to do with the knife? Is she smiling? Is that a genuine smile?

Blur—red blur in his eyes.

BANG!

Chapter 15

Cora's chest—it's open!

Torn flesh. Torn shirt. Her head is back. She's falling. Falling toward MacLeod. A grunt-cry-whimper issues from parted lips.

Her eyes widen. She's falling forward.

What the hell?!

There's a scream from somewhere.

Her body hits the floor. Her nose and face hit, bouncing.

Clattering comes from an item—the knife—that strikes the floor near his boot and slides away.

Screaming.

Her fingers are on the tile floor, curled and trembling.

On the patio, Josh and Enrique are down on the deck. They alternate wild-eyed stares toward the forest and back toward Cora. Breathing rapidly. Panic. One of them is calling her name.

MacLeod blinks. At his feet, Cora is face-down. She is still. A wisp of smoke curls up from her spine. A hole there is surrounded by a patch of darkness. Below her, a puddle spreads, creeping larger. Dark red. His left boot is in it.

Commotion to his right. Arturo crawls into view, his unfastened belt buckle hanging. He was in the bathroom.

He looks at his brother. He looks at Cora, his eyes wide and glistening.

MacLeod's face itches. His cheek.

Arturo turns on him. "What did you do?" he roars.

He crawls to Cora and puts a hand on her shoulder. A little shake. Nothing. A harder shake. No response.

Face-down, he screeches something unintelligible.

BANG!

To MacLeod's right, an object falls to the floor. White pieces. The elephant lamp has shattered.

Why?

Something itches. MacLeod touches the left side of his face. He has to lean over and raise his shoulder to do it. Red smears on his knuckles. Blood. Cora's blood. When she was shot. On his face. In his eye. He wipes it off as well as possible.

She was shot!

He looks down at her again. At Arturo, whose eyes are focused in the direction of Enrique and Josh. No, not on them. On something *beyond* them.

Wait, what the hell!? She was shot! By whom? From where?

All three of them are down on the floor, taking cover. Moving and looking and staying low.

Get your head down, you idiot!

MacLeod pitches over to the right. He crashes on the floor, pinching his shoulder. His knee is getting wet, he realizes. He's close to Arturo's feet. One of those brown hiking boots kicks him in the forehead.

What the—

Commotion. "No you don't!"

111

Arturo. He has scrambled to get something.

He's instantly over MacLeod, holding an object near his left eye. It's the knife.

"You will pay for this," he hisses.

The point of the knife pokes skin at the outside corner of MacLeod's eye.

He's cutting my eye out! He thought I was going for Cora's knife and now she's dead and he's taking it out on me!

"No, no, Hermano!"

The knife point pulls away.

Thank God.

Arturo focuses forward again. "Where is he?"

"I don't know," Enrique shouts back.

"Cora," Josh moans, looking at her. His face is wet.

"Cállete," Enrique commands.

BANG!

Josh rolls over and spider-crawls away from the railing. One of the white posts has buckled.

A bullet hit it?

Josh yells out. He could be hit.

"We gotta move," Enrique says, hurrying into the house. Josh scrambles after him.

As soon as they get inside, Arturo races into another room on hands and knees. Quickly, he returns with bags trailing him. He throws the strap for one bag over MacLeod's head.

112

"Vámanos!"

"With that guy out there?"

Arturo puts the tip of a weapon against Josh's nose. "Want it to end right here? I can help you with that. If not, we go!"

His eyes will tolerate no argument. MacLeod compliantly follows when they scoot towards the front door. The house is intensely quiet, other than four men breathing heavy. There's no sound of jeeps rolling up or approaching soldiers from outside.

When Arturo is ready with the AK-47, Enrique opens the front door a crack. He sneaks a device through and looks. It's a mirror attached to a post that telescopes. It's angled. MacLeod has seen it before in a movie, something with Navy SEALs. Enrique looks all around, changing the angle and shifting his body to see everything.

"Nothing. Clear," he reports in a whisper.

"You three," Arturo says, getting ready, "get to the big tree across the path. Enrique, spotter."

Enrique nods, putting the small rod between his teeth. They haul MacLeod to his feet.

Jesus. What if he's right outside, ready to mow us down? But how could he get to the house that quickly?

Another quick scan. Arturo tells them to go.

Outside, they hurry across a narrow path to a fallen tree. Silence all around. The jungle is deceptively silent.

Josh forces MacLeod down behind the gray branches and thick leaves of the tree. Enrique is with them, standing behind cover. He's looking back up the path through his telescope. The mirror hangs from the end at a funny angle, all

113

part of one device. Five yards away, Arturo waits at the house's designer front door, looking in the same direction. He checks the other way, and back. The way he grips the rifle, it's clear he's going to shoot.

Moments of stillness pass. Enrique shakes his head slowly. Arturo nods. MacLeod turns away.

RAT-A-TAT explodes in his ears. It lasts about three seconds. When MacLeod looks, Arturo's changing out the long clip. He pops in the new one, checks something and fires again.

Is he just firing randomly—hoping to hit our pursuer?

He's emptied the clip again. He changes it out and looks at Enrique. He sweeps the rifle forward. Josh hauls MacLeod to his feet.

"It's just one guy," Enrique says, slipping the telescope into his pocket. "If it was more than one, I would've seen something."

"You sure?" Josh asks. They're hustling down the trail, away from the house.

"Yeah, I'm sure. Maybe 'Turo got him."

Arturo catches up. He grabs the leash and hands the rifle to Enrique. It must be sizzling hot, as Enrique almost takes it by the barrel and adjusts to take it by the stock. He goes first, rifle forward. Then Josh with two bags, the shotgun's handle sticking out. Then Arturo, holding the leash and his pistol, followed by MacLeod as a human shield.

Under the hoodie, with his broken-form jog and electrifying fear, he's sweating buckets. He just watched a woman get killed, her chest blown out by a sniper's bullet. The man almost got Josh. Now he's after them.

Who?

114

Suddenly, Arturo turns, puts his gun arm over MacLeod's shoulder and fires several shots back toward the house. MacLeod can hardly stay upright with the jarring, loud motions. Arturo backpedals so they don't collide—a skill from the soccer pitch.

Thank God for the silencer. Does he sense someone, or is he firing at random?

Arturo turns and continues forward.

I'm a shield. Someone aiming for them is going to hit me, *first.*

"Who is it?" MacLeod asks.

"Keep moving!"

He must resemble a duck trying to hurry. They're covering ground, turning around a clump of trees. The jungle gets darker. The trail has moved away from the sunlit clearing of the lake. Now he can't see the sky at all.

"Who's after us?"

"I don't know!"

"Move your ass, MacLeod!" Enrique hisses.

The captive's legs loathe the binds. He glances for sharp edges as they hurry along. It makes little sense to restrict him during flight.

"Move it back there!"

"Get this thing off me!"

"No."

"I can move faster!"

No response. They continue.

115

Josh pauses and coughs. He's not prepared for this kind of work. MacLeod would rather pause to wait, so Josh's madness and shotgun can stay in front.

Can't those things go off on their own?

Enrique looks back, annoyed. "Come on, Amigo!"

Josh presses on. After topping a short ridge, the men pause in a spot bracketed by dense jungle.

"What the *fuck* happened?" Arturo asks. He approaches MacLeod, his gun pointed down.

A shrug, a blank look.

"How did they find us?" Enrique asks.

The men look at MacLeod.

"I don't know! Why are you looking at *me?*"

"We changed your shoes, dumped your cell phone and wallet." Arturo is looking him over. "Did we check his pants?"

"My pants? For what?"

"For a tracking device, man," Josh says—like this should be obvious. "Yeah, we did."

A tracking device?

"His body?" Arturo asks, circling MacLeod slowly. "Are you *chipped,* man?"

"You mean, like a *microchip?*"

Arturo clenches his teeth, canines showing.

"We checked," Enrique says.

"All the way down to his junk."

Briefly, MacLeod allows himself to picture Cora going over his unconscious form with latex gloves, perhaps resisting temptation to tear off his nuts.

She's dead, now. But she knew*!*

"I haven't been *chipped*," he tells Arturo, truthfully. "Not that I remember."

Enrique looks skeptical.

"You guys are watching too many James Bond movies."

Arturo gets in his face. "If they can insert a *chip* for a rich lady's prized cockapoo, they can do the same for a famous football star! Got it?"

"It would be in the neck or the hip, man," Josh says. "She didn't see any, uh, incision marks."

"She didn't," Arturo says, still in MacLeod's face but with his gaze rolling toward Josh.

"We're a thousand kilometers from Ciudad Panama," Enrique mutters. "How did they find us?"

"I don't know," Arturo says. "Move out!"

Enrique waves forward. Josh grabs a shoulder of MacLeod's hoodie. They hustle on, minus Arturo. He could be waiting to shoot anyone who comes over the rise, MacLeod reasons.

My rescuer? Were they right—that it's just one guy? How do they know? Whoever he was, he saw Cora. She was carrying the knife. Yes, she was carrying it. It fell when her chest...oh God...when she was shot. That was...one minute you're here, the next you're...

She was holding the knife and coming toward him. Hadn't she just joked about cutting out his tongue?

She was joking—I think. Cora. I'll never know. It doesn't matter now.

He's being hurried through the wild jungle. A girl is dead because someone—whoever they were—saw her carrying a knife and approaching him. They deemed her a threat. They fired.

Someone's looking out for me. But how did they get onto us?

"Hey, what about those crocodiles?" MacLeod asks.

"Crocodiles?"

"Yeah. That was yesterday, right? At the rope bridge?"

"What about it, hombre?" Enrique says. "Please don't tell me you're a granola crunchy worried about offing two lizards! I don't think I could handle that right now," he warns.

"That's not what I mean. God, these damned binds! Can you cut them off?"

"No," Enrique says. "Josh, go behind him."

Josh stands aside, arms directing the captive past.

"No, those crocodiles. What if they float?"

"What about it?"

"Well," MacLeod starts, thinking. "If you're a regular guy or a soldier in the jungle, and you see two crocodiles floating in the water...and it's obvious they didn't pick a fight with a larger croc...what would you think?"

"What do you mean, what would *I* think?"

"Enrique, two dead crocodiles...they've been shot...they haven't been skinned, or whatever those trophy hunters do...I

118

mean, wouldn't it be kind of obvious that something weird was going on?"

He looks back as they hurry along.

"There was blood on the riverbank, wasn't there? Did you guys cover it up?"

"We tried, man! Dirt. What's your point?"

"None. I don't know."

"Yes, you do. Speak! What are you getting at?"

"Uh," he starts, and can't finish. A new danger has begun blaring between his ears.

"Uh, never mind."

Enrique stops and sticks the end of the rifle under MacLeod's chin. It's still hot. "If I think, for a minute, you're saying it's *my* fault that *my* friend is dead, I will remove your face right now! Got it, Superstar?"

He whirls on a tree, prepared to turn it into Swiss cheese. "Fuck!" he barks, clenching the rifle. "Vámanos. Ahora!"

Josh nudges MacLeod's shoulder, leash in hand.

"Another beautiful day in the neighborhood," Josh sings.

Chapter 16

They wait under cover as another helicopter passes by. This one is closer than the last, about three hundred feet up. At that height, Enrique speculated earlier, it's more of a sweep than an intensive search. The jungle's too thick to effectively search by air. MacLeod has a sinking feeling he's correct, even if it's supposition. Searching the forests of Alaska would seem no less untenable.

Once, when he was eleven or twelve, he helped his younger sister Janice look for toys by pretending to be a rescue helicopter. Searching this way and that, slowly, roving without malevolence. She loved it, though the desired object—a dark green squeaky frog among rainbow-colored Legos, stickers and bits of Playdoh—ultimately proved impossible to locate. Back and forth he went, determined. He made a tearful Janice giggle when a stuffy bear became King Kong and grabbed the search helicopter. Then a different kind of mission had ensued— soldiers with special rotten-banana cannons and so on.

These were memories that got MacLeod through all those endless nights of reading, memorizing, studying. All those times catching a sunrise—not by choice—the Midwestern orange and yellow hues on snow, icicles, Formica diner tabletops.

For what, he often wondered. To prove he could do it, could survive the grind, spit out the correct answer or segment of boilerplate? That he could categorically memorize everything in a deposition?

MacLeod smirks to himself. Whatever the chopper's occupants hope to see, they can't truly expect to find it in the endless miles and seven shades of *verde* under a cloudy sky. And with the thick canopy, the four of them could be wearing construction orange with bright yellow boots and people *still* wouldn't spot them.

Enrique's hand is on MacLeod's chest to stop him, looking back the way they came. All is quiet. MacLeod hears nothing at first. Then, footsteps.

A pink object lands on the trail near them. It's a small toy car. Josh and Enrique relax.

"Enrique?"

"Sí. Sano y salvo."

Arturo comes around the bend, pistol forward. He puts it away and collects his signal car.

"You all make too much noise," he says. "Like mooses."

MacLeod thinks it would be unwise to correct him.

"Did you get him?"

"No. Crafty bastard. Seems to know when I'm waiting around a corner for him."

"You didn't see him?"

Arturo looks annoyed. "No, Josh, I didn't. He's a real predator," he adds.

So how do you know he's there?

Enrique chews on his lower lip.

Josh looks worried. "So how do you know he's back there, man? He could be a phantom."

Arturo appears to check his anger before speaking. "You know when a gnat is buzzing near your ear, but you can never turn fast enough to catch him? And he keeps at it as soon as you look away? That's how."

"Alone?" Enrique asks.

"Sí. Could be a mercenary."

"A mercenary?"

Arturo looks at MacLeod. "That's right," he sneers. "This is not Cleveland. We have *rogue elements* down here. Sometimes crawling through the jungle. Or showing up in a village to knock out a family. You never see them. Like sharks."

Rogue elements? Someone who's going to do whatever they want, like shoot a woman from behind?

They get moving, Enrique out front with the AK-47.

Josh comes up next to MacLeod with the leash wrapped around his wrist. "Look at this. Did I show you this?" he asks, holding up a black object.

Small metal binoculars. There's an odd crease in the middle.

"I brought these for watching natives. The women don't wear much, you know? And these saved me from being shot."

"Oh?"

He traces the odd crease with his near-black fingernail. "They were around my neck and must've gotten behind me when we took cover. I think the bullet punched through the railing board and hit that instead of hitting me. It ricocheted! Otherwise, that motherfucker would've gotten me, too! I'd have a big…"

He doesn't finish, his eyes suddenly tracking back. Arturo is behind them, bringing up the rear.

"Well, cosmic, man. Karma," he whispers. "My lucky day!"

He steps back behind. Rustling sounds are him putting the lucky binoculars away.

Cosmic is right. I would've preferred Cora. Still, the devil's boots don't creak, as they say.

***

"That place is getting worse all the time," Emma said, slicing shallots for a late dinner. "Now they've pulled the free coffee."

MacLeod looked up from one of the 4,100 emails in his work inbox. "You're kidding."

"Nope. It was shit, it wasn't Starbucks. But at least it was there. *Too expensive,* they say. What a load of kaka! I see the books, every penny that comes out of that place. Fuel, new shocks, twenty-packs of rubber floor mats, that claim for Jorgensen's shoulder. The C-F-O's making twice what *you* make, and they don't have seventeen hundred for a year of office coffee? Liars!"

MacLeod set down his phone on the counter, thoughts on the morning's Franklin deposition forcibly pushed back.

Emma wore her powder-blue Peace Corps T-shirt and khaki shorts. He knew this shirt to be particularly soft and cool to his fingertips—the utter opposite of how his wife was obviously feeling.

"Geordie said he's thinking about moving on. Find somebody else's books to work on." She dumped the shallots and chopped red onion in the skillet.

"Isn't he the one who was in Tanzania with you?"

"Yup." She offers a contrite look. "You'd like him, really sweet guy. Nuts about David Gray and Bragg. I don't think he knows a thing about soccer, though."

123

"Is the company in trouble?"

"Maybe. Nobody's saying it, but maybe things aren't as good as the Head Office makes out."

"Hmm," he said, touching her shoulder. "Why don't you think about pulling the ripcord? If that place is going downhill, why get dragged down with them?"

"What, seriously?"

"Sure," he said, shrugging. "Take some time, think about what you'd like to do differently."

"Maybe open my own. 'Emma MacLeod, Personalized Accounting.' Yeah, that's a thought. Or teach at Cuyahoga," she added optimistically.

"Yeah. Doesn't that sound good? Besides, don't you think I carry enough stress for the both of us?"

A warm smile, an embrace. The happy hiss of vegetables cooking in oil.

***

The downpour is so thick the world is drowning in curtains of gray, rain that's painful on bare skin. At a piss break, utterly soaked in stiff clothes, MacLeod wonders about mudslides. If the earth before him gives way, will freedom become realized in a brown roller coaster?

Twenty seconds after they return to the trail, the rain shuts off. Sunbeams appear, earning sarcastic laughter from Josh and Enrique. Of course, they will not be pausing in the sun to dry off a little. Under bloated clothes and water-logged bags, they trudge on.

124

'Definitely smashing, Darling.' Isn't that what Cora would've said?

Somehow, Lady Lucinda had put Cora in the crosshairs in that moment. Or someone did. If one of the four had to die—courtesy of dark forces in the world—why did it have to be her? Not the lunatic, not Latino Yosemite Sam. Not their leader, her lover, who has all the charm of a drug lord. *What did she see in him that was worth it?* It could've been more than a certain virility MacLeod doesn't want to guess about. But the American-type desires of humor, a stable income, kindness—those remain under cover, it would seem. Arturo is all purpose. His mission carries on though his girlfriend lies dead on the floor of someone's vacation house. When MacLeod looked at her still form for the last time, her unmoving dark locks could've belonged to a mannequin.

What would her rich father think? Is it possible he even knows where on Earth she is? Or where she's been? Her mother, he recalls, didn't even warrant a mention.

People like Cora come from somewhere, he muses. *Pandora's Box has participants.*

"Look at the size of that beast!" It's Josh, pointing to a tree above them.

The mental image of a dead girl on a bloody floor recedes as MacLeod snaps to. He and Enrique follow Josh's finger up. Four yards away, a great green thing is working its way around a complex tree. It is easily thicker than MacLeod's arm, with a length approaching twenty feet.

He wonders if this could be the famed anaconda, creature of legend. Are they *close* to the Amazon? Enrique said they're a thousand kilometers from Panama. Is it more than six hundred miles from there to the Amazon basin?

"I would like to know," Josh says, "*how* that thing can sneak up on a tapir or something. How's it quick enough to wrap

125

around it? That is a snake that kills by crushing and strangulation, right Enrique?"

"Think so. I don't know, Amigo. You'd think something that big and heavy wouldn't move so fast."

"Yes, that's what I mean. How?"

"Jaguars. Jaguars are built for speed. That's how *they* do it. Vicious. Scare the shit out of me. You'd see nothing—a flash of fur and then it's got you by the throat."

That's an image MacLeod can warm up to—Enrique on his back, struggling in vain to keep one of those killers from snapping his neck. Blood. Snarling.

As a kid, MacLeod read books on the big cats cover-to-cover. Once, researchers tracked a jaguar dragging a horse for six miles to feed her cubs. A thousand pounds of horse, dragged for three hours over terrain. For years, moments in the weight room or PT torture chamber made him wonder about that jaguar's determination.

"Are you ladies done pissing and watching the wildlife? We got to go."

"*You* qualify as wildlife, don't you, Arturo? Rrrowww!"

"I'm not in the mood, Josh!"

"He's cranky," Josh mutters as they get going. "Should've brought some tequila. I could go for a nice glass of it right now. Couldn't you, Enrique?"

Under the circumstances, MacLeod would go for a big swig, too. Anything to make this a *smidge* more tolerable, as his teammate Tony would say.

How far are they going today? Where's the next place? *Is* there one? The vacation house is now gone, so they might be doomed to roam the jungle in a random direction. It tracks that

126

they're on their way to somewhere, but the 'where' and 'why' are beyond the imagination of a middle-class man from Cleveland.

"Rápido," Arturo commands.

They pick up the pace, with Josh holding the leash. Enrique stretches his lead to twenty yards, so he can pause and look and aim, and get moving before the rest are on his heels. This goes on for a while, around curves and up and down gullies. Despite the weight and band, and hunched over to preserve his manhood, MacLeod manages to keep pace. This, he imagines, disappoints Enrique.

"Come on, Hero! Pick up the pace! How did you ever catch that ball?" he chides. He has to prove his manliness, spurred by another shower.

Catch that ball?

MacLeod can tell from the changing slack on his leash that Josh is having a harder time.

He hasn't been through what I've been through. Not even close.

The rain stops as they approach a river, which opens wide in front of them.

"Rio," Enrique calls out.

Arturo comes forward, checking his map. "Josh, hold him," he commands.

Josh tightens the leash, so MacLeod forces himself to relax. The black ribbon is almost eighteen yards across, goalie box line to keeper. The water moves lazily, sky and forest reflected on its surface. Clearly, depth is an issue, as Arturo puts his hand on the climbing rope in one bag.

After a moment, he apparently changes his mind and grabs a small tree branch. He tears lesser branches from it, mumbling something to Enrique. MacLeod could almost admire his efficiency, moving into the water without fear or question. He uses the four-foot stick to poke the river bottom before him, fording steadily. Enrique and his rifle watch the water.

Soon, Arturo's up to his waist. "Anything?" he calls.

"No. Good," his brother replies.

When he emerges on the other side, MacLeod realizes he's been biting his lower lip. Expecting something bad would happen—hoping it would. He feels pathetic. Fortune isn't smiling on him today.

Arturo spends a moment looking around with his gun, his spread fingers calling for them to be silent and still.

"Okay," Enrique says. "Josh, you two."

"Fuck, seriously?" Josh complains under his breath.

Are you nervous, you lunatic?

Josh watches the water intently. He pulls MacLeod forward until their boots are submerged. Then he stops. His eyes dart about upriver. He swears something in Czech.

"Now, Josh. Right now!"

"Fuck it," Josh mutters. Without requesting permission, he pulls the shotgun from his bag.

"We're watching, Josh. We've got it," Enrique encourages.

MacLeod tries to focus on the river bottom and not on the weapon. There's a sinking feeling *this* is the way his life ends—accidentally blown in half by a madman's twitchy finger.

"Goddammit, man," Josh mutters again, wrapping the leash around his wrist. With the same hand, he grabs MacLeod's hoodie by the front and leads him. The footing underneath is unstable. He licks his lips nervously as they progress. His eyes are all over the place. MacLeod's too, though they keep coming back to Babushka's direction of fire.

Maybe you should encourage him. That's all he needs.

"It's okay, Josh. They're watching. Arturo is on it."

He leers at the captive. "Please don't, MacLeod. Not from you."

What did I say?

They progress slowly.

"No, I—that's not how I mean it. I mean…you know…they're watching the water and…I think we're okay, man."

He laughs. "Reassurance from a dead man. That's a good—sh!"

He's slipped.

We're both going under!

"Don't you," he starts with a growl, regaining his footing.

However it's happened, MacLeod's down on his knees on the bottom. His chin is just above the surface. Pain shrieks up from below, the cord wracking him. He blinks rapidly, white worms of light crawling about. Otherwise, he can't move, focused solely on the quarter-size opening of a gun barrel seventeen inches away.

Josh is standing over him, teeth bared, hair wet. The shotgun is pointed at MacLeod's face, trembling in his grip.

This is it! Buggered!

Through the pain, he hears Enrique call out from somewhere. "Chill, Amigo."

"Josh, relax! Everything is okay." That was Arturo.

"Chill out. You're good, you're good!"

MacLeod can't breathe. A drop of water falls from the metal tube, white in this world's dead light. Will it be the last thing he ever sees?

Josh closes his eyes and slowly withdraws the gun. He fights to control his own shivering. His expression changes, a crack of daylight in darkness. It—whatever it is for Josh—seems to pass. He hauls MacLeod to his feet. "Get the fuck across this river!"

They make it across in seconds. Arturo helps pull them out. He slaps Josh on the shoulder. MacLeod fights off tears— that contemptible itching—while Emma's sweet face hovers before him. The last thing he would've seen before his head was burst like a watermelon.

Arturo waves for his brother to come and Josh doubles over, forcing MacLeod to stand close. Bags slip off, clunking on the earth. The shotgun is pointed down.

MacLeod bites his tongue against the pain from his crotch. Splashing tells him Enrique has made it across without incident.

"It's okay. We all made it," he tells Josh.

Josh stands upright and forces a smile, though he looks nauseous.

"Never again! Goddamned crocodiles. Swear on the Bible, never again in my life." He shakes it off.

"Nothing there," Enrique says to his brother, as if they've gotten lucky.

Lucky this time.

"Well, now," Josh shouts at MacLeod, adjusting his bags and weapon. "That was fun! Let's try not to do it again, eh?"

Shaking, MacLeod takes a deep breath. Pain coupled with relief. He gets moving, wet boots and clothes, as there's safety in routine. Relief that he's looking at passing plants and trees, and not up a dark tube towards death.

Chapter 17

How? How *did I get into this mess?*

He's a regular guy—smart, sort of handsome, athletic, American. Always done exactly what he's supposed to do. He hit the books, learned the lingo, filed all those briefs. *How* does this happen?

Because an enemy found you when you didn't know one was there.

That's the only explanation that fits.

The deposition.

If MacLeod could go back and alter a few hours of his life, it would be sitting in that attorney's office. If a carnival fortune-teller had taken his two dollars and prophesized his future would hinge on his flying to San José and sitting in an air-conditioned Costa Rican conference room—who could believe that? But over the hours of this adventure, the mental tumblers have repeatedly fallen into place with the word 'Deposition' stamped in metal.

Candance DeMeers, when they met, had seemed both calm and full of boundless energy. Plump and pretty in a homey Midwestern kind of way, she did not present as a 'retired' tech manager who saw 90-hour weeks as the norm. But that perception changed as soon as she began relating her story, and it was huge.

Her hands shook with anticipation, her strawberry-blond curls trembled. This thing *needed* to come out of her, for it had a life of its own. At 10:07 a.m., after introductions were made and ice water dispensed and the door closed, MacLeod's new paralegal Bruni switched on the audio recorders. His pad and pen were ready, but everything would be captured on two recorders.

Ms. DeMeers glanced at the pricey native art pieces Counselor Ramirez had selected for his conference room. She confessed she didn't know where to start. The pile of curled pages before her resembled a journalist's treasure trove.

Familiar with these proceedings, MacLeod knew how to prompt her. "You're here. We're here. Tell us a story. Where did you go to college?"

It was enough. He knew this info already, having studied her dossier on the southbound American Airlines flight. He probably knew more about her than she'd be comfortable with. But this was a tell-all, and Ms. DeMeers had stated she couldn't stay silent any longer. Whether spurred strictly by conscious or moral rectitude, one could hardly argue that it was damned heroic. Her former employer was Quazidyne, the fourth-largest tech company (by revenue) in the world.

She laid out the company's seven departments and her locations within (managers frequently moved around). Her time in the enterprise division saw a jumble of stories, which spilled out over the next five hours. They worked through lunch (catered tamales) and on. MacLeod had probably drunk a gallon of ice water and his hand hurt from scribbling. His work spread to a second notepad, with Bruni trying to sort info as they went. Though it all seemed unbelievable, in the expressive sense, he didn't doubt the veracity of a single word.

In Manila, a Quazidyne platform compliance specialist and security officer were both stabbed during a drugs-for-hookers scheme gone wrong. The security man nearly bled to death, and the platform guy spent three weeks in the hospital. It *wasn't* a bad stomach bug.

Another female manager was bribed into 'retirement' after she complained about Hawaii. During a conference in Lahaina, she and a cohort took their Mai Tais up to the boss' suite and found half-a-dozen high school girls partying with coke on the kitchenette counter. People had to run interference when one girl's parents came to the hotel, GPS-tracking her phone.

133

A South African software engineer fell from a sixth-floor balcony in Ibiza. According to Ms. DeMeers, the company pinned it on a room-service waiter and even planted evidence of anti-Dutch sentiment on the poor guy's laptop. The two coworkers partying with the deceased engineer, of course, saw the waiter do it and even saw him sneaking a few sips earlier in the evening. The company itself came to the waiter's rescue, getting him cleared with what amounted to a misdemeanor—after a seven-month jail stint and trial. He lost his job, but was compensated with $200,000 cash and a fancy piece of "scrubbed" tech. He also had to relocate to Tenerife, sworn to silence.

In Paris, the poor accountant who lost his leg was *not* clipped by a drunken taxi driver, despite what the official story said. "The vehicle he was struck by," Ms. DeMeers said, "happened to be a forklift—moving freight—at the cargo terminal of Charles De Gaulle Airport." This happened around midnight, because the accountant and his idiot cohorts got so high at a nightclub they fancied stealing a police car. They did so, quickly wrecked it behind an auto-body place, and proceeded to climb through a hole in the security fencing by an air freight depot. The cover story was so silky smooth, according to her, that the Metro Paris police were chasing a phantom Algerian cab driver for three days. Congressman Connors even weighed in at an unrelated press conference, stoking a ridiculous amount of right-wing anti-European (*"Aren't they all the same over there?"*) fervor in the accountant's home state of Oklahoma. He, the accountant, also got a quasi-hero's welcome a week later at the Stillwater airport because he'd once served five months in the Air Force Reserve.

"I mean, is this the fucking *Onion* or is this real life?!" Ms. DeMeers asked.

To his surprise—for he'd never felt like a cynic—MacLeod speculated, *Only an American company would try to get away with this stuff.*

It was an American company that had just reported third-quarter earnings of $7.1 billion. Enough money to buy a small country. Certainly enough to bribe a few people, manipulate judicial proceedings and trounce (or devour) smaller competing firms.

Enough to capture me and march me off to God-Knows-Where, or just kill me, MacLeod thinks, skirting a stand of bamboo stalks. He shakes his head, freshly flabbergasted. Nobody else notices.

Surprise, the joke's on you guys. When this shakes out—

"So, MacLeod, who's your favorite?"

What the hell is this, a rolling interview? A couple questions, shoot some crocodiles. A couple more questions, gunfight at the O.K. Corral. Hit the road, continue.

He glances at Josh, who's at his shoulder again. "My favorite?" he asks.

"Yeah, man. Your favorite player. Who would *you* want to be paired up with?"

He'd better play it cool. Invention time. Who would he want in the passenger seat of the orange Land Rover (not his silver Highlander) talking strategy on the way to the game?

"Either León or Zabić."

"León at Man-U? Aw, he's crazy, man. Those spin moves are wicked."

Good call, Counselor!

No exaggeration, León has skills, MacLeod knows. He's a 5'5" blur in home red, working the ball through defenders until Harris or Lucia are open for the shot. His speed can embarrass people.

"Why Zabić?"

The big Serb, all 6'4" of him, is a hard-working machine (from the clips). "He's a lot harder to defend than players give him credit for—he just doesn't have the flashy stats to prove it. Some lovely crosses that just haven't converted. Even if he has a career full of coulda-beens, I think that's something."

"Okay, okay. What about Patrice, from Nigeria? That bicycle against City—so sweet!"

Patrice...Patrice from Nigeria... "Sure, him too. He's had some nice takes."

Good cover, Dork.

They're climbing again. The hoodie is becoming a thick wool blanket, but he trudges on with his duck-style waddling. The thugs have done this to him, called the tune he has to play. How he would kill, though, to get this stupid rubber band off his legs and go sprinting across a wide, flat pitch.

Unlikely any of his captors managed to grab the soccer ball on the way out of the house. Too rushed by flying bullets and other concerns.

Who was that? Did Arturo get him? Will I ever find out?

Late afternoon sun breaks through. The canopy has gotten thinner as they've climbed, and now there are sunny views of mountainous green country. At another saddle, where they pause under cover, MacLeod begins to understand why people take the risk to come hike this land.

Josh is winded. The three of them drink water from canteens.

Play a card. Don't be a dead man.

"So," MacLeod starts, ignoring his thirst, "if you don't mind my asking, how are the ransom negotiations going?"

"What?"

"Your guy on the phone. He's, uh, isn't he sorting out the ransom details? My side pays enough money, and then I can go free?"

Arturo grins, looking into his binoculars. "No, that is not his job."

"Oh, okay. Someone else, then. We get to the next hideout, or whatever, and there's an update waiting for you. Isn't that how it works?"

"Ransom negotiations? There is no ransom to negotiate, Mister MacLeod."

A weird pain goes off behind his left eye, like someone has deposited a pebble in the soft tissue there. He wrinkles his face at it, trying to scratch an impossible itch.

"What?" he asks, trying to keep his voice even.

"Ah, let me explain," Enrique cuts in. "You see, in a ransom, you pay money so someone else can do something, like let the prisoner go. Correct?"

MacLeod nods. The tone of Enrique's voice— MacLeod's eye is twitching harder.

"Right. This time, you, MacLeod, will be paying for something *you* have already done."

What?

"It's a simple transaction, give and take," Enrique says, waving his hands.

Okay, what the hell does that mean?

"Guys, look," Josh says, pointing.

A rainbow arcs across the valley, soaring from bulging green humps and through steel-gray clouds.

"Es bonita, no?" Josh asks Enrique.

Enrique nods, smiling at Josh's silliness.

MacLeod fixates on Enrique's face.

What do you mean, paying? I am paying. Aren't I?

"Which end do you think the pot of gold is at?" Josh asks.

Enrique points.

"That's settled," Josh starts, ready to move. "Let's go! Arturo, what do you see?" he sings.

"Rebels."

They all freeze and look at him.

"Fuck."

"Cuántos?" Enrique asks, quickly raising his own binoculars.

"Twenty…five…thirty…forty."

"H—how do you know they're rebels?" MacLeod asks.

Arturo gives him a *you idiot* look and returns to monitoring. "Boots and bandoliers, MacLeod. That is not the Colombia Sanitation Department out for a work party."

"About a mile and a half," Enrique reports.

Rebels. Now look what you've gotten us into, you fucking imbeciles!

Whatever these guys have in store for him, there's no way rebels *wouldn't* make it worse. If they're caught, will they be killed on the spot? Or would *all of them* be taken hostage, followed by God knows what?

He can't hold it any longer. Another huge, staggering flaw in the plan. *These nitwits thought they'd accounted for everything.* "I'm sorry, didn't you say something about *rogue elements?*"

Arturo's head whips toward MacLeod. Nuclear heat radiates from his eyes. His jaw is clenched so tight he could crack his own molars.

Here it comes. Shouldn't have said anything, Fool!

"You," he whispers in MacLeod's face, "are lucky!"

When he exhales, MacLeod can smell the mint from the breakfast bar.

"Are they coming this way?" Josh asks quietly.

"No. Slow pace. I think we're running parallel," Enrique says.

Arturo checks his handgun's ammo clip. "Let's go."

They head downhill quickly.

"Rebels, rebels," Josh is muttering behind MacLeod. "Faaack, this is not good."

For once, MacLeod agrees. There's no conceivable way *any* encounter with rebels could be positive. They have their politics, their cause and their weapons. He doesn't understand the current versions of the first two, and he's admittedly quite afraid of the third. He imagines they also have wily tactics on their side. To survive this long—however long they've been at it—takes more than guts.

With luck, Arturo's correct and they won't be running into that group. With a hell of a lot of luck, the two parties won't get within a mile of each other.

But is there that much karma in the universe? For me?

He wishes this were a nightmare. Nightmares end.

Chapter 18

MacLeod wasn't supposed to be in Costa Rica at all. In their Edmonds, Washington, kitchen, he'd told Emma, "Rickman's got a bad stomach flu. He can't even get out of bed. I've got to go." She asked if she should come with him. "It's a lot of flying book-ending a deposition and a night working in a hotel. I don't think you'd have any fun."

"Costa Rica. That's pretty safe, right?"

San José, he reassured her, was far from narcos and *chupacabra* and the *Azuliqapavor.* "Sure it is. People go vacation there all the time. A lot of expats live in the area. Brazil would be another story. That place is going down the toilet."

Emma's expression said she had little argument. After clerking and six years of mind-numbing arbitration hearings—MacLeod hadn't found an opening in environmental law, yet—his reward was joining Petersen Gupta O'Malley Gonzalez just before Christmas. Nine weeks after escaping the drudgery of yo-yo meaningless work (his prior firm had sent him all over the country) and uprooting for Seattle, MacLeod is the sub in a case so big the particulars were unknown. But when a former manager at a company that important says meet me and my lawyer friend in Costa Rica, you go. When the man next in line to become partner is soiling his own bedsheets with illness—according to his wife—you get on a plane. You show up and do your job.

And then you get nabbed because…

***

It doesn't take long.

141

Ten minutes' climb from a dark grove with crunchy-looking dirt cones of red ants, Arturo stops with his hand raised. They all go silent. MacLeod's preoccupation with the hives they avoided (ten thousand little bastards in each—enough to eat a person alive) ends as abruptly as if King Kong was standing before him. But it's worse.

They're on a narrow path, climbing around a hill's shoulder. On MacLeod's left is a rock wall. To the right, the land drops away sharply, long grass and shadows, then forest. Trouble is coming, palpable in the warm breeze.

Josh grips the leash and steps in front of him. A scan confirms it: They have nowhere to go. Single-file, out in the open. Sitting ducks.

The crackle of a radio sounds ahead.

Sweat trickles down MacLeod's chest. Behind him, Enrique has moved close, doing something with a heavy object.

He whispers, "If Arturo bends over like to tie his boot, that's my signal, okay?"

MacLeod nods. *Signal to what?*

"Josh," Enrique whispers.

Josh gives a quick thumbs-up, pointed left.

The captor wishes he knew what Arturo was thinking right now. It seems too late to have regrets—for any of them.

The absence of noise is disconcerting. Either MacLeod's imagining things, or the boots of approaching men have stopped. They must be around a corner ahead, just out of sight.

Rebels. Shit, what were these guys thinking?

"Hola. Quién es?"

142

"Amigos," Arturo replies, carefully.

A rifle appears first, pointed in Arturo's direction. Two men in green and ball-caps appear. One has a mustache, the other long hair and a map of scars on his face. Both look older. Among them are bandoliers, machetes and equipment belts.

Jesus, what's going to happen? Are we dead meat?

Arturo's open hands are raised to chest-level. He speaks to them, calmly, in Spanish. He's five yards ahead, too far for MacLeod to make out. The rebels reply with questions. Arturo responds, agreeably and even-toned.

The long-haired one looks past him to Josh and MacLeod. Under his fatigues, he's wearing a yellow shirt with a bright-green collar. It is likely an old Brazil jersey.

The conversation continues. MacLeod avoids the gaze of the curious one. He makes out the words 'misión' and 'dólares.'

Whatever he's doing, as long as it works...

The rebels look calm. The lead one glances at the captive and says something to his partner. Arturo says something else slowly, then something that comes out faster, like it's casual, joking about a retarded cousin. The long-haired man, looking tired, wipes sweat out of his eye with his palm.

Relaxed enough. This is a good sign.

Arturo says a few words and the lead rebel nods. Fingers tighten their grip on the left side of MacLeod's hoodie. Arturo says something else casual, bending over.

Rush of movement.

What's happening?!

RAT-A-TAT-A-TAT!

143

Pinned against the rock, MacLeod feels the gunfire rushing past his back—like bullets exploding in his head. Josh has thrown him left against the wall while Enrique, no longer concealed, unleashed the AK-47. When he looks, the two men in green are falling. One has a torn-up chest.

Arturo has rolled aside and drawn his gun.

MacLeod winces, pulling his cheek off the rock. As he gets his balance, impressed by Josh's sudden strength, Enrique hurries to the fallen men.

BANG!

One for the man on the left, in the face.

BANG!

One for the other, shattering his head. It's like broken pottery.

Why did I look?

"Finale," Josh gushes.

MacLeod's stomach heaves, but he swallows against it. Nothing feels right in the world. There's but a paucity of human kindness left, and most of that departed with a terrified orphan boy two days ago.

Enrique flicks something on his smoking rifle. He puts a hand on Arturo's head, and it comes away bloody. Standing up, Arturo is covered in red.

"That was smooth, Bro," Enrique says. "Dad would be proud."

Arturo wipes blood from his ear and puts his weapon away. Apparently, none of the blood is his. He nudges a rebel with his boot.

"We shouldn't have had to kill these men. A waste."

The brothers turn to their captive, glaring. Arturo wipes body fluids away from his mouth and spits.

"I sure hope you're worth all this trouble, MacLeod."

"Sí."

"Hey, don't we need to get out of here?" Josh looks joyously excited.

"Yes. This was a patrol. Freddy was wrong—this area is crawling with rebels."

Freddy?

"How long do we have?" Enrique asks.

Arturo looks up the trail. "Not enough time to ask again. Vámanos!"

Like practiced thieves, the brothers take machetes, a knife and a handgun off the two bodies. Both men are a mess.

This is what war looks like—dirt and red and green.

Odors of smoked meat rise up. On the second man's chest, a torn flap of the yellow jersey has wrinkled and pulled serpentine.

"Wait wait wait," Josh almost shouts, hurrying to the bodies.

"No time for sentimental bullshit, Amigo," Enrique says, one foot on the slope down.

They watch Josh take an item off one of the dead men's belts.

Arturo has the leash. "Josh, we are going!"

145

"I saw this on the BBC, once," Josh says, pulling part of the item from the rest. He carefully positions the item underneath the body.

Don't ask, just run!

"Now we need to go," he says, ecstatic.

Arturo's eyes are wide. He and MacLeod almost tumble down the steep slope after Enrique. Josh hops after them.

Enrique brakes himself against a tree. "Was that a live…" he hisses, scared.

"You bet your ass it was," Josh says, nearly crashing on top of them.

Those eyes—he's Loki incarnate.

"Loco," Arturo says, pulling MacLeod's lower leg out from under him. They're now both seated, and moving. "Slide, you donkey!"

They do—all four of them. Sliding on their asses in mud and green. Out of control, but moving from danger. They come to a stop at a fallen log above a creek.

There are voices behind them, somewhere way up the hillside.

Arturo signals for silence. He and Enrique climb over the log's branches, as if to take cover. Josh helps MacLeod over. It's awkward, so he lands on his elbows and knee.

CRACK—FOOM!

The branch in front of MacLeod's nose shifts.

That was a grenade! This crazy motherfucker Josh just set a grenade as a booby trap. I have to get away from him.

146

Wild screaming rings out from above. A man is badly injured.

"Probably his legs or feet," Enrique mutters. "Good idea, you loco!"

Josh gives him an eager, toothy thumbs-up.

God, can someone please kill that guy? Take him out of his misery so we don't have to listen to this? Come on, Arturo, be a sport!

Arturo watches carefully. It looks like he's focused on listening, since he can't see anything up there. They must've dropped two hundred feet from the trail.

The screams of agony continue. There is no second voice yelling or trying to help.

That poor man, whoever he is.

"Good," Arturo says. "One at a time, let's cross."

They make it across the creek in near-silence. MacLeod is getting better at not splashing with his boots. No looks or reprimands this time.

The man is still howling behind them.

They're off the trail, now. Arturo puts a hand on his new machete, but declines to use it. MacLeod wonders if they make a distinct noise or cut an obvious path to follow. They've just killed three rebels, and now they want to disappear.

Josh is in the rear, exactly where he shouldn't be.

You just mutilated a man with a grenade, you maniac. You set the bomb in the van. And I bet that was you torching that apartment complex after we left. Christ, who raised this freak?!

Arturo leads the party on with a mixture of speed and caution, frequently checking a compass that's taped to the bottom of his binoculars. He heads left.

"Arturo," Enrique whispers.

Arturo stops and looks back, his eyes searching. "It stopped."

"Suddenly," Enrique says, looking worried.

"No shot? Maybe a rock," Josh speculates.

Enrique shrugs. "I didn't hear any sounds of talking. The cries were the same, and then they cut off."

Couldn't the poor bastard have just bled to death?

MacLeod pictures a man rolling side to side, his legs ending in crimson shreds.

Arturo waves. They press on, faster.

Oh God, the mercenary? Or whoever he is?

If so, the man's obviously persistent. How long has he been tracking them? Since yesterday? The day before? And who is he after—the captors or MacLeod?

Either way, doesn't it mean he's on my side? The 'enemy of my enemy' idea?

MacLeod wonders if he could be American or British, a secret agent. People that countries aren't supposed to have anymore, but most likely still do. The only way that works out, MacLeod reckons, is if there was an agent just hanging around Latin America, waiting for something big to happen.

Now I'm fuckin' dreaming. Nobody's coming to save me.

It's starting to get dark. He wonders how Arturo will handle this. He's too smart to use a flashlight.

148

MacLeod glances down at the jungle floor, at the big plants they're stepping around. If any have sharp edges or points to cut his rubber band, he sees them too late. He's had the thing on for twenty-four hours straight—since yesterday's little practice session.

"Pick it up, boys," Enrique says from his rear position. "We need to reach the next hideout."

"Before darkness?" Josh asks. "I hope your brother has his magic hideout finder stick, then."

"We're in the jungle, Josh. Magic is everywhere."

Chapter 19

"The keeper blocks it! Unbelievable! Ball comes out to Spazzio on the right. A try—and it's blocked! Carpenter got it again! Sensational! Ball's out to Ferguson. And he's seen something 'cause he launches it downfield. It's MacLeod. Could this be another miracle? Streaking past the Italians! Free in the middle. They might have something here. The ball drops to MacLeod..."

Morning. In a jungle lean-to.

It was almost dark when Arturo saw twin trees with markings, and the party descended another slope. That *was* a kind of magic. The alternative might have been to walk the forest until morning.

If MacLeod believed in any higher power—at this point, Shiva the Destroyer would do—he'd thank them aloud and light an array of candles. This hideout amounts to a bunch of planks roped to other planks in the crook of a huge tree—somebody's do-it-yourself project gone comically awry. But at least they had a wood floor to sleep on. That was critical, as it staved off one of those dire warnings echoing through the ages: *Don't* ever *sleep on the jungle floor.* Grateful for the semi-clean, semi-dry flatness, he'd pulled his hood tight around his face. He tried not to imagine centipedes—*Thanks, Mr. Ian Fleming!*—or great hairy spiders snuggling up to his body heat. All he could do was shut his eyes, ignore sounds, and journey back to various moments on the pitch. He may have slept.

If finding this place required a little magic, the rest of the adventure still fell into the 'Madness' bucket. The place was free of squatters, again, because nobody could possibly find it. No sane person, he's convinced, would try this.

Who plans an overland journey from Jungle Hell West to Jungle Hell Elsewhere, Colombia? We offer deluxe accommodations, plus amenities. Dead Cora—a pity. Mercenary—a big unknown. Rebels—not an unknown, and they sure as hell will be looking for whoever killed three of their comrades. Plus the local wildlife. Awesome vacation. Remind me to sign off on the brochures.

MacLeod shuts his eyes to wait. He once fed a sweet thread-the-needle pass to a short Iraqi named Uday (best assist ever), and Susan served up a juicy bicycle in the drizzle.

And the dream he keeps having. Mistake or not, this has to be about the World Cup—the final with Italy.

But these guys are not going to listen to me at all. They're someone's disciples.

***

The day was like trial by fire. Rather, trial by rain and wind. The pitch Uncle Mortimer took them to sat within spitting distance of the Clyde—twenty feet beyond a rock berm. The gray chop sent spray onto the turf, with winds so strong they'd have kept any ball from going in the drink. The men the MacLeods were to play with held a similar amount of charm. "Rangers men use their elbows," Aunt Molly had warned. After ten minutes of grumbly boot-around, they set to playing nine-on-nine with small goals and no keepers. Uncle took the other side, so he could watch the boys. They were talented high-school players, yes. Could they compete? Probably. Though none of the three would say it aloud, each knew the true purpose of this was to see what the younger twin could really do. Acknowledging greatness can be a bitter pill.

Rufus MacLeod's first four passes were crap, but then he calmed down. A deep run ended with him being thrown to the pitch. The man who helped him up afterward didn't say anything, which was good. No molly-coddled whelps, here. He got a number of elbows and dealt with them in silence. Soon, things started to click—his internal clock meshing with that of the live game.

"You're in, you're in, Roof," Mitch shouted and heeled a ball in to Rufus, who turned and shot. A defender with a lopsided mustache clapped his hands in frustration. As if drawn to a beacon, Mitch started going after him. A few feints and spins, using his own man with a quick cut to trap him off, two easy goals. Uncle Mortimer was impressed.

In the afternoon game, Mitch leaned heavily on his speed on give-and-goes. One man named Fenders or Flanders was spot-on with his release passes, and Mitch started drawing a lot of double-teams down deep. "That's one way you know you're hitting it," Uncle said. When the threat is so real they've got to shift one to help block you. Then you simply thread the needle inside and let your uncle or your twin brother blast it home. The MacLeods must've been involved in eight goals that game.

That night, Aunt and Uncle took the boys to a pub in Dunbarton to meet their friends. The one with the beard, Charlie or Drummond, asked a lot about the States, life in Cleveland and all. He soaked up the boys' lovable-losers bit about the Cleveland Browns, as he was a Hull man himself (consigned to rooting for a bottom-third team).

While the boys worked through pork chops and apples, the conversation bounced around. Rufus was enjoying his fare (and eyeing two plates of haggis warily) when Uncle accused them of having a charmed life.

"Mortimer, that's not true! What a pile of rubbish," Aunt Molly chided.

One of the others signaled that Uncle had had quite a few pints.

Us? A charmed life? Rufus wondered.

Uncle knew damned well, after all, that it was his own kid brother who'd decided to bail on fatherhood when the twins were four.

"It is true," Uncle said. "Next fall, they're off to university."

"Which they'll have to pay for! Just because the boys want to use their sharp brains instead of being a blockhead like you doesn't make 'em soft." Molly, red-faced, gave Rufus a reassuring look.

"You should get a job while you're there," Uncle said. "Books don't teach you everything."

"Aye," Charlie agreed.

"Stay out of it, *Charles*," Molly warned. "Your own girls are doing just fine *not* working in the yards. Am I wrong?"

"I'll get another round," Drummond said, looking to make a getaway.

Molly turned to Mitch and said, "Never you mind this rubbish. Your uncle's just trying to make up for not being there to set your dad straight. Think nothing of it."

"Maybe he's right, though," Rufus said, catching his aunt off-guard.

"O' course I'm right, Roof! Couple years slinging cement will help build you up, so you can shove those defenders off. Am I right?"

Charlie banged Uncle's mug with his own, spilling a bit.

"It's not the eighties anymore, Mortimer. Mitch and Rufus are going to school so they don't *have to* sling crap in a damned factory, right? As if that ever made anyone a better person."

"It would give 'em a taste of the life," Uncle said. "The other life, I mean." Uncle leaned toward Rufus, the "older" of the twins. "Believe me, having both perspectives would do ya some good. Be good for all your countrymen," he proclaimed. Sitting back, he said, "Maybe then you wouldn't have so many thieves. The bankers and lawyers. They knew what it was like to work hard, change their wicked ways."

"Now your uncle's just spouting 'cause he didn't get a choice," Aunt Molly told the boys. "That old saw. Pay it no mind."

"Connie and Liam didn't get a choice," Charlie said conversationally.

"That's right," Uncle agreed.

"Christ, not again," Aunt Molly said.

Drummond returned with more drinks. "Connie and Liam. No they didn't, no sir."

"They followed…" Aunt Molly's voice trailed off with a look from Uncle. "The money," she finished in a whisper, for Rufus.

The air in their corner of the pub seemed to have gotten colder, though it looked like Uncle was burning up with something. Rufus didn't know who Connie or Liam were. More importantly, judging from expressions around the table, he didn't know what had happened to them.

Uncle must've read his confusion. "Good chaps," he explained. "Lost on Piper Alpha."

All Rufus could offer was a blank look.

154

"What was that?" Mitch asked. Like Rufus, he was just a curious seventeen-year-old. The world was wide open.

"Bad oil rig fire. The worst," Molly told him, leaning close as if to crimp a water hose ahead of a flood. "Tell you later," she added, with a look to Rufus.

"To hell with Occidental," Charlie said, raising a glass. Uncle and Drummond raised theirs.

As if rehearsed, they chanted, "Fuck 'em hard and fuck 'em again!" They clinked glasses and drank. Molly drank as well, so the boys drank their sodas. It felt appropriate.

Later that night, when Uncle was blissfully out, Aunt Molly came to say goodnight to the brothers. Mitch was searching on his phone. She held out a book to Rufus. The cover showed a structure engulfed in flames. "Don't let it give you nightmares," she said. "I've had a few."

***

"Wake up, Josh. Enrique?"

MacLeod opens his eyes. It's later, now. Lighter. The wait has worked. Arturo is standing over him, with the cold toe of his boot against MacLeod's chin. There's a shower of white flowers and vines above him, up in the canopy.

"Time, MacLeod."

He nods slowly, his head hurting. Birds are squawking somewhere in the morning's dead light.

"You snore," Arturo says. He swipes a bug or something off MacLeod's hood and hauls him to his feet. "We piss, then we go. How much do you weigh?"

155

"One-seventy-five. Probably less, now," he says, trying to steady himself.

Arturo smirks. "Xavientar would break you in half," he states.

"Aye."

Xavientar? Who the hell is that?

They eat bars for breakfast while Arturo takes a call. He talks quietly, holding up a map. Enrique scans the environs with binoculars. When they're done, the bar wrappers go into a Ziploc bag in Enrique's duffel.

"Why don't you guys just let me go?"

That sounded reasonable. It can't hurt to ask, can it?

Enrique chuckles into his binoculars. "Nothing wrong with your sense of humor, man."

"Well, could you tell me where we're going, at least?"

"Southeast. That's all you need to know, now."

What's 'southeast' mean? What's there?

"To where?"

"Relax," Enrique mutters. "You'll find out."

Arturo hangs up the phone.

"You still have blood on you," Josh observes.

Arturo shrugs it off. "He'll meet us at Rio Negro," he tells Enrique. "Diez kilometers."

"Bueno," Enrique replies.

MacLeod watches the men check their weapons, wondering who the *he* is. If it's Satan himself—all fiery evil and rivers-of-dead-fetuses bullshit—at least MacLeod is better prepared.

Those men on Piper Alpha didn't have an opt-out clause, either.

Chapter 20

"Fantástico," Enrique mutters—his voice dripping with sarcasm. Beside him, Josh is elated.

The banana plants have parted to show them a gorge with sheer walls. Crossing it, strung 80 feet above a rocky river, is a wood-and-rope bridge straight from Hollywood films. Vines spider-web the granite façade, meeting a tangled mane of pink flowers. They've followed Arturo's map and compass accurately, so this path is no accident.

Brilliant. Death by plummet. Objection: Abuse of process, Your Honor.

"I will go first," Josh says.

"Be my guest," Enrique says, eyeing the drop.

The rope anchors are trees, one of which has fallen. MacLeod tries to compare the twelve-foot log's bulk to that of an overturned truck. He arrives at a guestimate of seven thousand pounds, with comparable friction potential based on the log's depression in the soil. It should hold.

Josh puts the machete away, licking his lips. He grips a rope railing and shakes it. The whole bridge sways a little. He pulls on the near rope with both hands. "Probably one at a time," he reports.

Enrique makes a noise. Josh gives them a big foolish grin and starts with baby steps.

If he falls, what happens? If the bridge fails while he's on it, does he die? Do I want him to die?

Either way, it would delay the all-important rendezvous at Rio Negro. That must be a good thing, as it's unlikely this is all leading to a surprise birthday party a la *The Game*.

Didn't Cora say I'm paying for my crimes? No, victories. *I have to pay the price for my victory. This has got to be about beating Italy, when we won it all. But this is a hell-of-a-lot of work for retribution.*

They still believe they've got Mitch. Cora knew—she saw it. I don't have the wicked scar on my side from that knife attack in Brighton. Mitch does. She covered it up when I was shirtless. She must've thought Arturo would go nuclear if he found out. In his shoes, I think I would.

Josh is halfway across, over the white water. He's walking on the rope itself, with a wide stance. Though the rope looks slick, there are no telltale signs of fraying. He's farther. Soon, he steps off the bridge onto solid ground and starts dancing.

To MacLeod, watching him celebrate is like studying a gray-green rotten peach you almost want to bite into—to experience the disgust you suspect is there simply because it's alien. The abyss, however, is not going to pull this bizarre creature over.

Be like Gollum, you freak, and dance your way right over the ledge. Give us a show.

Enrique mutters "piece of cake," and starts across. He uses baby steps, too. Carrying two bags over his shoulder, he goes slowly and clenches the ropes. The ancient planks look false and fragile, tested by his muscled bulk.

MacLeod squares-up to the bridge, now. The ropes are a yard apart, calling for a wide stance. The rubber band around his legs will not accommodate that.

Arturo's gun prods his back. "Don't get any ideas," he says.

"Cut my binds, please."

"What?"

Slowly, MacLeod turns to show him his stretched stance. The distance between his boots is six inches shy of the rope span. "Look at this. I don't want to fall!"

Enrique is across.

"You can do it."

"Arturo, please. Where am I going to go?"

Arturo rolls his eyes. "No tricks," he warns, slipping his own boot between MacLeod's legs and pressing down on the rubber band.

Why don't you cut it?

Carefully, practiced, the captive slips his right foot back and out, then the left one.

"I know you're hoping I would cut it off, as if I don't have a second one in my bag. Or that I would leave it on your foot, for you to drop as a clue halfway across the bridge. Too bad. We're always two steps ahead of you, MacLeod. Move!"

Mimicking the others, while desiring one clean shot at Arturo's sneering face, MacLeod sets his boots on the rope. He can't put a hand on each side, thanks to the binds. Instead, he grips the guide rope on the left, white-knuckle, finds his posture won't accommodate. He decides to go laterally on one rope.

If I slip, will Arturo be compelled to come rescue me? Jackass scheme!

A bird takes flight farther up the gorge. The leash cord clicks on each wood plank as he progresses. If he looks down, he'll throw up.

This one's only eighty feet. I might survive that!

The bridge starts tilting—with MacLeod pitching forward. He changes his grip from overhand to underhand and pushes in panic.

"Hold it," Enrique shouts.

To MacLeod's right, across the abyss, Josh is pushing the bottom rope he's not using. Enrique is crouched down at the other ropes, a hand on each, working to keep them vertically aligned with his body.

The water below is frothy. Sweat runs down MacLeod's sides.

"Keep going," Arturo commands.

Fuck you, Amigo!

Fighting off the urge to wail like a child, he slides his right foot over. Then his left. Shift grip. Repeat. Breathe.

Like Riley that time at school—breathing through the pain after someone crushed his world.

It takes a while, he imagines, but that's irrelevant. He's a man who's trying not to imagine the feeling of his forehead smashing against rock below. He edges his way over.

Finally, his boots are over rock. His fists, super-tight around the rope, are close to a browner hand.

Enrique grunts, "Come on! Be done with this."

MacLeod steps off, right into Josh's arms.

Behind him, Enrique grabs the leash and collapses on weeds. "You'd better be worth all this trouble, MacLeod!"

"I don't know if I am," he replies. "Why don't you guys just let me go? Get back to your normal lives."

161

Enrique laughs hard, and Josh joins in. Arturo makes his way across like a monkey, his face stern as ever.

"You really should have a career in comedy," Enrique says. "If you didn't have this date with destiny."

Feeling cheeky, now.

"Well, is she cute? A nice rack?"

"Ah, the comedian. Like you said," Josh reports.

Arturo slams MacLeod in the gut with a hard thing. White lights. He doubles over, wincing through coughs.

"I very much look forward to getting rid of you," he hisses in the captive's ear. "*Then* I can go on with my normal life, Cão!"

***

Why was I thinking of Riley up there, MacLeod wonders. *It's been years since I...since he...*

It comes back, a slate shard pushing through the gelatinous layers of briefs, hearings, mugs of ineffectual coffee at the kitchen table, tender moments with Emma, throw-in combination plays that occasionally worked out. A hard alien thing coming forth through a downpour, unperturbed by weather or years.

MacLeod was home on a laundry-grocery run one spring break. He didn't mind not having a car since he could roadtrip with Ellis and Priscilla from Youngstown (Soundgarden and Garbage the whole way). On a Sunday morning, while his mother and sister were at church, he went for a jog in the rain. A Zen-like freedom took over—time away from dry text and lamplight and cold dinners—and the miles stretched on. Soaked to the bone after 90 minutes, he was meandering home when he passed Riley's house. There'd been no draw or intent that he was aware of, but there it was, navy with white trim and a cherry tree blooming.

There in the driveway was Riley, shooting baskets. The net was graying and droopy, and the box was all but faded into white nothing. Somehow, this seemed to fit the shooter. Stooped and tired, no hop in his shot. From twenty yards away, MacLeod almost called his name. He didn't know what he'd say, other than a quick hello. Riley was not an old friend.

He didn't notice and MacLeod kept on running with heavy feet. In his periphery, the basketball clanged off the rim and plunked off the green Explorer, rolling into the yard. He paused before trudging to get it, appearing defeated.

MacLeod didn't think of Riley again (he believes) until years later, when someone forwarded him a Facebook post for Riley's memorial service. The page was populated with high-school names MacLeod remembered (Schenk was not among them) along with links for addiction services and the dangers of methamphetamines. Riley, it turned out, had walked into a live construction site in Cincinnati and was decapitated by a swinging crane load.

The tax litigation speaker droned on. Fellow conference attendees checked their watches, counting the minutes until an overpriced if lousy lunch would commence. Hopelessly lost in business-expense minutiae, MacLeod was puzzled by the sensation of stinging eyes.

Chapter 21

Rio Negro—a calm, blue ribbon that curves away into flat, emerald-hued country. This is the least challenging land he's seen on this journey. Where are they? This waterway could be in a hundred places on Earth.

So why here? What's so important about this spot?

The answer must lie with the cluster of posts and planks that someone might call a dock below them. Hardly big enough to stand on. It's a safe bet the President of Colombia will not be disembarking here.

They wait in the trees, under thick canopy, thirty yards from the dock. They're safely hidden from helicopters, like the one that flew by ten minutes ago. Military. It had missile launchers on the sides. To no surprise, it neither turned nor made a second pass. The party remained unseen, while the chopper moved either toward or away from trouble. Wondering which, MacLeod thinks of Herrera, at the old office. His *esposa* was an expert on South American history and politics. She could be MacLeod's on-site Wikipedia, having completed her dissertation on The Disappeared.

Right now, I've disappeared. The United States is looking for me. The world. The President. Navy SEALs are doing their thing. Soldiers in faraway listening outposts are combing through cell-phone conversations and volumes of data.

Or it's all a bullshit snow-job in the interest of keeping up appearances. Either way, I think I'm still fucked.

Across the river, small monkeys navigate a cracked tree. From here, the three of them look cute, harmless. Could there have been a fourth in the group—caught or slain by a hunter? The *serpiente* dude from their first day likely has no idea how close he was to being killed for convenience, or that a dire situation was playing out. Perhaps he didn't even know the name MacLeod.

The singular drop of a distant falling thing punctuates the swaying of palm fronds in breeze. To kill time, all MacLeod can do is wonder who the head honcho is. Is he the mystery man who came up with the plan, ordered everything, set up the houses and hideouts, the route, the men (and woman)? The guy with all the answers.

This jerk-off better be really impressive.

They wait. Nothing happens—no sounds of approaching vehicles. The monkeys leap away, off to better fruit or vantage point. A dragonfly hovers about the dock.

"Did they say anything else about those mudslides in Bangladesh?"

"It's bad," Arturo responds. "A thousand. Two thousand. Who knows?"

"I feel bad for those people, you know?" Enrique stretches his leg. "They're just trying to get by in mud huts. God says, 'Nothing personal, but here's another typhoon up your nose.' That's it."

"It's forsaken land," Josh chimes in. "There's too many of them, and there's nowhere to go. So they cling to the riverbanks like rats clawing their way to stability. There's no permanence anywhere."

Rats trying to get back into the prison. That's *permanence.*

Nearby, a bird takes flight for the other side of the river. Blue with yellow markings.

Maybe it's going to find a dead kid to scavenge, MacLeod decides.

165

Soon, a peculiar droning noise rises up, becoming distinct. It gets louder and changes pitch, becoming a boat motor.

"Here he is," Enrique reports.

A forest-green speedboat emerges from the bend in the river. The driver throttles down the engine to idle as it gets closer. He is alone, an older man in camouflage. A beard, salt-and-pepper hair, red sunglasses. His Latino complexion is expected, like a deeper tan than Arturo's. Waves lap the shore as he pulls up to the dock's remains. Appearing to be inexperienced with boats, he turns the craft this way and that on approach.

Arturo heads down to help. The interior of the boat appears to be navy blue—all of it. A dark tarp covers something in the front. The chrome parts have been painted in the ugly forest-green of the hull. There isn't a white or light-colored speck on the craft. MacLeod had never imagined camouflaging a boat like this, so it must have purpose.

Arturo eases the boat to a halt against the pylons. The man throws a mooring line over one post and climbs out in boots. He's chubby. The swagger in his walk marks him as someone with wealth. MacLeod finds such people easy to recognize.

The man and Arturo embrace. He claps Arturo on the back and kisses his cheek. Then he laughs.

"You have done well, Nephew!"

"Thank you."

"The road in was a little rough?" His accent is thicker than theirs.

"Nothing we couldn't handle."

They walk toward the party on shore.

"And your girl?"

166

Arturo makes a tight-lipped face. "She knew the risks."

"Sim, que pena. Enrique. Como você está!?"

"Ótimo, Obrigado!" They embrace.

"You are being a good soldier and listening to your brother?"

That's not Spanish, it's Portuguese. And isn't this just a cute love fest?

Enrique says, "He hasn't led me wrong, yet!"

"Ótimo, ótimo. And you must be *Josh*."

They shake hands.

"I'm along for the party, Sir."

"Good man."

The stranger turns an evil eye on MacLeod through his red sunglasses. His smug face is too nominally handsome to stand out. MacLeod chooses not to say anything. The man sneers and turns to give directions.

"That one," he says, jerking a thumb in MacLeod's direction, "under the covers. Bags and supplies. Everyone aboard!"

Josh and Enrique guide MacLeod to the boat. Enrique gets in first, feet squelching in the mud. The rubber bind fights MacLeod's step up. With effort, the men get him in without throwing him face-first. There are towels for their feet, two swivel chairs and a bench seat at the rear.

The old man pulls up the tarp, revealing crates of food, water, camping supplies and what looks like a folded-up blanket. There's a lane between the two rows. The uncle repeatedly glances at the sky.

167

"Get in there," Arturo says, hauling MacLeod forward. A wave of body odor hits. Enrique jams his gut with something heavy.

MacLeod bends over, coughing. All air has left him.

Fucker! Was that necessary?

They get him down onto the deck of the boat, face-down. When he opens his eyes, he's being shoved until his cranium bumps the fiberglass hull. It smells like finger paint from his old church preschool. Mrs. Marquez and Goldfish and "Jellybean Junction."

Enrique remarks and they stop pushing. Someone sets a heavy crate on his ass, and the world gets darker. The deck's textured pattern presses into MacLeod's cheek. His bound hands are stuck under his crotch. His feet are banded together, and he's hemmed in by crates on three sides. He forces himself to take a deep breath, to control the fear that's creeping over him like wicked spiders.

"I was delayed," the old man growls. "Rebels cut trees at the stream. I had to go around. Filthy bastards."

"Are you worried they could mistake you for someone else?"

"You mean, like a regular army colonel?" Squeaking is him monkeying with a chair. "No worries. From what I hear, those fat cats would be riding around with a flag and a full detachment. I'm better off looking like a kingpin. Nobody messes with them."

The old man throttles up and they're moving. A tease of wind sneaks up MacLeod's left pants leg, while the rest of him is starting to get hot.

What's the point of all this? Where are we going? Why are we going there? It doesn't make any goddamned sense!

The boat turns this way and that. Things clink and shift in the crates.

Enrique said he better be worth it. All the work to get him somewhere safely—that's what he was talking about. But the ransom idea has worn through—the reward risked ten times on this trip, already.

If it isn't about a cash payout, why worry about getting him somewhere safely? Why not just kill him on the spot, in Ciudad Panama?

Because I'm going to be used for something, MacLeod concludes. *Probably not anything too cheery, either.*

In heat and darkness, he retreats, shutting out the madness of this world.

Chapter 22

"The keeper blocks it! Unbelievable! Ball comes out to Spazzio on the right. A try—and it's blocked! Carpenter got it again! Sensational! Ball's out to Ferguson. And he's seen something 'cause he launches it downfield. It's MacLeod. Could this be another miracle? Streaking past the Italians! Free in the middle. They might have something here. The ball drops to MacLeod. Little deft touch to the—OH! He hammers it home! What a brilliant strike! Rizzi never had a chance at it! The Americans have scored! The Americans have scored! They're in front of Italy with but a minute left in the game! Do you believe it?! Mitch MacLeod again!"

Joyous pandemonium filled the world of Americans and soccer fans everywhere.

It has been anointed The Greatest Play of All Time. And The Miracle, and Payback, and The Catastrophic Counter. Since the play was actually a sequence of five individually crucial moments of action, sport columnists debated which was the most important.

In what was arguably a stupid call, Pappas was flagged for fouling Enrico Gandolfini *in* the box deep in stoppage time. Though people the world over were crying foul (the so-called flop happened at the *edge*, on the line) it appeared that an Italian penalty kick would deliver the World Cup trophy to the *Azzurri*. The American side would settle for runners-up, no small feat considering it was their best campaign ever. Fate was written.

The PK was set. Dan Carpenter, son of a sheet-metal worker and a special-ed teacher—and a man who'd admitted on film how much he loathed penalty shots—guessed correctly. He blocked Gandolfini's laser with his elbows. The ball bounced out, to where Julius Spazzio had muscled inside of midfielder

170

Gutierrez. Spazzio didn't get a clean take—the ball popped off his shin-guard. Carpenter, on the ground, followed his training and lifted his leg in the air. Spazzio's shot caromed off Carpenter's toe and looped out to left-back Ferguson. Stunned fans, behind horrified or elated faces, believed they were looking at an overtime game. Instead, what appeared to be Ferguson's All-World Clear became the most brilliant pass in history.

Striker Mitchell James MacLeod, waiting at the halfway line, took off. It was verified by seven different camera angles that he sprang into action faster than the two Italian defenders, who were gawking at the blown penalty. Onside and with a bubble, MacLeod raced from the center circle toward right goal post. By all accounts, Ferguson's ball arced 87 yards through the air. It dropped to MacLeod two strides from the penalty spot. MacLeod, a lefty in full sprint, deftly popped it up with his right foot. When the ball descended to inches off the turf, he hammered it with his left. Rizzi, the Italian keeper, never had a real chance at blocking it. The spinning orb punched the back of the goal net and MacLeod checked the near-side line judge to see that his off-sides flag had not been raised. He was quickly buried under celebratory teammates, then carried off the field.

Eventually, the referee regained enough control to officially end it with a kick-off. Gandolfini was so disgusted he kicked the ball into the stands.

MacLeod and Carpenter made the cover of most every large publication across the globe. U.S. magazines ran special second-by-second breakdown sections. Headlines featured 'Magical' and 'Unbelievable' and 'Victorious' to go with gushing interviews and team-of-destiny flavor stories. It was, people said, the antithesis of 9/11—a stunning, improbable victory carried out by a multicultural cast of heroes and reserves (including MacLeod, despite his Brazil goals) previously ranked 21st in the world. Even British columnists (whose Three Lions had made the quarterfinals) admitted that it was a greater upset than Leicester City taking the 2016 E.P.L. crown.

Cartoons the world over displayed the final seconds, frequently showing the *Azzurri* defenders getting lap dances or enjoying poolside drinks while a blurry U.S. flag races through. Half the Italian squad went into hiding (keeper Rizzi was rumored to have been thrown into an Indonesian volcano or was taking inventory at an Antarctic science station).

In America, books and magazines and posters sold out. The *blacks* were so popular they had to be purchased on eBay. ESPN's SportsCenter changed its opening to include MacLeod's shot. Equipment stores couldn't keep stock, and recreational soccer leagues swelled. Best of all, according to MacLeod, charities were raking it in. Food banks were inundated. Kids got coats, women's shelters expanded. MacLeod and right-mid Hasegawa were interviewed at a clouded leopard preserve in Thailand. The second it hit YouTube, an anonymous company donated $10 million each to the preserve and the World Wildlife Fund. In a grand ceremony (following the two million-strong victory parade in Chicago) U.S. Soccer handed over its World Cup purse to Children's Hospital. Everybody won.

Rufus Mortimer MacLeod, watching on a law-office conference room screen, couldn't believe it. A grid of briefs and notes covered the table—Sunday-afternoon preparation for a Monday hearing—and homemade chicken salad waited in a bowl. Emma had come for moral support, and so they could watch the game together. When the goal played out on the screen, the two of them danced around the room. It was simply too good to be true.

Then the team carrying Mitch. Then Gandolfini's act of frustrated concession. Then three lovely tweets, and glory.

For months, Rufus woke in darkness and heard the jubilant stadium roar. His feet hit the coarse area rug, and a sense of pride carried him toward the bathroom and his day.

My brother, the one and only Mitch MacLeod.

Ironically, Mitch wasn't supposed to be one of the stars. Riggs was considered the *Yankees'* best weapon. He left the quarterfinal against Belgium with a bad shoulder. Carstens went in, resulting in an off-kilter attack. If Jackson hadn't played so brilliantly, reacting and lunging like a maniac, then there wouldn't have been any heroics against Brazil in the semis. The final wouldn't have happened.

Riggs. Carstens. Jackson. Gutierrez deflecting that Brazilian mid's top-of-the-key strike. Carpenter, again and again. Then Mitch. Right now, I suppose he's safe and pacing a room somewhere, behind twenty American guards with guns.

If you can hear me, Bro, would you point Lady Lucinda my way?

***

The engine throttles down. The boat slows as they turn.

"Fucking assholes," someone says.

Who, the rebels?

"Check the map." That was the old man.

"Enrique?"

"I got it. Nothing, yet."

"They just cut down the trees and don't watch?" Josh.

"Sí. They want to give people headaches, that's all."

"Nothing," Enrique reports.

Thunder rumbles in the distance. MacLeod is surprised he can hear it over the motor.

173

If it is thunder. Shit, could those be explosions? Like with the rebels? Have these assholes dragged me all the way out here just to get killed by revolutionaries?

"I think we are blocked in," Arturo says. "If we go here or here, it takes us southwest. We won't get within thirty kilometers of the border."

"Shit! Those dogs."

Border? What border?

The boat is turning slowly. They seem to be idling, now.

"What do you want to do?"

A pause.

"We go on foot. We were going to have to do that, anyway."

"All right! The adventure continues." That was Josh.

Another turn. Then contact. It feels like the boat is pushing forward onto land. Things scrape underneath, then stop.

"Let's go," the old man says. "We'll get the mule to pull us in."

Someone chuckles. Movement. Someone has stepped off the boat.

A brief yearning to sleep—to be left alone—is incinerated by the world brightening quickly. The cover is now off.

"Come on, MacLeod," Enrique says. He pulls on the leash.

Motherfucker!

MacLeod is forced to get up on his knees, with the cord digging into his throat and crotch.

"Stand up, Hero!"

"Go fuck yourself."

"Oh, someone's going to get a lesson in *etiquette* before this is over."

"Save it, Hermano," Arturo says. The cord around MacLeod's neck slackens a bit. Arturo and Josh help him step out of the boat.

The shore is different here. They've moored the boat in a small spot between gnarled trees with thick roots. From here, it looks like the river narrows and disappears altogether beneath a huge fallen tree. Stark-white wood shows where it's been cut. His captors didn't think to bring their own axes.

Arturo puts a rope in MacLeod's hands. It's tied to the mooring ring on the front of the boat. "Trabajas," he says, pointing.

Work. Job. Fuck you. I have a job. It isn't what I want, but it beats this.

Still, he glances toward an opening among roots and puddles. A cloud of bugs hovers around the mud. The other men are off the boat. He gives Arturo an annoyed expression.

"Do you need convincing?" Arturo asks with dead eyes. "We brought the pliers."

Chinga tu madre, Asshole!

Following another second of hesitance—the sheer distaste of forced labor—MacLeod gets a tight grip on the rope and aligns himself with the front of the craft. Josh leads, casually waving at clouds of bugs.

175

He pulls. The boat is plenty heavy, but it isn't impossible. It has a flattened 'V' bottom made of fiberglass or aluminum.

Thinking of the seated rows he's done over the years—probably more than Mitch—he leans back and pulls. Back up, find stable footing, lean back and pull. Correct form or not, the boat comes. Again. Out of the water. It gets heavier, all the way out, now. The bottom slides over roots, exuding a watery-earth smell. He adjusts his footing again, aware of how Enrique and the new man watch with amusement. Arturo scans the area with his binoculars.

Farther back from the water, his boots find a little pond with squishy black mud. A few turtles are hanging out, being turtles. Though his path brings him near, he's careful to not run them over with the boat.

What does quicksand look like? If the turtles are on the mud, and aren't sinking, the ground must be okay, right? How much do these little guys weigh, anyway? Eight inches across, two pounds each?

His feet sink into the mud, up to his socks. He could feel ludicrous, a circus animal having to withdraw each foot and find better ground. He's squelching, for God's sake.

The boat fights him over a stump. He feels the slightest amount of pride when it relents and comes to a spot between two trees. Will a snapped rope indicate a small victory? His neck aches, chafing under the damnable leash. One more big pull.

"I think he's done, now," Josh calls to the others.

"Bueno," Arturo returns.

MacLeod has pulled the boat twenty-five feet from the water, one and-a-half lengths. His hollow victory becomes frail—the distance felt much farther.

When Josh leads him back over, the three Latinos are conversing in whispers. Their bags are on the grass. MacLeod's eyes fall on a new duffle stuffed with a rolled-up blanket. Its strange pattern includes turquoise, tan and red.

Why does he get the feeling his fate is tied to that blanket?

Lumps on the sides of another bag tell him there are cylindrical supplies, too. Like water.

"Water, please?" he asks no one in particular.

Enrique turns to him and laughs. "Seriously?"

MacLeod fights a new itch in his throat, studying the turf.

"I would like some agua, por favor."

"Drink the river, man."

He looks at Arturo and the old man, then beyond them to the waterway. A mouthful of that, he believes, would be a complimentary serving of Montezuma's Revenge.

Arturo verifies their course on the map.

"All right," the older man says. "Vámanos."

Enrique drapes two bags over MacLeod's shoulders this time, so he has one on each side. The right one is heavier—it has the bottles of water—while the old man carries the blanket bag. Enrique grabs the leash, and he and Josh walk behind MacLeod. Arturo leads, map and machete.

MacLeod can't help focusing on the blanket and the old man's weird red shades. It's become cloudy again, dark enough to suggest a wicked cold snap. After a few minutes, they reconnect with a trail that runs parallel to the river. MacLeod honestly has no idea which direction they're traveling, raising the question of what border somebody mentioned earlier. Venezuela and Brazil are his best guesses. Neither one seems more desirable than here.

Rumbling above, this time, is thunder. The sky opens up—rain coming down hard and hot.

Ignoring the ache around his neck from the cord, MacLeod tilts his head up and catches drops in his mouth. He's tired, beat. At the least, this offers a little parasite-free relief from the sky.

The old man—*Did someone call him Olivar?*—glances back through his red shades. He mentions something to Arturo, followed by laughter.

In the hot rain, they push deeper into Hell's heart.

Chapter 23

"What an amazing strike! Once again, MacLeod does it! Once again, this young man from Cleveland has snatched victory from the jaws of defeat! Cliché as that sounds, it is absolutely true. First, the Brazilians. Now, the Azzurri—*this time for that precious solid-gold cup down on that fancy stand. If you're watching this or listening and think you're dreaming, you are not!"*

The trek has continued for at least the length of a soccer game. Time out here has begun to feel elastic—and irrelevant. MacLeod stopped scanning for tripwires, animals or signs of rebels a while ago. Arturo would reach it first. At this point, introduction of a *rogue element* can't possibly make his situation worse. He's a pawn of revenge, and those people die.

Still, with each successive step, the alarm bells in the back of his head ring a tad louder. It's likely he's going to experience revenge—*real* hatred—at the old man's hands. 'Robbed of power,' someone once said of a king in a movie he can't place. That seems appropriate, now. Hunger and fatigue have bled his ability to care. Rain or no rain, his boots progress down the Death Road, down that path of military-industrial 1984-type order Pink Floyd warned about in a seminal album. "The Call of Ktulu" rolls on, antithetical to all the briefs filed early, hands shaken, volleys, step-over attacks, Christmas morning gift openings, kisses for a loved one.

How much of it matters, now? I'm here. Mitch is safe. Emma is safe, if in the dark. They'll eventually get on with their lives, no matter what happens to me.

It's too difficult to think of his wife 'moving on.' His cerebral cortex has thrown up a wall where questions bounce off harmlessly.

His mother will move on, as will Janice. They'll be the family members *of*, with stories to tell and interviews not-so-politely asking what it's like to have this happen to a son, an older brother.

And Mitch—his womb partner for all time, souls eternally coming up cat's eye in tic tac toe—he'll get on with life, too. A black armband (for both teams) and sympathy flowers and money directed to charities. His twin brother is set to become a "60 Minutes" episode.

A funny thought strikes him. That maybe this close call would convince Mitch to marry that hot barista, Lakshmi. She seems nice on the videos. Laid back, intelligent, tolerant of his antics.

Thanks for the va-jay-jay shot by the way, you dork. Great to have that pop up on my phone during an arbitration hearing.

An angular dark mass catches MacLeod's eye, as Arturo and the old man have stopped. Without having to shoot crocodiles or machete-chop snakes or dodge frantic monkeys or pterodactyls, they have reached the hideout.

A hundred yards down a slope sits a cabin with real walls and a floor and ceiling. Moss and ferns cover the roof. It's all in shades of brown and green, set back a few minutes from the trail. Arturo approaches first, leading with the gun. He quickly confirms the place is deserted, and the party descends into a gorge to reach it. This being Colombia, MacLeod reasons, this spot could be a kind of drug traffickers' rest stop.

This Olivar guy must be connected—a friend in the industry. Otherwise, the party would've walked into certain death as surely as if the rebels had found them. From what MacLeod has read, drug traffickers don't think of February (or any month) as the off season.

180

It stands to reason, as well, that there must be a road or an airfield nearby. Escape is a possibility.

Don't get ahead of yourself, MacLeod. You're forgetting the handcuffs, leash and four armed assholes surrounding you. Don't cue up the adventure music, yet.

Here and there, Enrique had waited back to watch and listen behind them. For the *rogue element*, perhaps. He doesn't seem as concerned as the day before. He might be thinking they ditched the phantom threat when they got in the boat. Without any concept of time elapsed, no estimates of distance are left. Whoever that pursuer is, he must be far, far behind now.

The plywood cabin has two day-lit rooms—a main room with shelves and overturned furniture, and a bedroom with metal bunk beds and old mattresses. Opposite the door, the walls are only stomach-high, with the open space above serving as glassless windows. It's like someone ran out of materials and just left it as-is.

Arturo is shooting something in the corner when MacLeod steps inside. Black licorice segments say it was a snake. The violence and dart-gun sounds of a silenced pistol seem routine, now. Enrique checks the bunk room. Droppings on the floor indicate the birds are happy with the window arrangement. Rolls of white at the top must be mosquito netting. MacLeod glances at the dead snake, wondering what kind it was and if that dictated its remaining lifespan, anyway. There's always something bigger, faster and more vicious in the jungle.

They let him wander to the open windows, where there's a view of the gorge beyond. A high waterfall off to the left feeds a rocky stream down below them. It disappears among ferns and other greenery. Maybe running toward Rio Negro. He's so turned around, he doesn't know which way to begin. That seems like a moot question, at this point.

Where is Emma, when she should be turning his chin and pointing out the potential of variegated layers? Peach begonias there, with blue hydrangeas behind them for contrast.

She's safe and sound. Sano y salvo. Probably going out of her mind, like Mom and Grandma and Janice. And Mitch.

"Piss break," Josh tells him, pulling the leash outside.

It's drizzling when he takes MacLeod a short distance from the cabin for business time. The diminished amount of urine is a harsh reminder of how little food he's consumed over the last few days. He's probably a little thinner, too.

"Another relaxing vacation spot," Josh says. "It might be nice to bring a lady here, and go rustic."

Play it cool. Maybe I can get some information from him.

"Yeah, if not for the drug dealers and all."

"That's true. I understand they are *slightly* possessive of their crap." He laughs at his own joke, not in any hurry to get back. "I don't know how Enrique's uncle is connected like this. I mean, it's one thing to have money, and he has a lot of it. Cell phones or something. But it's a different story to actually know a drug lord and say, 'Señor, do you mind if I borrow your pad for a couple days?' I mean, those people have a reputation for being so ruthless. I think you'd have to be halfway crazy just to approach one, you know? Unless he knows them through business."

Good, light. Coupla joes having a regular chat. Keep it going.

"That's probably what it is. In the States, all the big fat-cats are interconnected. They sit on each other's companies' board of directors and stuff. That's where they get a lot of their moolah."

Sounds good, approachable.

MacLeod glances around. "So, what's going on? Where are we?"

Josh glances behind him. "Mister Olivar said we're about five kilometers from the border. We're going to wait until tonight and go in the dark."

Something!

"The border of...Brazil?"

"That's right. Smart guy. Did you figure, we're heading southeast, we must be getting over to Brazil?"

Brazil? Why Brazil?

"Uh, lucky guess. I mean, we keep moving. We've got to be moving somewhere."

"Oh, I know. Otherwise, we're just lost souls wandering around the jungle, waiting for the spirits to come get us."

"Why do we cross in the dark? Over to Brazil."

"They said it's because of the government patrols in daytime. Like they sweep by with helicopters twice a day or something."

The rain picks up again, announced by half-hearted thunder.

"The Colombians or the Brazilians?"

"Brazilians. Personally, I don't think there's a chance in hell of that. Even if they see the rebels, what are they going to do about it? It's two hundred clicks of jungle in each direction, no roads. And the two governments aren't exactly buddy-buddy right now, so the Brazilians wouldn't help the Colombians find the rebels on this side. Probably moot, anyway."

183

"The helicopters we saw this morning."

"Exactly. Honestly, I wish Mister Olivar wasn't leading us right down the middle of rebel-held territory, but what are you going to do? A job is a job, man."

MacLeod pauses for a second, dining on information, hungry for more. The way things are shaping up, this could be his last chance.

"The job is…to capture me and trek across Colombia, to Brazil, right? Why? Is…is this about ransom? About the game?"

"Not about a ransom."

Fuck. Well that seals it.

MacLeod's hands are shaking, his flesh appearing strangely pale and vulnerable compared to the dark wood around. He glances about for the point of a log, anything to catch his leg band on.

What did Enrique say yesterday? They're not taking me across the border to ransom *me. If that's right…there's only one other reason why they'd do this. What else can you learn?*

"This is about beating Italy? About a football game?"

Don't panic, don't panic. Keep cool.

Josh shrugs. "Yeah."

"This is *not* about beating Italy," Enrique says, stepping out from behind a thick tree. He wears a sneer.

"Oh, right," Josh says, poking something with a stick.

"Then…will you tell me what it's about, Enrique?"

Enrique's fists are clenched as he circles the captive. "We would've *flattened* Italy, the way they played against you! They would have had *no* chance! None!" He's behind him, now.

184

"But, Diabo Norte appeared out of smoke and stole the game. And for that, he will pay."

Diabo Norte? What? What the hell is he talking about?

Wait wait wait…that word doesn't sound Spanish. It's 'diablo'. He's not pronouncing the 'l'. Unless that's not in Spanish, but in…Portuguese.

"Brazil," MacLeod blurts out. "Th-this is about beating Brazil? In the semifinal match?"

"Don't pretend you didn't know, MacLeod."

"Know? Of course I didn't know! Who—this—n-none of this makes any sense to me! To think that some guys would—"

"Now you talk like an American. 'I didn't know.' 'It doesn't make any sense to me.' Always pretending to be a step behind the pack in understanding. Pretending to be *innocent*. In reality," he says, gesturing to the sky, "the puppet masters."

MacLeod looks at him, not sure of what to say.

"How many puppet governments have you propped up? Twelve? Twenty? The Banana Republics. The Eastern Bloc. Iraq." He sneers again. "And to think you feel righteous enough to compete in the sacred game, in the sacred tournament."

"You've been…speaking Spanish," MacLeod observes, realizing how stupid it sounds in retrospect. "Your accent…I figured…"

"The language of the conquerors. Sí." Enrique sticks a thumb in his own chest. "My heart always belongs to Brasil. Arturo and I, we bleed with the people. We suffer with them. We have suffered long and hard…because of *you*."

"Ah, the *Azuliqapavor*," Josh says.

185

MacLeod forgot he's still here. Just watching this little show.

"That's right, Josh. *Azuliqapavor.*"

Azuliqapavor? Azuliqapavor. I've heard of that. Markets falling. Housing sell-off. Idle farmers. Those rioters near São Paulo...Oh, shit! Is that Mitch? They blame Mitch *for the whole country's depression?*

"Seriously?" he asks Enrique, who doesn't respond. "This is because...he won a game for our side?"

"The big one," Josh corrects.

Enrique says nothing. If he caught the word 'he' instead of 'I', it doesn't register.

"All this...about a football game? Come on! Seriously?" he asks Enrique, forcing a chuckle. "A football ga—"

Lightning-fast, Enrique grabs MacLeod by the front of his sweatshirt and hauls him somewhere.

Whoa! What?

His legs go out from under him. On his knees. Ahead of him is a cone nest.

Fire ants?!

The iron grip on MacLeod's throat and shoulder holds him suspended, inches from the miniscule mountain.

Oh God, don't!!! I'll be eaten alive!

Afraid to even breathe, MacLeod holds his bound arms down against his groin. He can't let them swing or touch anywhere near the nest.

A few of the little insects crawl about, off on their missions.

186

"The only reason I don't shove you in face-first is because Uncle wants you alive and in good health for the ritual. Got it? Otherwise, *adios Muchacho!*"

Enrique pulls him to his feet.

Thank God!

Once he's upright, Enrique jacks him in the face.

MacLeod falls backward, unable to help himself. He crashes on a fern, his sense of balance obliterated by a stinging nose. He can hardly see.

"Laugh about that," Enrique snarls. He rubs his knuckles and stomps off.

Have I landed on an ant nest?!

MacLeod frantically wiggles about, trying to see what he's on. It's just safe greenery, a crushed fern. He shakes his head to fight through the teary-eyed itch, the shame of a bloodied left nostril.

"Man, he tagged you," Josh gushes.

He's still here, watching? Of course he is. They can't leave me unguarded.

"Didn't they teach you how to fight in the Premier League? Bam! Boom!"

Ignoring him, MacLeod gingerly turns over and attempts to rise up. It takes a couple tries. Times when he was knocked flat on the pitch, there was always someone else's hand to help him stand. At his feet, the squashed plant looks rather sad.

There lay the great Roof MacLeod, twin of American hero and Culverhouse Crossing striker Mitch MacLeod...before they dragged his ass into Brazil for God knows whatever fate.

He fights against teary eyes and a quivering lip. He manages to wipe his bloody nose on his right sleeve. The pain is familiar, safe. Better than being eaten. The word 'deserve' flutters in his mind.

A helicopter passes in the distance.

"I think we're going to put you on trial or something," Josh says.

"Really? Sounds awesome."

"Arturo said it's important. Part of cleansing the land of your spirit. I think that's how he put it."

Might as well try.

"Josh, I'm not Mitch MacLeod." A pause. "I'm Rufus. Mitch's twin brother."

Josh looks up from his whittling. His narrowed eyes start to widen. An excited smile appears. He glances back toward the cabin.

"No shit? That's hilarious! I *knew* there was something off about you. You're too nice and polite to be a striker. I knew it. Ha!" Another glance at the cabin.

Is he contemplating a move?

"Oh man, this is big. The wrong guy. The wrong twin. Man, you can't make this stuff up!"

"We were both at the club," MacLeod explains, excitement lifting his voice. "We were both wearing the black T-shirts, the ones with the American flag."

"And we grabbed you by the bathroom and snuck out the fire exit, right into the van. Oh, that's funny."

Good, good. Keep it going. Maybe he can help me.

"I think Cora realized it."

He lowers his voice. "How?"

"The scar. Mitch has a bad knife scar, from when he was attacked in Brighton. On his side," MacLeod says, patting his own side. "He has it, but I don't. I'm not Mitch. She must've seen it when my shirt was off."

"Ah," he says, eyes full of glee. "That tracks. Smart girl. She would've figured it out, anyway. Women always know."

Try it.

"So, can you help me?"

Josh glances back at the cabin. "Well, that's too bad. Good luck convincing this group. They're committed. The reason Mister Olivar wears the red shades is so he doesn't get mesmerized by your *blue azul magic* or whatever."

What? Knowing I'm the wrong fucking guy and you still can't?

"Let me go. Please."

"Can't," he says. "They'd kill me so fast it would be pathetic." He shrugs. "Then they'd hunt you down and kill you. They'd probably still go through with the trial. I bet they would."

No no no.

MacLeod lets out a heavy sigh. A frayed rope is severed, dropping into the dark hole. "What...what trial?"

Josh jabs a thumb back toward the cabin. "For being the Diabo Norte."

MacLeod just stares back at him.

"Oh, I know," Josh says, whittling away. "I don't get a lot of this Charrúa Indian shit, either. Evil spirits and alignment

189

of the cosmos and all that. But," he adds, like he's arguing for the defense, "I told myself: It's a lot of money. And you'll get to be part of something crazy good, like capturing an international football star. Never get another chance to do that. And I definitely won't get another chance to see a person skinned alive, so...why not?"

What?!!!

Bile rises up. MacLeod coughs.

"What was that again?!"

"Skinned alive," Josh deadpans.

We're not choosing a breakfast cereal, you whacko! You're talking about...oh God, they can't! Me. Me!

"Oh, I guess you wouldn't know that part. Yeah, sorry. That's part of the ritual." He ticks off on his fingers. "There's the humiliation, the powerless bit, the regrets, something else." His dirty fingers dance in air. "I forget the order. I don't know. Maybe it's not important."

The world is spinning. MacLeod can barely stay on his feet.

"I *do* know we're going to cut through the fence and go a little ways into Brazil. And there's this stone altar. Do you call it a dais? And that's where you'll be sacrificed, at sunrise."

Sunrise. Sacrificed.

"C'est la vie," he says. "In my home country, we're pretty good about saying things like that. It's a holdover from the Soviet days, the Iron Fist. 'Where is Aunt Zuzana?' 'Oh, she died. A soldier shot her in the street. She looked at his uniform funny. C'est la vie! Stuff like that, man. Anyway."

I'm going to be skinned alive in Brazil! Oh God.

I can't resist. If I do, they'll just gag me and drag me.

Skinned alive?! Maybe they'll scalp me, first. If they do, won't I bleed to death quickly? What if they start with my chest? Or my fingers?

This can't be happening!

Arturo has come out.

"Mister Olivar is meditating right now," he says.

Drops of rain filter through his goatee.

Billions of rain drops fall here, falling on me. Will they cool me off when these men are cutting me open? Will they do anything to soothe the burning?

"When he is ready, we will commence your trial."

"My trial?"

"*Azuliqapavor*. This is how it will be done, Diabo Norte. The land will be cleansed of your wickedry, and then you will meet your end."

He grabs the leash and walks. MacLeod stands still.

Arturo senses the resistance. He wears a pernicious grin when he yanks MacLeod over to the ground.

Fuck you. Choke me to death, you pig!

The pain is intense—crotch and throat and spine. He closes his eyes against it, wondering how long it will take to succumb.

Arturo growls with joyous labor. Catching on to the ploy, he grabs MacLeod under one arm and drags him over. A sturdy tree leans over the hideout. He tries the metal ring that's been affixed to the trunk. Satisfied, he removes the pulley-system connection and loops the leash through it. With a demonic growl, he hauls MacLeod to his feet and pins him against the trunk.

No no no, choke me out. Kill me now!

Before MacLeod can see the ring and get the gist, Arturo tightens the slack and ties a knot. MacLeod finds he has just enough slack to stand next to the tree and lean. Not enough slack to sit down. Red-faced and sweating, he pulls on it. Pain—crotch and throat.

Trembling with rage and agony, MacLeod stops pulling.

No, I can't do it! I'm not strong enough. Who…what was the name of that emperor in that Marlowe play…Tamburlaine? Bajazeth. That was it. He brained himself. So did his wife. Strong enough. I'm…not strong enough.

Josh has followed. He finds a rock to sit on, and continues whittling in the pouring rain.

MacLeod studies his new spot, the metal ring drug traffickers must've affixed to hang things.

These bastards have thought of everything. They can't even let me off myself!

"North Devil," MacLeod mutters in disgust. "Diabo Norte."

It's ridiculous. It's ridiculous. It's all fucked. The world is fucked up. Nothing makes sense. And ridiculous people have plans, and all the power.

"You've got bad pizzazz, man!"

He pulls on the binds again. Any chance of breaking free, or throttling Josh?

A small lightbulb goes on, that he missed the fact that Arturo and Enrique are Brazilian rather than Hispanic. It's almost funny, his missing that. With the accents and Spanish conversation, it's no wonder he couldn't tell the difference. Voices were never his strong suit. He supposes it must be easy for some, being fluent in both languages.

What's it matter? We all swung the trees from Ethiopia, anyway.

A weird smoke smell comes from the cabin, acrid and sharp among the wet vegetation. It must be Olivar's bullshit meditation. MacLeod's remaining life is down to minutes. He's pretty well buggered. William Wallace looked so brave and defiant in that Mel Gibson movie.

Not me. I'll be screaming and wailing like…like a man being tortured to death.

He looks up the slope, through the green and rain. He can't even find the spot where they left the trail. Who could ever find him down here, awaiting his fate?

Whoever that guy was, I guess he won't get to be my hero. Well, he can say he tried.

Son of a bitch. I'm going to die here, in the jungle, and there's nothing I or anyone else can do about it.

Snot and blood and rain—*torture soup* down his face. He doesn't resemble the brave, defiant American. Not like this.

Neither did Riley, he recalls, staring at popping puddles in his driveway.

MacLeod growls at himself. He growls at both a past and a future he seems powerless to alter.

Okay Mitch…I'll be taking one for the team today. Make it count.

He shuts his eyes, listening to the river of the downpour.

Chapter 24

Somehow, they are paired. Inseparable. One's failure, the other's ultimate victory. They are chained together, hanging off either side of a pinnacle. The modern history of the MacLeods: Roof's silence-filled falling when he was on the rise; Mitch's sudden skyrocketing from passed-over reserve to team savior, national hero.

The irony of a trapped, determined man having no effect swinging a sledge hammer. The irony of Mitch's Magic Moment—the greatest play in sports history—*not* being the reason an American is tied up and doomed in Latin America.

It was his 93rd-minute goal to beat Brazil that did it. Mitch making his move, trying to find Jackson, the crazy ricochets. Then Mitch being shoved over, taking a desperate shot with his right, and bouncing it right under the keeper's arm.

It was a seminal moment for U.S. Soccer, for underdog teams everywhere. The *Yankees* got past *a seleção* when most analysts thought it was Brazil's year. History written. Millions and millions of people stopping to take notice, daring to wonder What If. Across the globe, it seemed, people lined up to root for America in the final. The sentiment was particularly strong in non-Italian Europe, partly because of Italian striker Spazzio's well-documented dirty play (a flagrant, uncalled hand-ball against Germany didn't help). What had seemed utterly improbable became a surprise tidal wave of red-white-and-blue support, everywhere.

Except in Brazil, where they began falling apart at the seams.

Your twin brother is seen as a true hero. The play the whole world remembers—inconsequential to these men because he denied them the chance to play Italy for the gold. Madness.

194

Movement. Someone is untying him. Enrique.

My time is up. No, first I have this stupid trial thing.

MacLeod doesn't protest when he's led into the cabin. A primal voice tells him to save his energy. That there will be a better time.

He may have nodded off, half-leaning on a tree. There's no agony roaring from his crotch. Maybe his levels of discomfort have been 'recalibrated for the conditions,' as his friend says. Which friend? He can't remember. That face and voice reside in the domain of the old world.

The cabin stinks from incense burning, and the paltry furniture has been removed. On the floor by the window is a red box, done with spray paint. A cluster of bird droppings there echoes his sentiments. This has all the legitimacy of an unqualified real-estate billionaire thinking he could run a country, no matter who put him there. Enrique leads him to the box.

The old man, Olivar, comes out of the other room, followed by Arturo. Olivar wears a kind of headdress with colorful feathers. Combined with his weird sunglasses and a tan-colored shawl over his shoulders, it could be a third-grader's Halloween outfit. He walks slowly, carrying a rolled-up scroll. Arturo, unadorned, carries another.

Olivar speaks in a language MacLeod doesn't recognize. It's a short phrase.

Arturo says, "Diabo Norte will kneel for its trial."

MacLeod glances at Enrique, who'd apparently like nothing better than to apply a club. Slowly, he drops to his knees in the box. Enrique takes the leash and hooks it to something above. It's tight, but MacLeod can breathe. There must be a hook or ring in the ceiling, like the one outside.

195

Enrique joins his brother and uncle at the front of the room, five yards from the defendant. Five yards from his black-and-rose granite kitchen island to the living room's bay window. During their condo hunting, Emma asked him to think in square feet, instead of yards, as realtors only dealt in square footage. Josh nimbly drops to a cross-legged seat by the door to the other room. He laces his dirty fingers under his chin, curious.

They're trying me. I'm a real lawyer. Fucking hilarious.

Olivar opens his scroll. So does Arturo.

Olivar speaks more in the strange language. Arturo waits until he's done. "The trial of the insufferable Diabo Norte now begins."

Chapter 25

Jesus, are they serious? These grown men are actually doing this? What a crock of shit.

Arturo seems to repeat his line in Portuguese. It isn't Spanish, MacLeod knows, so he supplies his own dialogue for sanity's sake.

Cleveland International Airport is a non-smoking facility. All unattended bags will be confiscated. Thank you for your cooperation. El aeropuerto internacional de Cleveland es...

Olivar speaks a line.

"Diabo Norte will only reply when spoken to," Arturo says in English. Then in Portuguese.

Olivar speaks.

"We will hear the grievances." Then in Portuguese.

Just relax, Counselor. This is going to take a while.

He forces himself to sit compliantly on his heels. No fire ants. No crocodiles. *Just rusty nails, bird shit, snake guts in the corner, faded spray-paint pricing from Home Depot Bogotá East.* And waiting.

Olivar speaks. Then Arturo. "Diabo Norte will own up to its crimes. First, that it knowingly used deceit and trickery to score in a football match against the benevolent peoples of Brazil." Again in Portuguese.

Olivar.

Arturo. "How does Diabo Norte answer?" Repeat.

They all look at MacLeod.

I didn't do anything wrong. Neither did Mitch. He won a soccer game.

MacLeod shakes his head. "No. No I didn't…"

Enrique comes over, something metal and blue in his hand.

It's a tool. Pliers! What is he—

He grabs MacLeod's hand, his right middle finger. The nail. With the pliers.

Oh fuck-fuck-fuck!

The captive screams out, fire ripping through his hand and arm. He pulls against the leash and is choked by the cord.

Enrique opens the pliers. A white and red object drops to the wood floor. MacLeod is panting. The pain is an angry thing behind his navel. A phantom dribble of pee has escaped into his underwear.

Try to block it out, Roof. You can make it better. Stay still. Breathe. Focus on the floor.

With effort, he steadies himself and the pull on his throat gets better. The tiny object on the floor is his fingernail. Smooth curve. Torn skin. Blood. His body part, removed.

Enrique is still standing over him.

Olivar speaks. Arturo follows him. "Diabo Norte will remain silent during this trial."

"Hear that?" Enrique asks, clicking the pliers before his face. "You have nine more fingernails. Keep disagreeing, and maybe I'll take your tongue next."

Blinking through tears, MacLeod glares up at him.

198

Enrique returns to his post. Olivar reads a line. "How does Diabo Norte answer to the first crime?"

You are reduced. Your finger is still attached. Toe the line or you'll lose it!

Keeping his eyes on them, trying to ignore the insult and cries betrayal from his wringing hands, MacLeod nods slowly.

Olivar. "Second, Diabo Norte committed fouls against the players of the benevolent peoples of Brazil."

A nod.

Olivar. "Third, Diabo Norte knowingly and intentionally cheated in using an unfair play to defeat the team from the land of Italia."

What the hell is he talking about?

It doesn't matter. Just nod, you fool.

A nod.

Olivar. "Fourth, Diabo Norte knowingly and deceitfully took advantage of sloppy play by players from the land of Italia to steal what rightfully belonged to the benevolent peoples of Brazil."

A nod.

Olivar. "Fifth, Diabo Norte will agree to return to the benevolent peoples of Brazil what it has stolen with these wicked actions."

How?

A nod.

Olivar. "Diabo Norte has accepted responsibility for these crimes. Diabo Norte will be punished accordingly."

MacLeod watches them, not sure if he's supposed to nod.

Is this done with, now?

Olivar clears his throat and reads, followed by Arturo in English. "Now, Diabo Norte will answer to crimes committed by the devils from his wicked nation. First, that the devils from the wicked nation to the north have made war on unsuspecting and innocent peoples in the surrounding lands."

MacLeod watches them. Enrique gives him a look, perhaps hoping for disagreement and subsequent entertainment.

A nod.

Olivar. "Second, that the devils from the wicked nation to the north have used agents of deceit to improperly learn knowledge about the benevolent peoples in the surrounding lands."

Spies. Who doesn't?

A nod.

Josh has gotten up and gone into the other room.

Maybe he's bored. Too much like school for an ADD kid.

Olivar. "Third, that the devils from the wicked nation to the north have removed from power those who disagree with the wicked nation's political agenda and machines of commerce."

A nod.

Olivar. "Fourth, that the devils from the wicked nation to the north have put into power the selected agents, regardless of the peoples' wishes, who submit to and further the wicked nation's political agenda and machines of commerce."

A nod.

Olivar. "Fifth, that the devils from the wicked nation to the north have engaged in the illegal and poisonous practice known as 'nation-building.'"

Okay, yeah, we've done that.

A nod.

Olivar. "Sixth, that the devils from the wicked nation to the north have used economic force to dominate and strangle the benevolent farmers and laborers of this land and surrounding lands."

Yeah, that too.

A nod.

Olivar. "Seventh, that the devils from the wicked nation to the north have made war on the benevolent peoples of the faraway lands of Vietnam, Afghanistan and Iraq."

A nod.

Olivar. "Eighth, that the devils from the wicked nation to the north will continue to make war on benevolent peoples and use economic coercion to satisfy their own political and commercial needs."

A nod.

Olivar. "So ends the list of grievances against the devils from the wicked nation to the north."

They wait. Enrique is looking at his uncle's scroll.

Are we done, yet?

Olivar. "Now, Diabo Norte will have the opportunity to accept and understand the criminality of its actions. Does Diabo Norte submit to this part of the trial?"

Do I have a choice?

A nod.

Olivar reads. "The court asks if Diabo Norte regrets its actions during the aforementioned football contest with the players of the country of Brazil." Repeat.

A nod. What else can be done?

Olivar. "The court hears this regret. Next, the court asks if Diabo Norte regrets its actions during the aforementioned football contest with the players of the land of Italia."

A nod.

Olivar. "The court hears this regret. Next, the court asks if Diabo Norte feels it has any power left to harm, deceive, make war or defend its way of life."

No, Assholes, you've pretty much taken all the power I have.

MacLeod shakes his head slowly.

Olivar. "The court hears Diabo Norte acknowledge that it has lost its power. Next, the court asks if Diabo Norte chooses to yield to the judgment and sentence rendered by this court."

MacLeod nods slowly.

Olivar reads, followed by Arturo. "The court hears and accepts this decision by Diabo Norte."

The defendant shuts his eyes, fearing the worst.

Okay, here it comes!

Olivar spews his part. Arturo seems to relish his part, magnanimously repeating the so-called 'sentence' in English. "It is the judgment of this court that Diabo Norte is guilty of these heard grievances. The correct punishment for these grievances is—"

PLINK-BONK.

Chapter 26

Something has rolled across the floor. It sounded metal.

There. Don't look!

It's rolling away from MacLeod.

BANG!

A brilliant flash tears at his eyelids. The sound fills everything he knows. Hot air.

It's a bomb!

What's happened?

Open your eyes and find out.

Sparks and smoke have appeared on the floor. Enrique is standing at the door, covering his ears.

MacLeod is dizzy, everything off-kilter, aware that he's falling over.

Something is happening. Something—

Enrique comes flying backward across the room, toward him.

A blast of air fills the world. The roar is deadened, muffled.

Another explosion?

Something wet hits MacLeod's forehead and finger.

Arturo is fleeing.

There's a sharp, acrid smell.

Enrique lands near him. He flops like a fish, close to MacLeod's elevated knees.

The cord is tighter around his neck.

I'm being choked.

There's blood all over the place.

I'm choking.

Olivar is trying to flee, hands over his ears. His headdress is crumpled on the floor.

Enrique is still. There's blood everywhere—on his chest and neck and chin and cheek.

I'm choking.

There's a man at the open door, holding a shotgun. Dark clothing. Camouflage. Dark complexion. Boots. Equipped. Shotgun. Something alien to focus on.

His eyes pass over MacLeod.

He's turning left, aiming at Olivar.

He fires. A flash.

A blast of air fills the room.

I'm choking.

Olivar's leg erupts in dark red.

The dark man spins around the open door.

He faces MacLeod and aims.

No! Not me!!!

A muzzle flash.

Force.

Something explodes nearby. Hot air hits his face.

Am I hit?

The burst was above him, he realizes.

Enrique's eye has rolled to look at MacLeod, half-shut. A raspberry-jam crater covers his chest.

Bits of wood rain down. The cord isn't choking MacLeod. It's gotten looser.

Olivar appears to be howling. He is gripping his right thigh, which ends in a scarlet stump. MacLeod can't hear his cries.

Next to him, the dark man is looking to the left. He takes a step toward MacLeod. He shoots left, around the open door, toward the other room. The force pushes the door away from him. Wood splinters on the wall by the doorway.

MacLeod is going over backward, off-balance, falling. Things drop on him—bits, splinters of wood, dust, his leash, a metal ring. It pings off his cheekbone.

What? Did he shoot the ceiling?

The man takes another step toward him, pumping the shotgun. His focus and body are still turned toward the other room.

He fires again. This time MacLeod feels it, pushing against him. On the floor, Enrique is utterly still, eyes half shut.

On the other side, in his periphery, Olivar is raising a hand to his head. Falling over.

The dark man—tall, Latin, gloves, stern face—pumps and fires again. He is upon MacLeod.

Enrique is dead. He's after Josh and Arturo.

He has released the shotgun. It is falling to the floor, pointed away.

What in the hell is he doing? He just—

The steely, stubble-faced man grabs MacLeod by the upper arms. He lifts him up.

He's picking me up like this? Yes, I'm upright.

MacLeod's arms are pinned to his sides. In a display of strength, he's being lifted and carried.

Whoa—going backward, now. Why?

The backs of his legs hit the window sill. The man is cringing, his eyes focused.

I'm going out?

Falling backward, now. Turning sideways.

The man has released his grip and is reaching for something else, turning away.

MacLeod falls through the air.

Chapter 27

The cabin window and the foreign man roll out of view.

Shit, what's below me?

He crashes onto plants and earth, ferns and green spin. During his tumble down the slope, he briefly glimpses the cabin again. A dark object seemed to be in the air, coming out the window. Not the man, his rescuer. Something small.

What is that?

His car-accident disorientation is exacerbated by the silence. He doesn't understand why his hearing is gone.

The object—do I want it? I must want it.

He can't stop moving. Another, faster glimpse of the cabin.

There's no sign of his rescuer, but it seems like part of the window frame is splintered and red.

Where is the item he threw out?

Things claw his face. His hands, surprisingly free, grab at bushes and plants and earth. Pain shouts from all over.

Finally, he stops, his feet swinging down into a tree trunk.

Where is it—whatever it is?

Trying to keep his head from spinning, he glances around.

Thank God Arturo removed the pulley cord. My grapes would be squashed by now. There!

In a fern three yards uphill sits a long, dark case. He lunges for it with the clumsiness of a drunken man. It's in a black case and has a green-and-white bubble compass on the blunt end.

A knife!

It feels supreme in his hands, an instrument of weight and intent.

He scrambles down behind the tree. His legs resist, caught on something. He's still wearing the rubber band. The knife case has a Velcro strap, which is tough to open like it's never been used. His fingers don't want to work—his right hand whimpers displeasure—but he gets it open on the second try. The weapon is a jagged beast of a thing, seven inches long.

He knows enough to swipe away from his body when he cuts the rubber band.

My legs are free. They can move freely.

He starts to turn the blade around, focusing on the hand tie.

No, run! Worry about your hands later.

He glances up at the cabin. No movement. The ruined, red-splotched window piece stands out ominously in the afternoon light. His rescuer isn't coming along.

He takes off, halfway down the slope. The stream is below. Across from him, the hill climbs steeply. Nearly jubilant, he bounds down toward the stream, trying not to slip in the mud. The leash trails behind him.

Don't catch on anything, you bastard.

The frothy stream weaves among slick, black boulders. The water is warm. He nearly face-plants, trying to hurry across.

On solid ground, he glances back at the cabin. If someone's taking aim to shoot, he needs to know.

Josh and Arturo are at the window, scanning.

Fuck!

Josh points. MacLeod returns to the work of climbing the slope. Loose, wet earth. A log slides under his feet. He grabs at a thick-stemmed plant, which holds. He stays upright and bites his tongue, the leash choking him.

Vibrations. Things hit the bushes nearby. They're shooting.

MacLeod's loose, scrambling up and away from danger. The top is thick with bushes. He plunges in, knowing he needs to put as much stuff between him and the pursuers as possible.

Run like hell, man.

His leash snags on something, almost hanging him again. He wrenches it free and shoves it down the front of his pants.

Find a way to deal with that later.

He hurries on. The bushes and trees are thick. Leaves scrape his cheeks. He must be making a lot of noise. Maybe the rain can help deaden the sound, flatten things out. Hope will have to be good enough, as he still can't hear a thing.

What in the hell was that thing that guy used? If it was a grenade, wouldn't I have been blown to bits?

MacLeod knows he must be leaving a trail as if a bull came through. Arturo always seemed comfortable with the jungle. He probably has tracking skills.

A view opens up. He's reached a little cut below his rock ledge. He heads down to the right, scanning for trouble. He seems to be alone. Could this be a good spot to get free?

This rock is like one of those boulders on that hiking trail in Washington. The glaciers carried along fifty-ton chunks of rock and randomly deposited them on hillsides.

At the bottom, twenty feet below the ledge, he hooks a left and hugs the wall. His hearing seems to be better, recuperating from under-the-water dullness. He concentrates. It happened so fast. The bomb device, Enrique flying back, the rescuer blasting away and heaving him out the window.

His heart has been throbbing, he realizes, as if he'll be betrayed by a pulsing ricocheting off this rock. At the moment, he seems covered. A granite ledge cuts across the sky, becoming reddish earth fifty yards off. If Arturo and Josh get to the ledge, they probably can't see him.

But he won't know they're above him unless he can hear them coming. A moment of sheer quiet tells him that's a deceptive hope. He'll have to look.

Have I gone far enough for this?

Against the wall, he unsheathes the knife. It's an impressive blade. Slowly, he turns it toward himself.

This thing is made for stunning violence, removing organs and life force.

The plastic tie that binds his wrists is thin. Polyethylene terephthalate—sturdy material. The gap between his wrists is a half-inch at most. Much of that space was occupied by the metal cord that kept him crippled, the one that kept wracking him.

Insane device. Brilliant, but insane. Must've been Cora's.

The knife ought to go through the plastic tie easily enough. Sawing will be safer than pressing the blade against it, he figures. Pressing, if the blade pops through, he could disembowel himself with this monster.

In a bizarre mental spot between panic and prudence, he sets the blade between his thighs and clenches. After a moment, rubbing his wrists against it, his hands are free. The weapon's wicked capability has been confirmed. He gazes at it.

Will I actually use this on one of them? Do I want that?

He slides the knife back in its case, unable to picture himself going through the act—that blade plunging into flesh.

Wait, what was that? A noise?

He hugs the wall and freezes. So still he can hear his own heartbeat in the rain.

Are you hearing things? Phantoms? Or is there something there?

He can't look. If he comes out to look, he might see Josh's shotgun pointed down at him. The end.

Of all our senses, the ears have the best ability to deceive us.

Was it a physics professor who said that? He and Mitch had that survey class together.

He waits, listening. Nothing. The reality is, he can't hear enough of anything. Without this sense—or guidance—he's blind.

The weapon is weighty in his hand. It is an instrument of potential, for those with enough malice or desperation in their bones. In the movies, it looks so easy. The good guy hides behind a tree or a wall. The bad guy passes. The good guy sneaks up behind him and strikes.

Yeah, but you're not James Bond or Rambo. You're a lawyer who couldn't even sneak up on a toddler. You've never attacked a person in your whole life.

The voice is right. Any thoughts of heroism are predicated on Josh and Arturo coming down from the ledge and *not* looking behind them, *not* sensing or hearing him before he creeps up and acts faster than a gun.

Utterly impossible. I'd be dead, right there by those bushes.

After a few deep breaths, he sneaks out from the rock, trying not to trip on anything. He risks a look, fear pulling his face tight. The ledge is clear. Shocked, he comes to his senses and scampers across to the other side of the gully.

Chapter 28

God, this is amazing—freedom like this. My body can move!

MacLeod races up the other side of the little valley and reaches a tree at the top. The rain pauses. From behind the tree, he risks a look back.

Nothing.

Wait—there!

Movement. Yes, someone's coming through the green, almost at the top of the ledge.

Thirty additional seconds of indecision, and he'd be dead right now. He slinks away, trying to be quiet. He stays low. The less space his form occupies in someone's vision, the better. And he probably won't get any kind of warning before bullets come through the leaves.

Now, hurry. Fast.

He glances at the knife's compass. Northwest seems to be the best way—moving away from Brazil.

The image of Enrique lying on the floor of the cabin, after the shooting started. All the blood, the huge hole in his chest. He was looking at MacLeod when he died. Did he have regrets?

Goddamned fanatic. Shotgun death, the real thing. And that Olivar guy, having his leg blown off.

A phantom pain pulsates through his hip and groin. His own body is empathizing. Could the men have found a tourniquet for Olivar, or was he done for?

MacLeod tries to keep quiet. There's no way of knowing if the others' hearing is just as depleted as his. Josh was in the other room when it all started. Arturo ducked away, caught unarmed.

Dense fog is rolling through a new cut. Soon, visibility drops to twenty feet. He could be on the edge of the Colombian Grand Canyon and not know it.

Arturo knows this terrain, and he doesn't have to be quiet. He's the seeker. Does it matter if he's heard? He must know MacLeod won't turn and face him, man to man. He's got a gun. He's probably got several guns.

Shit, what am I doing? The guy's practically a soldier.

The jungle stops, opening onto a grassy slope that narrows on the left. More cover on the other side, a hundred yards away. In the grassy area between, he'll stand out like a strobe light.

Is there a choice? Stand and fight? No.

Gritting his teeth, he bursts out onto the grass and runs as fast as he can. A section of bamboo looks solid ahead, calling out to him. He dodges around it and goes five yards deep before nerves force him to look. From a spot with good cover, he peers back through a gap in the leaves.

Josh emerges onto the grass, carrying his shotgun and wearing a backpack.

Josh. So where is Arturo? There goes the wild hope that maybe the two would've run into each other and mistakenly fired. Damn. Arturo may hate him—that scene at the first hideout—but they're allied in getting me.

Josh is walking slowly, looking around MacLeod's section of greenery. It seems too quiet.

MacLeod can't wait. He turns and creeps away. If he can move from tree to tree, he might maintain the distance.

It's getting darker in here. He's completely lost track of the day's hours. Is nighttime close?

A dog bark comes from somewhere.

Dog bark?

Bits of wood splinter off a tree trunk to his left, twelve feet away. Leaves are ripped.

Not a dog bark, you idiot! It was Josh's Babushka, or whatever the hell he called it.

He runs.

Was he firing blind, or did he hear me?

Something pops in his left ear. The world becomes noisier. He hurries from tree to tree, grateful for any solid mass between himself and the madman.

Was Arturo with him? MacLeod wishes he knew for certain, and that he's not going to run into him in here. Could Arturo have gotten around in front of him somehow? Hasn't he been moving too fast for that? In the cut where he sawed through his binds, he had a few minutes' wait. It didn't seem like there was a decent way around, though. Arturo might've passed by on a different route, then. There's simply no telling.

Move faster. You don't want this to end now.

The hoodie is heavy with rainwater and sweat. He wonders if he should've taken it off earlier, as he'd certainly be a step faster without it. But now it would be a clear marker to follow. He's better off with the illusion of protection, at least.

Any second, Arturo could appear out of nowhere and start shooting. MacLeod will have no hope then. He can't outrun bullets. Trees and plants won't become obstructions to honor the number of times he and Emma have donated to environmental causes. That maybe they'll shift and obstruct a few bullets.

God, you're thinking nonsense. Just run!

The land rises and falls and twists. There's a mountain off to the right, though it looks too far away to provide an escape. For a man whose life of late has become death by twelve-point courier font, overland distance is hard to judge.

He'll have to rely on speed and Lady Lucinda.

Chapter 29

How fast can MacLeod cover a mile in this jungle? Ten minutes? Nine? If it takes the others twelve minutes, that would put him a ways ahead. Twenty minutes, give or take, since he saw Josh.

Water.

The rain faucet has turned off, yet he still hears rushing water. As if called, he turns toward it and ducks a few spider webs. If he finds rushing river rapids, will he have the guts to try a crossing?

Hoping it's something significantly smaller, he bounds to the top of a shaded ridge. Down a ravine is a gushing creek. It looks to be five yards across, broken up by rock islands. Off to his left, fifty yards away, is a waterfall. It drops in several tiers. At the base, the riot of white water stands out against a dark patch. To a man in desperate need of harbor, it looks promising.

It could also be a trap, he concedes—one way in, one way out. The urge to try this solution billows, as night is coming on quickly. This isn't like the time he flooded the toilet and, panicking, tore off his old rugby shirt to contain the mess.

He looks back for a moment and catches nothing. In a perfect world, he'd be able to check that he hasn't left behind any kind of trail—snapped plant stems or footprints in the mud. In a perfect world, he wouldn't be relying on a primordial ravine to save his life. And if Arturo and Josh find this place, he will have made the mother of all mistakes.

You're a hundred miles from the nearest city or coast. Do something!

Sure enough, the base of the waterfall is near-black behind hanging vines. It's a cave. There are no crocodiles in sight.

His minutes of advantage have probably bled down to seconds. Taking hold of his leash—he's not faking out a defender, here—he leapfrogs across the rock islands, banging his shin on the way. When he lands safely, biting his lower lip against crying out, his hand is on a two-inch-thick tree branch. It's fairly straight.

Do I have time?

The wood of the branch seems strong, so he works like a madman. With the serrated knife, it takes only a couple minutes to saw through. He checks both the ridge and the cave, convinced danger should be right on top of him. When he takes the branch piece, a spot of stark-white wood is left. It stands out like bone—an obvious sign of disturbance. He shifts it away and covers it with fallen leaves and a rock. Blood throbbing in his ears, he does his best to scatter the shavings with his boot.

Holding the branch and knife, he creeps over head-sized rocks to the base of the falls. Beyond, the cave is a black maw among the brown-gray rock wall. Spaghetti-thin snakes hanging over its entrance are really just vines. Anything could be inside, though.

There doesn't seem to be time for caution. He hustles to a spot behind the waterfall, hoping for concealment.

In his hand, the shaft of wood is mostly straight, almost four feet long.

Now, how did Josh do this?

Gripping the branch with his right hand—he and Mitch are both lefties—he hacks at it with the knife. It isn't the same as peeling sweet potatoes, he realizes, and he doesn't know what angle to use. Nature favors forty-dive degrees for mountain

219

angles, so he aims for that. Peaks look plenty sharp from a distance.

After a few minutes, he gets one end of the branch into a sharp point. It looks decent enough to inflict damage. Looking out through the pouring water, he sees no threats and continues.

Some insane motherfucker stabs my brother with a steak knife in a nightclub in downtown Brighton. Now I'm here—a sane man—trying to carve a spear out of a tree branch in the jungle, hoping I don't have to use it.

Quickly, he whittles the other end into a point. Now he's got the knife and a two-ended spear—a quasi-impressive hunter of old. It will have to be good enough.

Glancing back, he approaches the cave, sore feet feeling for stable rocks. He can't see anything inside.

Hearing is returning. With another pop, the waterfall fills his ears with noise. With the rejuvenated sense, he listens for any pitch change or movement. That may be all the warning he gets.

The yawning cave is like a test of courage. His teeth chatter, as he's soaked to the bone. Even through the heat of fear, the opening feels refrigerator cold.

No crocs in here—too bloody cold. With drug-runners or smugglers, there'd be signs of human life. What about leopards or jaguars? Would a cat make its den in a cave like this? Bears in Colombia? Fuck, this is insanity.

He hears nothing different, which means nothing by itself. Slowly, his eyes adjust. He can see variations and shapes in the dark. The mouth floor is littered with granite baseballs. Thinking he'd rather face a surprise than learn of it from behind, he chucks a rock. It clatters off brethren. No reaction. A second time, farther. It bounces off a wall and other rocks. Nothing moves.

220

What else is in here? Scorpions and spiders? Bats? Centipedes?

Nothing has reacted so far, that he can see. He doesn't want to guess any more about creatures that scurry in darkness. He takes a few more steps. Nothing. Maddening nothingness. His eyes and ears discern only emptiness and rock. Waiting out the night in this place seems better than being *out there* in the true jungle.

An illusion of protection, but it's all he's got. He doesn't want to sleep, but he *needs* to sleep. If there is a tomorrow, he can't face it hallucinatory-zombie-tired. Jurgens, at the office, when his daughter was born. The poor guy stood during meetings, slurping coffee, for fear that to sit down was to nod off and incur unholy wrath from Missavit.

As darkness advances behind him, MacLeod approaches the unknown with his weapons. For an act of lunacy, this cave represents his basket of options. Five yards from the entrance, before the cave jogs left, is a rock that has potential. He cannot literally stand on his feet all night. If there *is* a tomorrow, he'll have to get there by waiting on this rock. Waiting in shadows and darkness, behind a waterfall. Waiting with a homemade spear and his new knife—the gift from a stranger.

After he shot Cora. After he saved my miserable life...and gave up his own. That was bravery! Tracking us that far—however the hell he did it. Outnumbered four-to-one in a rescue operation. He must've known. Whoever you are, man, I hope your family gets a colossal payout and a medal.

Peering out at the darkening world, he feels reduced by the genuine courage of this ultimate cost-benefit ratio question. MacLeod is alive because someone else did what *he* believed was right. This unnamed hero chose to kill, and risk being killed, because MacLeod's life was deemed invaluable. A lawyer and husband. A soccer star (by mistake). An American.

221

From now on, every deposit in a barista's tip jar or pedestrian soccer pass or response to a charity cold call better measure up.

Chapter 30

Son of a bitch, MacLeod thought, gawking up at the union building's TV.

On another Saturday gobbled up by the Notre Dame library, he'd taken a quick break to hit the union cafeteria for a sandwich. Students were massed under the three screens, mostly focused on the Irish's game at Navy. But MacLeod glanced up in time to see Mel Schenker taking off his helmet on the Purdue sideline. Elated, he was being congratulated by teammates. He'd just made his third interception of the day against Northwestern. A rowdy S-C-H-E-N-K fan club in the stands sported mushroom-shaped wigs to go with their painted chests and #31 signs. A mug of Schenk—with the same over-confident smile MacLeod remembered—floated up on the screen comparing him to other defensive backs in the country.

The bastard made it.

MacLeod had the exact same sentiment five years later when Schenk made a "textbook" interception against a rookie Detroit Lions quarterback. It was his third season in the NFL. No arrests for driving under the influence or battery, a clean nose. A paid professional. Like Mitch.

What would've happened, though? If I'd reported that beat-down of Riley, would Purdue have rescinded their scholarship offer?

MacLeod had no idea, of course, if there even *was* a scholarship at stake. Schenk could've walked on the team, and paid for school with the usual basket of student loans. Would *anything* have happened if he'd spoken up? People back home might just chalk it up to a football star blowing off some steam. (Three-year lettermen, it reasoned, were afforded such liberties with their aggression.)

Hadn't Riley deserved it? The guy was a prick.

Was it the question of loyalty that nagged him like an invisible splinter in the flesh of his palm? Had he liked Schenk that much? They'd palled around at malls and parties. Never really close, but never any disagreements. The guy's confidence and enthusiasm were infectious—someone cool not named Mitch. He was all right. Coleman, too. Obviously, since MacLeod had never said anything, he was square with what had happened. Riley *was* a pain in the ass.

Still, if I'd said something...

Maybe Riley wouldn't have "fallen into the meth trap" as Madison had put it on the phone. Maybe he wouldn't have swayed into a construction site in Columbus—deliriously high— and gotten his head taken off by a swinging crane-load of pipes.

Phuong, at the new office, is fond of that term *cost-benefit ratio*. Everything breaks down to that, she says (ingrained after fifteen years in product-safety work). Costs weighed against benefits for everything in life. "Apply the filter, MacLeod. *Trust* it."

Missavit howling at Bettancourt because she'd played a gamble, stepped out-of-line. Cost: Vocational jeopardy via volcanic superior. Benefit: Augmented reputation through slick maneuvering.

Candance DeMeers wanting to give her deposition 3,000 miles from her former employer. Cost: The revulsion and therapy associated with her managerial job. Benefit: Safety, peace of mind. *(Candance. Can-dance—freely, safely.)*

Uncle Mort's friends who'd obediently mustered into a "safe" island amid an inferno on the North Sea. Cost: Worry, fear, their lives. Benefit: None.

MacLeod pausing at the high school vice principal's door, the scene of Riley's beating by Schenk on his mind, and choosing to walk away. Cost: A classmate's psyche, a man's future. Benefit: No disturbance in the river, no awkward pause in the typical school drama.

Emma's fallen expression when he told her he'd have to skip the Pittsburgh theatre festival and work all weekend to catch up. Cost: Spousal sadness and disappointment, missed bistro food and romance and hilarity. Benefit. *Benefit...*

The cursor in his brain blinks expectantly. A phantom of the $3,700 swing (seventeen billable hours versus not splurging $1,500 over a carefree trip) hovers in the darkness of the screen, itself aware of lost relevance. The line, instead, remains empty, the cursor moved elsewhere.

He did as he was told (faithfully, steadfastly).

Benefit: None.

Toe the line, toe the line, toe the line.

Chapter 31

Roof MacLeod, you've been bought and sold to settle someone else's debt. The wrong people are dead—it's supposed to be you back there—and two nut-jobs are hunting for you. Thank you, Azuliqapavor. *Really.*

The stone under his seat—cursed. The water running outside—cursed. The rocks at his feet—cursed. The terrible bogeyman *Azuliqapavor* holds sway here, a Voodoo-armed demigod wearing a necklace of children's skulls.

How can I escape this? I'm so fucked!

Sitting in this cave, still on the Colombia side, he's probably 300 miles from Rio de Janeiro. *Not that it matters. These maniacs believe in the* Azuliqapavor *and carry it with them. Their madness will find me.*

A sigh escapes his lips. This new tempest in his life had been wrought by a bad myth. The *Azuliqapavor.* A whispered thing, like *chupacabra* or *yeti.* You know it's out there. It doesn't really have a place, a home, except *down here.* One of those nebulous folktale things that provides color in an airplane magazine or late-night news show. Spooking, maiming, crushing.

Working ninety-hour weeks, MacLeod's life has barely made room for Emma. There simply wasn't time to follow another country's economic decline—not with the Russians flexing their tank-tattooed arms and Malaysian terrorist concerns filling the air.

There were the riots in São Paulo and Recife, he recalls. Police crackdowns sent scores to the hospital. Some died when police used tear gas to disperse a massive town-square protest of the government. Corruption and bribery bred chaos.

Blame your elected officials, not me.

If the whole of Brazil fell into a nationwide funk—the Azuliqapavor—thanks to an unfavorable soccer game, it seems crazy. His rec-squad teammate Tony said a lot of it was a holdover from the disappointment of the 2014 Cup. The country had spent gobs of money on stadiums and airports, exorbitant piles. More was supposed to go to education and infrastructure, but the poor essentially got nothing out of '14. Then *a seleção* got trounced in an "early" exit and the Rio Olympics set another burner going under the pot. Eventually, something had to blow.

So Mitch and Company beats the national team four years later and it sets off a depression across Brazil? Because Americans did it?

Other nonsense had surfaced. A row with native tribes on the Amazon, with the United Nations issuing an edict. Things had deteriorated in the favelas. Mitch said Culverhouse Crossing and other teams delivered a bunch of signed soccer balls and shoes to those kids (a safe option, rather than risk insult with food or textbooks, which might've been burned).

Retirement communities were threatened, as well. Big crowds marching up the driveways with pitchforks and Molotov cocktails, stopped at the gates by panicky guards and their machine guns. Residents deserved to celebrate Thanksgiving normally, as their fellow Americans back north would.

MacLeod's mother has gotten the brochures. Brazil wanted in on the action—the droves of American retirees who passed up the Sunshine State for Mexico and Costa Rica. She said there's at least three big retirement centers north of Fortaleza, on the Atlantic coast. Thousands of Americans and Canadians in each (plus a number of Germans). Casinos, fine dining, golf, the works. A new, small airport (dubbed Condy-Orange after Orange County in Anaheim) welcomed people from Miami and Dallas-Fort Worth. To those shouting protesters—the ones without jobs or prospects or decent food, the pundits had said—Turkey Day gorging on Brazilian soil must've seemed like a kick in the groin.

Then Brazilian Army helicopters showed up with rubber bullets for crowd dispersal…no wonder these guys are so pissed at me, or Mitch. Arturo'd probably like to throttle any Yankee he could get his hands on.

Try me, Diabo Norte. Skin me alive on Homeland soil. Demon dispelled, the land is free. Makes sense.

He fights another shivering spell, stamping his feet on the uneven stones. Hopeful that no danger is upon him—that he won't see Arturo's goatee and glare appear beyond the water—he puts the spear between his numb thighs and crosses his arms.

On the soccer pitch, it was always so easy. His thin, muscular body had always revved the engine-heater for the Beautiful Game. Twelve degrees and snowing once, and they still gathered enough lads for a five-on-five. Players were there to play, not bitch about weather. Get your gloves on and get on with it.

Can't he pretend, now?

Don't be such a molly-coddled bairn. Of course you can!

That's right, Uncle. I may not be Mitch, but I'm Roof, a MacLeod. I can hack it. Boy, Dad's going to feel like shit for bugging out on us. Mom's got to be going out of her mind, whichever truth she's heard.

There are two truths, he figures. In the grand scheme of things, certain information was made public and the rest was withheld. It has to happen that way. Public-relations fiascos are a popular item at law conferences. Who's *supposed* to know *what* and who *definitely should not* know *what?*

It reasons that Mitch himself or a teammate realized immediately that something bad was up. A guy doesn't take

228

fifteen minutes in the bathroom for a leak. Considering all the people coming in and out, Arturo's window of opportunity was probably mere seconds. Less than a minute to grab a man, throw a hood over his head, and wrestle him down a hall and out a guarded side door. The van doors shut and nobody's the wiser.

He can't recall any tingling or alarm in his head competing with the lime vodka tonic. No sensation that anything might be amiss as he rinsed amaretto soap off his hands and dried them with a paper towel.

My fate was changed in the span of seconds. Mere bad luck.

No, not bad luck. Of course.

It was a Panamanian nightclub, and the Men's Team players went unannounced. So Cora, Enrique and Arturo blended anonymously among the dozens already there. Either directed before the fact or given up during the entourage ride there, some unit of the team staff knew. Suspicions ran to an unnamed member of Security—a man who could reliably point a bunch of thick-wallet bachelors toward a spot with the prettiest chicas. Easy enough. It had an upstairs corner spot in what had seemed like an upscale part of town.

They nabbed me faster than the SAS could've. Brilliant.

With limited exposure to law-enforcement standards, he's had to ponder fleeting summations of the aftermath. It feels likely that Mitch himself and company were quietly whisked away to their deluxe hotel, protected by many guns. Hours after an extensive search turned up nothing—*At least they would've done that for me*—the team president decided to release the fact that Mitch *was* taken. It generates instant concern and worry, it mobilizes forces all the way up the chain—*that* Mitch MacLeod is missing—and it maintains a ruse rather than destabilize a situation further. Mitch, at least, would be removed from danger.

A game of decoys and information trading probably ensued, so the organization could identify who the inside man was. Mitch was no doubt back in the States, probably holed up in a room at the Airport Hilton and forbidden from outside contact. Meanwhile, the rest of the world believes he's been abducted.

Probably the top news item across the globe. Highlight reels and interviews and conjecture running 24/7. Can't beat that, Bro.

By nature, the taking of Mitch overshadowed another huge question for a few people: Where was Roof?

Bruni, his paralegal, would've been the first to know something was up. After the deposition was finished, they went back to the hotel. It was around 4:30 when they parted in the lobby. He gave her the afternoon off, and she'd fly back the following morning. He spent the afternoon organizing information (the case required strategy) and got room-service empeñadas around 6. Data and minutes flew by until it was time to hit the airport for his 8:15 flight to Panama.

Bruni would've called him twice the following morning. The lack of a callback or text would've set things in motion for his little corner of the world. Sitting chief atop that world, and by necessity kept in the dark, was Emma.

I bet they couldn't tell her the goddamned truth. My wife doesn't know why my cell goes unanswered, why I'm not back in Seattle, why none of my friends or people at the office know where I am.

Don't be a dolt, Roof. Of course she knows! All the bullshit on the news about Mitch. You've gone missing—his identical twin brother has gone missing. She must be climbing the walls, now.

Has a representative team come to their apartment? FBI and members of the U.S. Men's National Team and the State Department, come to discuss the prudence of her not blabbing

230

suspicions to everyone she knows? Have they looked through the place, checked out the queen-sized bed, picked through the unpacked moving boxes stacked high in the den and second bedroom?

She's playing Scrabble with Lola to tea and Vivaldi at the place. Jazz on the radio while the car warms up. She's going to the new yoga studio, doing her stretches, keeping her secret, letting sweat mask her tears.

There's a pillow of solace, he supposes, in knowing she can't be certain what's happened to him the past few days. Her imagination isn't that concrete. Crocodiles, druggies, Josh. Telling her later won't be the same as her living it now, like he is. Later, he can share everything.

Later? Good one, Roof. How do you figure on getting out of here to secure that dazzling, rainbow-sprinkle later*?!*

Hide and run—it's all he can do. What else does a man like him have, when his law degree and soccer skills and egalitarian beliefs can't be filed under the 'assets' heading?

Mitchy, if you don't have the most stellar fucking life from here on, I'm gonna return from the spirit world and give you a wedgie for the ages!

***

Quazidyne and Diabo Norte. Where did the two camps meet? How were they connected? If the tech company wanted him dead—clearly, they were *that* well connected—they could've just poisoned his hotel food.

Then this bunch wouldn't have their Diabo Norte to sacrifice.

Where and how? Someone was common to both causes—Mitch's doom and Quazidyne's fate. Who?

MacLeod's head feels as dense as the rock he's sitting on. The puzzle's edges keep shifting, sliding away, morphing into non-edge pieces.

The only reason this whole thing worked was because of a link—someone who knew he was coming down here and tipped off Olivar. Or that someone was even more integral— perhaps responsible for the entirety of the plot. Who else knew?

Rickman knew. The partner was out sick with the stomach flu. *Maybe*, he concedes. At this point, a lot of things formerly concrete are becoming suspect. Certain bridges shouldn't be crossed carelessly. If Rickman was playing hooky because he felt danger, or because he was told to, that would explain a lot. It was a big case. It *is* a big case. After seven-plus years of comparatively low-stakes arbitration, MacLeod hasn't yet grasped the 'when' and 'how' a lawyer should sense danger in their job. Sixth sense—or something else?

Through the fog of faces and facts swarming at the fore of his brain, MacLeod spies an amazing thing. A chameleon has navigated a branch near the waterfall's spray. Its curled-up tail is what initially drew his eye—concentric circle patterns being one of those oddities of life. The creature's a pure emerald green, water droplets glistening on a surface he'd like to touch. He'd like to know.

In high school, a visiting wildlife expert draped ten feet of yellow python over his neck. While a few girls squirmed and recoiled, he stood firm under its bulk. Its tail wrapped slowly about his arm. Its head swayed slowly, flicking its tongue, smelling the world. He felt no sense of malice or danger, no micro vibes that the snake might, in fact, try to constrict him. Its skin was cool (not freezing in the chilly classroom) and deceptively smooth. Bumps beneath the surface, little imperfections, irked him. It was like wanting to run your hand down a polished wood railing, but knowing you might get a whopper of a splinter lancing the helpless fleshy chunk on your middle finger.

Outside, the chameleon takes a leaf and retreats back up the branch.

How do you know when to stay still and when to stay hidden? What's your biological radar? Is the answer in the trillions of water particles that fall here?

He returns to his search, mentally flipping through the partner V-cards he'd studied in the murderously long week before coming to Seattle. Gupta was clean. Tall, bronze complexion, silver goatee matching his suits. Gonzalez seemed clean. The only guilt by association at play would've been in name alone. A bit on the pudgy and pale and unkempt side, the amiable tax litigator had already solicited MacLeod's help for the upcoming summer barbecues. "Chasing sundresses and tennis skirts, guilty as charged," he'd said over a vodka tonic at an Anthony's Homeport lunch. The guy held all the menace of a basset hound.

Petersen, who was absent at the lunch, swung by and introduced himself late one night. He'd just flown in from Istanbul. Short but with a drill-sergeant's handshake and voice. He must've been the bulldog of the group. "I understand you have a famous brother," he said—in a voice which stated, without a doubt, this was merely an ice-breaker. No further information was required or needed. "Yes, sir," was Roof's reply. The meaning was clear: The name MacLeod didn't matter shit to Petersen Gupta O'Malley Gonzalez. Hours mattered. Effort mattered. Petersen had ties to a Swiss conglomerate that owned hotels across Europe. Divorced twice, no kids, a $350 hourly rate. He was more likely to be found arguing a subsidy on a direct flight *across the pond* than worrying about a Brazilian's soccer-vengeance dreams.

O'Malley, though. There was something mildly suspect about him, a nebulous taint he couldn't shake. It was in the way he feigned surprise when they'd first met at the office. "Oh my,

233

that MacLeod is your brother. Of course," he'd added sounding false and antiquated.

'That MacLeod?' Not to be confused with a fictional New York senator, tool manufacturer CEO or the sword-swinging star of a movie series. Yes, I'm the brother of the Mitch MacLeod. Hard to believe? When you wake every morning to see that face in the mirror, to hear the exultant roar of 80,000 people when your feet hit the floor. Someone very close to you caused that celebration. Someone close to you—your twin brother—but not you.

And every goddamned time a barista or box-office jockey thinks they recognize you? Irritating as hell. No, I'm not that MacLeod. I'm just a sad-sap attorney. But I have his face.

No, the chances that O'Malley didn't know exactly who new counselor Rufus Mortimer MacLeod was were paper thin.

His adversary, he felt confident, was Ronald Thomas O'Malley. Born December 1, 1959, in Syracuse, New York. Parents were Michael and Maria, a telephone line worker and a seamstress. Two younger sisters. The family moved to Poughkeepsie in 1967, then Pasadena in 1973 when Michael O'Malley died from work-related injuries. College at UCLA, summa cum laude, class of '79. Work began with Frost Swindell Sword. In 1983, O'Malley transferred to Sao Paulo, Brazil office, where he worked on real-estate holdings until 1988.

That's it. Got you now, you fucker.

A picture floats up: A younger but cocky O'Malley in shades and a Hawaiian shirt celebrating a just-caught marlin. On the other side of the strung-up silver-hued monster is Olivar. Same bad chin and lopsided smile. *The* Mister Olivar.

The tumblers now click into place as if it was in their nature to do so. A hot-shot California lawyer comes to the biggest city in Latin America and meets all kinds of legitimate land kings. With one of them, he forms a separate partnership, a friendship that lasts for decades. He hears how his friend is sick in the heart over his country (to an unknown degree) and he definitely hears the name (repeatedly) of a reserve striker who came on in the second half and scored two dazzling goals, knocking Brazil off their presumptive championship train.

How far back does this go? Everyone knows CONCACAF starts up in February. Was O'Malley just waiting for the right alignment of calendars? He didn't set up this Quazidyne business—that all feels too legit. Candance wasn't spinning a yard.

It's all speculation, parts of it elastically unreasonable to far-fetched. He isn't even sure how much would hold up before a grand jury with a skeptical judge. He is, however, hiding in a cave in Colombia with the blood of two other people spattered on his rented clothes. The domino train that put him here had to be kicked over somewhere, by someone.

Right now, that miserable bastard is snorkeling off Papeete, probably ruminating about bikini bodies and colonial fair trades. A Seattle winter for drinks in the tropics, a junior litigator for an old debt and a whopping, sympathy-augmented judgment against a tech juggernaut.

He better hope I never find him alone.

***

The night is coming alive with birdcalls and other wildlife. MacLeod really doesn't want to imagine what chitinous or hairy creatures will be slinking and skulking and crawling around out there. The cave seems dodgy enough.

Mitch, you just had to go and score some fancy goals and win a world championship and put me in this spot.

235

It's not true, though. Even if it was something short of wholly unfair, it would be an inaccurate indictment. Mitch has racked up 71 goals for his E.P.L. squad, Culverhouse Crossing. *Including a few absolutely sick beauties!* He worked like a maniac to earn a roster spot on the US National Team and chipped in three assists from a reserve spot during the run. His status was limited to electrifying potential, though (with the exception of all of Cleveland) until the 70th minute against Brazil in the semifinal. Then, like a fresh-legs jaguar, he streaked down the left side, cut in, back outside to beat his man and played a splendid give-and-go to net the equalizer.

All he's done is to be his best. I still owe six autographs to people back in Ohio.

Nobody at the new office, so far, has lost face by requesting an autograph from the twin brother of a star. Perhaps it's more widely known that Mitch MacLeod spends his time in England, tearing it up in the Premier League.

I guess enough people knew you'd be back in this hemisphere for World Cup qualifying.

The U.S.M.N.T. was expected to at least cruise—if not outright slaughter—their way through C.O.N.C.A.C.A.F. after winning the whole thing two-and-a-half years earlier. Mitch and Company didn't disappoint, trouncing Panama 4-1. MacLeod had caught the highlights at the San José Airport, waiting on his flight. (Enough people stared at him that he wondered what Emma would think of his growing a goatee.) He'd been looking forward to hanging with his brother—it had been since July, with Mitch missing Christmas because of tight bookend games.

Opening and closing his fists, an age-old habit, he assembles the chain of events—amino acids, navy puzzle pieces, bullets in a bandolier—which best fits the predicament.

It couldn't have been Miss Scarlet with the wrench in the billiard room because she was busy polishing Mustard's brass knob in the upstairs bath. Okay, for real, here we go.

236

He stands. Hands open and close—the pursuit of warmth and clarity.

Thirty months ago, the one-and-only Mitchell James MacLeod enters the FIFA World Cup semifinal in the 68th minute, sees an opportunity (or a less-than-frisky defense) and produces a stellar goal. Twenty-five minutes later, in stoppage time, he knocks in a pinball shot that stuns the world and stops the hearts of Brazilians everywhere. Days later, when the US beats Italy on Mitch's spectacular game-winner, it's like a dagger to the back of an entire nation. Azuliquapavor grips the country, depression ensues, countless problems finally come to light. Mitch is recast as Diabo Norte, and must therefore be eliminated to liberate the shining land of Brazil.

Still a bit looney-tunes, but okay. Mr. Olivar, among others, sets his sights on Mitch and mentions this to business partner, Ronald O'Malley. O'Malley may or may not have a hand in securing the addition of Rufus MacLeod—mi!—to his Seattle law firm. Either way, with the offending star's identical twin brought into the fold, possibilities open up. Meanwhile Candance DeMeers, several months removed from an international management position with tech giant Quazidyne, feels ready to unburden her conscience about corporate shenanigans. From the spatial safety of her parents' Costa Rican abode, she contacts friend-of-a-friend Theo Rickman at PGOG. Rickman makes arrangements for a deposition in San José, but either gets sick or is poisoned or is coerced into not making the flight.

As a stand-in, fresh-off-the-arbitration-boat Counselor Rufus MacLeod gets the call for the substitution opportunity of a lifetime. While Rickman is yakking his guts up on a couch, O'Malley and Olivar make three dozen phone calls and (one of them) puts into place the master plan of a lifetime. Details are hammered out. "Sure, there are places in the jungle you can use." "Why risk having an inbound plane searched by Brazilian narcotics officers? We can just drive his ass into Colombia and take the scenic route. He is, after all, world famous. Let's make sure nobody can find him." "Rebels? Pah, no problem. They're not operating in these parts, anyway."

The men and materials, the weapons, the route and hideouts. This thing, MacLeod is certain, has been in the works for a while.

And it all works like a dream. O'Malley delivers and hops a flight to the South Pacific. Olivar and his disciples—nephews, whatever—believe they have the dreaded Diabo Norte in their grasp. After all, he's a dead ringer who's wearing the same flashy-insulting black T-shirt. Grab him and throw him in the work van. The only problem is, the real Mitch MacLeod gets reprioritized to a hotel suite behind wary suit-wearing American security agents. He knows his brother is missing, but he's prevented from so much as looking at a phone for fear that a bizarre ordeal could actually deteriorate. No Emma, no Mom or Janice. Fortunately for the stand-in, an element of American covert operations gets on the tale of the surly hikers. He sees the victim being threatened, pops the offending woman, and avoids madness while pursuing said hikers. After a day or two, the trail of carnage leads him to Mister Nucking-Futs Olivar and his show trial of whatever quasi-indigenous tomfoolery. He strikes, perishes ... and I'm freed.

Alive, for now.

Chapter 32

"One minute left in extra time, now. If the score stays knotted at one apiece, the Americans and Brazilians will step off for a drink and a stretch, and then come back for an additional— oh wait a minute!

"Herzog plays a deep cross to left. It goes to Trujillo, back to MacLeod. He finds Jackson—no! Blocked again! Ball comes out, Silva's got it—no, Trujillo nabbed it. To Herzog, beats his man, up to Jackson. Over to MacLeod. It's in! The US has scored! This is not to be believed! In the ninety-third minute, Mitch MacLeod becomes the American savior. He takes a lovely volley off Jackson's cranium, falling over to his left, and he pops it just past their keeper! What a sensational finish!"

Daylight. Morning.

A memory floats up, unannounced. A conference, a banquet hall. A dark-skinned man, western Africa, Dr. Kenneth or Dr. Kenny. Speaking calmly at the podium, pictures of soldiers and burned villages behind him. He worked for a place in Minnesota: The Center for the Victims of Torture. He'd survived it himself—beatings and solitary confinement. He wanted, chiefly, what any such victim wants: Acknowledgment. The Forgiveness process could begin once the perpetrator admitted what he'd done, and that it was wrong. Voices needed to cry out and be heard.

A connection is made between the once-broken man in the memory and the sledgehammer man and MacLeod's body— unbroken, yet. Pain comes swiftly.

My arse! It stings!

Instinctively, MacLeod stands and steps away from the rock. Bolts of lightning race up his spine and through his legs, making him stumble. He catches himself without going completely over. In the cold and unknown, his body shakes. Inexplicably, he bites his tongue trying to regulate his breathing. Injury to insult.

There's nothing on his body. No critters used his body heat or clothes for their own comfort. Defying logic, he has escaped attack while passing the night in spurts of troubled sleep, elbows on knees, head in hands.

That dream. The semifinal against Brazil. That rather huge event in my life. To think, he wasn't a starter, either. He subbed in at sixty-five.

Amazingly, there's no sign of Arturo and Josh. His enemies haven't wandered down here to ambush him. Darkness superseded bloodthirsty intent.

MacLeod checks the knife, still there, and reaches for the spear.

Two left. Cora is long-gone. Enrique is dead. Olivar *must* be dead—all that blood from his blown-off leg. Just Josh and Arturo. And their guns.

Trying to urinate produces feelings of pathetic hollowness. There's nothing left to piss out. Food and beer are phantom desires belonging to another man's past. Even his clothes are dry.

Deep cracked-throat thirst strikes him, as if on cue. It hurts to breathe. Clutching the knife, eyes roving, he creeps to the waterfall. The gushing is constant, just as it probably went all night long, and will go all day and all night after that. It will still be going after his fate—what length of life, or what kind of death—has been decided. The spatter of it from his open hand is energizing, bodily molecules remembering what purpose they are supposed to be serving. He takes four handfuls, grateful for relief and a wet sleeve.

Above on the rim, there are no signs of danger. Shreds of sky are a dull, pale blue-gray. It's almost as if his body sensed the lightness and declared, without doubt, that he should be at the office.

Maybe this is my chance to get away. If they're still asleep. But where to?

The blackness of the cave around him suddenly feels like a beacon. It will call to Arturo and Josh. He found it easily enough. How long could it possibly be before one of them feels the pull of this obvious hiding place? All they have to do is glimpse it the way he did—yawning in daylight—and the game is up. One way in, one way out. He can't stay.

Coincidentally, almost paradoxically, he *knows* that no rescuers would find him here. Not in a chunk of jungle as big as Ohio. Miles off any footpaths, it would probably take thousands of men in search lines to find this place, barring any local help (which he hasn't seen or heard).

Rescuers, what rescuers? The Navy SEALs? Colombian Army? U.S. Marshalls? Who would come for the man who isn't *Mitch MacLeod?*

At the rim above the waterfall gorge, he steps as he would through a minefield. It *could be* a minefield, for all he knows. Take three steps, listen. Take two steps, listen. Sunrise, somewhere off to his right, has been overtaken by thick fog. The goddess of the world is ticking up the screen brightness one notch at a time, nothing more. His hearing is better—the jungle is loud with sharp clarity. Could it be that his nose can help, too?

Josh should reek like a cadaver and vodka? And what does a great big pulsating ball of rage smell like? Plus cologne?

Rage is a new concept, foreign territory, really. He's had a few guys take a swing at him on the pitch, but he'd always chalked those up to assholes being assholes who lost their cool for a minute. He didn't draw yellow cards (or reds), and he wasn't the target of sustained anger. Even Missavit, the Dark Lord from his first firm, had radiated a general disdain for him— nothing deserved, nothing more than his own basic dissatisfaction with life. No crosshairs on him.

MacLeod himself has felt the usual various rejections and slights. Hearing racist remarks got his hackles up (*enough already!*). He'd fantasized over the satisfaction to be gained by grabbing an offender by the throat and hurling him to the ground, but these moments were brief and empty. He got angry at a litigation professor for undue trashing in a couple classes— limited to fuming and commiserating with others. He kept a reservoir of malice for the swindlers who'd cold-call his grandmother, trying to con her into all kinds of bullshit scams. Almost equally guilty were the grownup kids of Alzheimer's sufferers who weren't paying enough attention to stop these thefts from happening (his law-school friend Gabriella was buried in undoing this kind of damage).

But *rage*? Never before, and not at him. Two days ago, he wasn't truly aware of what it really meant—to be the focus of rage, to have it yourself.

Now, picking through huge-leaf plants in fog, he senses a foreign distasteful emotion building steadily within.

A tech company with so much dirty laundry they'd kill to keep it from being aired.

The boss who'd sell out a lesser lawyer at his own firm, knowing it meant torture and death.

The assholes looking for me—for Mitch—to purify the land via another person's blood. Who cares if it's a cultural thing? This goes way beyond reason.

My brother? My American hero *soccer star brother? No way.*

The knife and spear in his grip feel powerful. Weapons. Tools of intent. Facing men with guns, they are *something*, at least.

And if one of the guilty emerges from the stand of thick, emerald-green bamboo he's approaching, he'll swing for the face. It would feel good to draw blood and crack bone.

And then what? Are you strong enough to kill, Roof?

The thought makes him pause and turn a full three-sixty. Unrelenting forest in all directions. No sign of an open space, or a road, or a village. He's been out here, with them, for four or five days. How is it possible to not run across a road or village in all this time? Doesn't anybody live in this corner of the world?

Rebels do. They are the locals. Met some the other day.

After ten minutes' travel, he finds a clearing. The thinning fog shows him fifty yards of sloping grass, with palm trees uphill on the left. No sign of his pursuers.

Staying low, he hurries across the wet green. There's a trickling stream in the middle, running down what is apparently a gully. The cloud of fog pulls away, revealing the deepening gully and a cluster of bushes at the bottom.

Shit!

Figures emerge from the bushes. Josh and Arturo are coming out, like they camped there for the night.

Fuck, I've run right into them!

MacLeod reaches the trees and ducks under a spider web. Three yards deep and ridiculously noisy, he turns and looks from cover. The men are ninety yards downhill, almost a football field away.

243

Josh is aiming his shotgun.

They saw me!

MacLeod flattens himself on the earth.

BOOM!

Shots hit the leaves above. He can hear Josh pumping the shotgun as he pushes his knuckles into the cool mud and turns to fly.

Goddammit—goddammit—goddammit! How?!

It doesn't matter. Run or die!

He runs with the spear in his left hand, pinned up against his body, using his right arm to clear branches out of the way.

You're back on the training pitch, dodging in and out of tight cones. You don't need arms for balance. There is no whistle. There is no end.

Cool, wet leaves slice across his cheek. He reaches a dirt lane that cuts through the jungle. Where it comes from doesn't matter. It leads away from here, away from *them*. That's all he needs to know. Tunnel vision takes over—a goal, no teammates. Forward is all that matters.

The sense of freedom sweeps through him. MacLeod was always fast—even a fingernail faster than his world-famous brother (proven several times in parks). Mitch caught that ball against Italy.

I could have, too. Those fucking yoga stretches and Arhea's insistence and Herdoñez's boot-in-ass coaching.

It is a pleasure to run on this path. Running from two madmen. Running from their guns. Running from death. He's faster. Every footrace against a challenger, going back to first grade, including grown-ups. His clothes are not stiff and

244

heavy—they are just colors painted on him, part of his lean body. He wills them to move more freely. Light steps, gazelle steps.

The track leads to a small, glaringly white structure. It appears to be a roadside chapel, just enough room for two people to kneel under cover before a ceramic Jesus. The kind of thing American couples trek to for kitsch photos in a magazine.

Won't help me.

He flies past. Hiding behind it would be ludicrous. Pausing to consider it would be stupid.

He's off the track. It ended at the chapel. He's back to flying through jungle, now. Leaves and mossy roots and plants and butter-yellow flowers—the kind that lure unwary travelers in for a sniff so the big beast can leap on them. He glances back, distractedly wondering what devout Catholics chose *that* spot for a little chapel—

Whoa! Something's happened. You're flying!

He has tripped on a log. He's airborne, facing forward as a dark blur races toward him.

Splash!

Shit! What did I do?

MacLeod is submerged in a dark pool of unknown nature. He's up to his chest in it. It's thick. It feels like mud, smells like rot and sand. Bits of it in his short hair. His knife and spear have gone flying. In a panic, he looks around and finds the knife behind him—too far to reach.

There's a suction to this, pulling at him. His legs and feet can't find solid ground. It's hard to move in this sludge.

Is this quicksand? Oh God, I'm fucked!

The killers are coming. The compass bubble of the knife peeks at him from the muck—seven feet away. Out of reach.

Be calm. Think!

He's half lying in this stuff. Momentum carried him far enough that his elbows and head are out of it, close to the shore. There's a chunk of tree branch in front of him—two feet long, four inches in diameter. It's heavy enough that it would be sinking too, unless it's on solid ground. That lumpy brown is just like the lumpy brown he's stuck in.

Act quickly or die!

The chunk of branch. He grabs for it, sinking him a little further, up to his armpits. His hands squeeze the solid wood, clenching against the suffocating panic in his head. He turns it on its end like a post. Concentrating, he digs down. Still soft—he's hitting the edge of the quicksand basin. He's in up to his shoulders, heart flailing against his tonsils. Teeth clenched, he tries again, a lunge forward and down. The wood spears in a couple inches and bites into solid ground.

Thank God!

With a white-knuckle grip on the shaft, he exerts pressure. The anchor holds. He slowly pulls himself forward— the temptation to move with haste countered by fear that the all-important chunk of shore will cave.

Don't crack. Don't give, now! Please!

The quicksand lessens his hold. At the speed of a sloth, his body's moving forward against the muck. He's coming free.

I will never again question all the lifting. Butterflies and bent-over rows and crunches. Shut up and do it!

Out to his knees, now. A new plant for his anchor. If he'd landed six inches shorter—if he hadn't been as fast, creating a shorter arc—he'd be a dead man. Lost forever.

Once he's out to his torso, he uses a rare dry spot on his forearm to wipe sweat from his brow. He reeks of beach sand and swamp. Close by, a pair of turtles are hanging out, near the edge of the chocolate-colored muck.

Don't go in there, Guys. You'll regret it.

One knee out. Exhaustion competing with the fear that Josh and Arturo must be near. Crawling forward, he's pulling his other foot free.

Freeze, you idiot! That's a wire!

Chapter 33

Right under his outstretched hand—a thin metal wire.

Holy shit!

He almost pushes off backwards to get away from it. His trembling fingers are so close he knows exactly what it would feel like.

This is a mine!

Rebels. They must've set it.

The wire runs across his path, strung between a tree on the right and a dark lump on his left. A dark lump packed with explosives and shrapnel. Five feet from his nose.

A nugget of dirty sand rolls down his jaw. The world is suddenly too quiet. Just MacLeod and a bomb.

Breathe.

Biting his lip, he slowly withdraws his hand. For a moment, he's a statue with his fingers in wet sand and mud. Cold earth won't betray him, not like a human device.

But they're coming! You've got to move!

He searches frantically. From this position, he can't see other wires. He starts crawling toward the right, away from the trip-wire.

These damned turtles probably crawl under the thing all the time, incapable of understanding the danger. How could you explain to an animal that there would be a flash and a loud boom, and then the animal would be in ten pieces? Unless its shell would protect it. Could a turtle's shell do that—withstand the force of a bomb? Are the shells made of chitin, like a beetle's exterior?

He cautiously gets to his feet, the clothes like weights on his frame. He's added twenty pounds of sand and muck. Shaking out what he can, he realizes it's best to ditch serious weight—the hoodie.

But what if they see it?

Want to make it out of here alive, Roof?

He hurriedly takes it off, pulling and tearing against all the soaked-in crap. When it's off, he's amazingly lighter. Shirtless in the jungle.

Smashing now, Darling.

He looks at the trip-wire.

Maybe you can get one of those bastards if you lay a trap.

The place where he tripped over a fallen log sits on a rise, six feet higher than where he's standing now. It makes sense. If they come over that way, and don't trip or fall into the quicksand, they'll have a likely path of travel.

He drops the hoodie a couple feet to one side of the trip-wire. With a little luck, they'll see it but not see the wire, and go right through.

He'd like to hear that explosion. Far behind him.

Now move! Get your spear, first.

Carefully, he steps over to the spear, mindful of the camouflaged lump at the far end of the wire.

Noise! They're coming. Run!

The sound of footfalls comes from the direction of the chapel. Buttery morning light makes everything dappled, hard to distinguish. He grabs the spear and takes off.

Fall in the quicksand! Set off the mine, you bastards!

He needs to hear it—a boom, cries of surprise and pain—but he can't wait. He's got to move, anywhere away from them. A hill climbs ahead of him—as good an option as any. He keeps low to the ground, watching for wires, hurrying as fast as he can. Probably leaving muddy footprints, but he can't worry about everything.

Too bad I can't just cover myself in mud and hide, like they do in the movies. Don't suppose there's a detachment of Bogota's Finest out looking for tax evaders and non-recyclers, here.

The trail becomes steep, the thick plants ending. Hoping to hear a bang and scream, he charges up the green slope, slipping in the dewy grass. He almost drops the spear. At the top, he takes cover behind prickly, almond-shaped leaves and turns to look back.

No sign, no explosion. The dawn world is so quiet, he'd be able to distinguish a cry of surprise from a distant birdcall.

Safe to assume your booby trap has failed.

When he whirls about to continue, a distant sliver of orange stands out among the green. It's too small to be a structure. A half-mile, if that. Scanning for wires and crocodiles, he bee-lines for the object. It vanishes in the jungle, but he knows to maintain direction.

Among the scents of forest and layered decay, the smell of oil pops up. Engine oil, comforting and familiar. Like the red-and-silver Honda lawnmower from his old house in Cleveland.

In a clearing, parked by a red-dirt road, is a red-orange excavator.

Here!?

It's empty, like it's been forgotten. There's no sign of anyone around, placing the construction monster outside the sphere of reason   and miles from any work site.

Mateo said there was magic down here. Maybe this is it.

MacLeod's eyes travel the Komatsu's thirty-foot arm to a wide, trough-like shovel resting on the ground. A hastily folded blue tarp sits beside it in the eight-inch grass. Beyond, a hundred yards off, the mystery road curls back into darkness.

He touches the engine housing—cool and smooth—as if the whole million-dollar vehicle is an alien ship requiring corporeal verification. At his feet, the ribbed tracks have left faint ridges in the grass and mud.

Please, give me something!

He steps up and opens the unlocked cab door. A neon orange vest is draped over the black chair. There's no key in the control box. The controls themselves are five long rods with knobs on the ends, some marked with worn letters. A radio has been mounted to the ceiling above him. He returns to the empty key slot among the gray plastic.

No key. Shit!

He doesn't know how to drive one of these machines. It shouldn't be that hard to figure out—with time, and the key. He has no hope of hot-wiring it, either. Cars were his dad's thing.

MacLeod's heart is banging at his sternum. Here's his chance to make a ridiculously slow getaway, and there's no key. An empty soda bottle, a little pink stuffed elephant in the seat, but no key—and no minutes to spare.

251

The pink elephant looks at him, imploring him to try something, anything.

Is it time to run?

He grabs the vest. Something heavy weighs down the pocket.

A walkie-talkie! Oh my God!

He handles it—cool, hard plastic—and hits the 'talk' button. Nothing.

Wait. First, check behind you!

Maybe it's instinct, but he turns to look instead of talking.

Is he really there? Arturo?

Either it's an illusion percolating through the warped, green-tinted glass, or someone is coming through the forest, a hundred fifty yards back.

Think fast!

The trees on the other edge of the clearing seem just as far away. If he runs, he'll be without cover for far too long. His pursuers will have a clean shot. Arturo was pretty steady with those squatters, with the rebels and crocodiles. He wouldn't miss. MacLeod doesn't have time to get out of sight.

Fuck-fuck-fuck! What do I do?!

He creeps out of the cab, closes the door quietly and quickly. Too quickly. He pinches his finger and bites his lower lip to stifle a yell.

Shit, you left the walkie-talkie!

He has to—there's no time.

Keeping the machine between himself and his pursuer, he focuses on the wide shovel and tarp. Competing options and commands bang each other in his brain, almost blinding him.

This is stupid—this is stupid—this is stupid! You're out of options!

He half-throws the tarp over the shovel, gets under the tarp and curls himself *in* the shovel. He fits, rough steel pressing against his scalp and ribs and bare arm. It's inexplicably cold.

All concentration goes toward lying still and silent. On his side in the shovel of an excavator, with a blue tarp hiding him. He holds the spear over him lengthwise, thoughts on striking quickly growing more ridiculous by the second.

This is stupid—this is stupid—this is stupid! Is all of me hidden?

The pocket world becomes warm and blue under the tarp. A pebble digs into his right shoulder as he adjusts. Blood slaps in his ears. He keeps his breathing silent, sucking in and breathing open-mouthed, the hide-and-seek way he learned as a kid.

Just like you hid when Schenk was beating up on Riley?

Someone approaches. Something metal clinks. It could be the ammo in a backpack. The man probably has both weapons—the AK-47 and the pistol. Is MacLeod about to get firsthand knowledge of their intended purpose?

The man is breathing hard, like he's been sprinting to catch up. He's alone.

FUT.

The sound of a boot on the step to the cab. The cab door squeaks open.

"Pô," he says. "Estúpido!"

253

Arturo. Come to take my life.

Don't let him see me.

Did Riley plead for mercy? Wasn't he crying out, 'No more?'

Arturo gets down—his body weight depresses the sod—and the cab door bangs shut.

I've gotta piss. If I do, will he hear me? Liquid dribbling? Or see it? He must be twelve feet away.

Another step.

Don't move!

A royal itch climbs up from the grains of sand in his crotch. Every fiber in his being is screaming for silence, for luck.

This is it—the worst idea ever. I'm almost thirty years old. I've got a juris doctorate, I'm a lawyer. Survived years of muck where I didn't even have time to make myself a goddamned sandwich. No vacations. Forget about seeing my own twin, the most famous soccer star on the planet. Got a lovely wife who puts up with me. Sorry, Emma, my luck has run out!

Footsteps.

They're linked on a chain, like pearls of death threaded by my own goddamned cable of apathy. Riley, beaten down. Riley, shooting basketball that morning in the rain. Riley, dead in a construction site! Me, waiting for death in a construction vehicle.

How long have I been tripping over this?

Footsteps.

MacLeod squeezes the spear and holds his breath. The second-to-last thing he sees will be the *azul* waffle pattern of this ridiculous Home Depot weekend-sale tarp.

Here it comes.

Azuliqapavor is smothering him…

Chapter 34

Movement, traveling away.

Past me?

It sounds like Arturo has stopped on the left, on the other side of the machine's arm.

Leave me alone! Go to the forest!

Clinking sounds.

He's running away. He's running away? This is too good to be true!

The clinking sounds retreat, twenty seconds, twenty-five. The sound of big leaves being brushed aside.

MacLeod lets out a long breath, listening.

Is this possible?

Hearing nothing else, he pulls the tarp back slowly. No Arturo. He sets the spear out first, letting it settle in the grass. Trying to make small, subtle movements, he eases his bare torso up from the rough metal scoop. Caution is paramount. He directs his focus to the patch of jungle where Arturo has apparently gone.

Nothing.

He's on his knees when leaves crash off to the right, from that direction.

Fuck-he's-coming-back!

MacLeod's fingers wrap around the spear. Clinking sounds, crashing and yells through the jungle. Arturo's coming back.

MacLeod hurries down the side of the machine and turns at the corner of the engine housing. Things explode around him. Sparks, dust, awful noise. The pops of gunfire seem to come afterward. A thing pecked his arm.

He can't breathe, gulping for air behind the big machine. He's trying to not cough out his heart. Pain and searing alarm take hold.

Red leaks from the side of his right arm. Steeling himself to look, he finds a short gouging wound. He's been nicked.

Lucky dog!

It's quiet, now. It sounds like Arturo's stopped approaching.

How close is he?

Rustling. Clinking. A zipper.

Shaking, MacLeod knows he needs to risk a look. He gets down to look under the body of the machine, through the gap between the monstrous tracks.

Arturo is stopped thirty feet from the excavator. Only his wide-stance legs up to his knees can be seen. He's not bending down to look back, so MacLeod reasons the clinking noise must be him changing the clip in his rifle.

Shit. This is where it ends, Bucko! Some hero. Any second, Josh is going to creep up behind you, and it's Babushka time!

"You cannot win, Diabo Norte!"

The enemy's legs take two steps closer. He probably knows exactly where MacLeod is.

At least he's a little afraid, too—keeping his distance like that.

"I won't make any more mistakes."

Suddenly, his knees go wider, like he's about to shoot.

MacLeod hops off the turf and gets behind the right track. Four shots come, pinging off the track. One hits the ground by his left foot, close enough to feel the grass protest.

Jesus, that was close!

"We can play this game all day, Amigo!"

MacLeod takes a couple steps back. No sign of Josh coming, yet.

How long can this go on? Try something!

"Arturo, I'm not the one you want."

"You are MacLeod, Diabo Norte, and you are a dead man!"

"Arturo, listen to me. I am Rufus. Roof. Mitch MacLeod is my twin brother." A pause. "Mitch MacLeod es mi hermano. You—you guys kidnapped the wrong man."

A slight pause. "You lie! Why should I believe you?"

"I'm a lawyer. How could I get a law degree if I was playing football in the U.K.? I got to the nightclub in Panama *after* the game. The guys put a black flag shirt on me. We're identical twins, me and Mitch. I went to the bathroom. You guys grabbed me instead of Mitch."

MacLeod can hear him shift, but can't see him.

Where is he? Where's he going to go? Fuck!

258

A pear-sized rock is wedged in the track in front of him. A weapon. Keeping his eyes up, he grasps at the rock. Stuck in a gap, it comes free after a couple yanks.

Where is he?

MacLeod senses movement. A click and footfall come just before shots. He moves left. Sparks and shrapnel erupt from the right side of the machine.

Fuck! Christ somebody help me!

There are smoking holes in the engine housing, inches from where his face was. The metal is puckered. Dull daylight shows through. MacLeod wants to touch his own cheek and forehead with the back of his hand, make sure his own face is still intact.

Just like lining up to take a penalty shot, Mitch. Nobody shanks that.

Three more shots come while he's bouncing on his feet behind the left track. Amazingly, none perforate his legs.

I can't do this anymore. I'm out of luck!

"Your luck is running out, MacLeod! No more lies. No more heroes are coming to save you. There's nobody else for Diabo Norte. Time to pay." The source of his voice changes, as if he's moving around. "Why don't you make it easier on yourself and give up?"

"No thanks!"

MacLeod watches for him. His grip on the spear is loose—slippery from sweat, damp wood. His heart needs to stop fluttering in his throat.

"Then we will do this the hard way. But it *will* happen. You will die." He is moving again. "My uncle. My brother. My country!"

MacLeod steps back a bit, far enough that he can see if Arturo's crawling *under* the machine to get him. If Arturo shoots his feet, he's a dead man.

"You don't need to be afraid, anymore. You know that, right? Give up."

Is he trying to distract me with conversation, like they do in the movies? Engage an adversary with questions, and charge in when it's the other person's turn to answer?

"Right," is the succinct answer, choked off by the taste of metallic grit.

Flying debris from a gun—watch out!

He gets a glimpse of leg to the right and hops left.

There's a noise of surprise coupled with rapid-fire shots.

Did he just hit the ground? Did he trip over the tarp or something?!

MacLeod chances a look through the tracks.

Yes, he's on the ground. Strike! Go!

He pulls back, can't do it.

"Fuck," Arturo barks, getting back to his feet.

Is he reloading? How many rounds are in that thing? Will I hear it when he reloads?

"Ah, you are smart. You've kept your head. A worthy target. That's going to make it sweeter when I finally get you!"

He moves again.

He's up on the track!

MacLeod jumps aside. Shots shatter the glass of the cab.

Pain! My shoulder!

Arturo swears.

With spiraling vision, MacLeod circles the machine to the right. Arturo is still up on the track. His attention focused on adjusting his rifle.

Before he reloads!

MacLeod hurls the rock at him, aiming for body. When Arturo looks up, the rock strikes his chin.

Ignoring the concerns of new wounds, he switches to circling left. There's a cry of pain mixed with shots. A bullet pings off somewhere near his body. He trips as the engine housing rattles with gunfire.

Get up! Finish it!

MacLeod's up and hurrying around the machine. When he turns the corner, spear raised, Arturo has gotten down, his back momentarily to his prey.

What the—

Throat! You're being hanged!

MacLeod stumbles and nearly falls on his face right into him. The cord is tight around his neck, caught in the track.

Arturo, bloodied, levels the rifle at him. "Diabo Norte."

A dribble of pee flows out of MacLeod.

Lunge. Get a foot out and block that try, Striker!

He puts the point of the spear *in* the tip of the rifle.

BANG!

A thing explodes.

261

Pain!

The spear flies right. It almost leaves his hand—his fingertips just saving possession.

What the fuck!?

Arturo's eyes are wide, intense white among the dark of blood. There's no second or third shot.

He had one round left!

A shrieking pain comes from MacLeod's ear. The animal in him tells him to ignore it, to flip the spear around as a stunned Arturo takes a step back. The broken, smoking end goes down and back. The sharp, perfect end comes over and forward.

Now thrust!

MacLeod jams the spear into Arturo's gut, hard as he can.

"Diabo!"

Oh God! Don't watch!

Arturo falls away, a horrible scream emanating from his red-rimmed mouth. The spear goes with him, stuck in, the wood vibrating out of MacLeod's grip. A glob of blood and spittle arcs onto the grass.

MacLeod grabs at the cord around his neck. It takes a couple attempts to unhook the leash from the excavator's track. His now-empty hands won't steady enough to do the job. He finally loosens it from around his neck.

Forgot it was there! I nearly hanged myself.

Arturo is grunting and rolling on the grass.

Backing away, MacLeod gets the cord off his neck. When his arm brushes his right ear, taking the leash off, the pain makes him seize up. He drops to one knee.

Get up and finish him!

As Arturo struggles back and forth, the spear moves like a windshield wiper.

Oh God!

MacLeod gets up, wincing. Everything hurts. The sight. The sound of Arturo growling—he has to get away from it.

No. Finish him!

But what will it feel like to pull that spear loose and stab him again?! Are you a monster, Roof?

On his side, Arturo looks at his own raised, blood-drenched hand. He seems freshly bewildered. The AK-47 is in the grass behind him.

I can't. I can't!

The weapon must be empty.

Grab it and club him. Brain him. You have to!

He fights off nausea and concentrates. The weapon is within reach. A wretched, bugs-under-your-skin itchiness consumes him. He has to flee.

Are you so afraid of upsetting the balance of the cosmos? Kill him. Save yourself!

MacLeod turns away. Beside him, the glass windows of the cab are gone, blown to a thousand pieces.

Maybe shards of it hit him in the face, but who cares?! Go!

He grabs the walkie-talkie from a splatter of bluish polygons.

BOOM!

Stuff erupts around the excavator.

Josh! Fly, you fool!

Falling back from the cab, he glimpses the form of Josh kneeling by the trees, maybe seventy yards away. His arm sliding down is the telltale pumping of a shotgun.

Chapter 35

Monozygotic separation and Japanese steakhouse feet and gorgeously rotating balls and too-tired-too-late-but-reaching keepers and I've done every fucking thing right to the fucking letter and this is the thanks I get—dumped in verde hell based on a whoopsy! Step aside, Mel Brooks. The Big Guy's still got you beat by a quarter mile. Un-fucking-real!

Back into the jungle. Plants rip past as he barrels downhill. Shirtless, weapon-less, he crashes through the emerald world. His grip on the radio must be tight enough to crack it. He wants the road, but he can't give Josh the psycho a clear shot. Babushka. Not now. Not after all he's been through.

He senses a clear spot running parallel on the left—the road has curved toward him. From the ruffled red-dirt track, he glances back, looking for Josh. MacLeod is far from the clearing—*that place of insanity!*—and the pain in his arm and ear is fading, supplanted by whistling freedom. Big trees arch overhead, sentinel gates to welcome his sprint.

The satellites and planes can see me now. I'm not wearing the hoodie anymore. Come on, guys! Shirtless, bleeding Caucasian guy running for his life. Come on, people. Doesn't it look noteworthy?

Faster. This is a genuinely good feeling—running as fast as he can, regardless of his state, down this road. Finally, freedom. He could be a gazelle, his leaden boots barely touching the earth.

Where somebody's driven an excavator, there must be a place it came from. A place with people. I'm getting out!

He glances back. No Josh.

Maybe he finished off Arturo for me.

Would Arturo let him, if Josh asked? Neither man is the type to believe in a mercy killing. Not if they really *were* going to skin him alive.

The excavator's tracks continue. Rumpled bushes and snapped-off tree branches show where its girth was an issue.

So where the hell did it come from?

He continues, scanning for trouble. He would pray for a helicopter or other people, now. Any kind of resolution to this.

Pain that will not be denied starts to come back—his arm, an ice-chunk-to-the-earlobe burn. He's still afraid to touch it, to find out if it's even gone from his head. Wind hurts. The heaviness of fatigue swarms up. Would he feel lighter—better, therefore—if he shed his soaked pants and boots?

The heavy thing in my hand—the walkie-talkie!

He clicks the 'on' switch. Nothing happens.

Oh no! Come on.

Pausing, he shakes it. It feels plenty heavy. He pops open the battery door to find four 'D's. One looks out of place. He pulls them all out for a quick inspection and finds no acid-burn decay. Excited, he drops one in the grass and has to swipe dirt off it with a less-sandy area of pants. Hurrying, he slides them back into their slots and replaces the battery door.

He clicks the 'on' switch again. Static.

Thank God!

Glancing back for Josh, he hits the 'talk' button.

What do I say?

"Mayday—mayday. Can anybody hear me?"

He continues running down the road.

266

Nothing.

He switches channels, wishing he knew more about how these things worked.

"Mayday—mayday. Can anybody hear me?"

"Qué?"

Oh thank God!

"This is MacLeod. Please help me!" His brain crackles. "Ay-ayudeme, por favor!"

"Who is this?" a voice asks in a heavy accent.

He slows to a jog. "Rufus MacLeod. I'm Rufus MacLeod! I'm lost in the jungle, in Colombia! Somebody please help me!"

The road has started to climb. The excavator tracks lead up toward a hill crest.

Civilization!

He looks back for Josh and sprints uphill. Swiping at sweat, he races up the curving slope.

There's no way he could catch me. I'm almost free! Keep going.

The road crests a ridge and drops quickly.

Oh thank God!

Below, situated on the side of a green slope, is a house. It's all alone, like a secluded vacation house or ranch.

A hacienda?

Help!

267

He starts downhill.

Wait! Something's not right.

The large compound is a couple hundred yards down the wider track. There are green jeeps parked outside, blocking a white SUV.

And people. With guns. Soldiers.

Chapter 36

Wait. Get low! Turn off the walkie-talkie.

The white SUV's brake lights are on.

MacLeod drops to his belly and crawls over to a bush by the road.

People are running about.

CRACK! CRACK-CRACK!

That was gunfire! What's going on here?!

His eyes are dropping into the weeds.

No-no-no. Are these rebels?

Two rifle-bearing men have come to the driver's side of the SUV. They try the door, then point at it. There's some yelling. Then the crack of gunfire. They've shot the door. Now they wrench it open.

The only normal people I've seen for days, and they turn out to be rebels?

The driver has long silver hair and a blue shirt. They drag him out by his hair.

Don't watch, Roof.

As the man stands there with hands raised, there's muzzle flash from the rebel's gun. The victim drops, clutching his legs. The shots are like hammers on plywood, followed by his wailing. MacLeod looks away. Three reports follow.

They killed that man. Whoever he was, they just murdered him.

Defeated, freedom canceled by the slamming of a heavy portcullis. He has no choice but one.

Stay low. Don't let them see you—or hear you.

There's no sign of Josh coming.

Wait, what's that?

Off to the right, maybe two miles away, a tan-colored structure points up from the trees. If it's a church, it's old and forgotten and broken. There's no telltale cross. Yet it looks like stone.

Could those be ruins?

It's got to be safer than the jungle. Go.

Fearing the noise—sounds bizarrely carried on the wind—he waits until he's creeping downhill in the forest to try the walkie-talkie again. He flicks a beetle off a fallen chunk of tree branch and hastily strips it down to a club. Before he hits the 'on' switch and 'talk' button, he checks in all directions. Nothing.

"Mayday mayday," he whispers. "This is MacLeod. Does someone read me? Over."

Isn't that what he's supposed to say? They didn't quite cover this in Litigation Tactics seminar.

There's a burst of static. Then, "MacLeod? MacLeod! This is Captain Pearson, U.S. Navy. Where are you?"

American. U.S. Navy! Thank God!

His eyes are watering. He blinks it away and looks around.

"I don't know. They said we're only a few miles from Brazil. In-in Colombia. The Colombia side." He walks a few

270

steps. "I'm about a mile from a rust-colored excavator in a field. One of the psychos is down, there. I hope he's still down!" A few more steps. "There's rebels here. I just left a hilltop above a hacienda. They executed the owner, or someone. You've got to get me out of here! Over."

He hears a lot of commotion in the background when the American voice comes back on. "We will, we will. We've got people on their way, now! Can you move? Can you get to a safe spot? Over."

Yes-yes-yes!

"It's not safe, here. I'm going to try to cut over to a tan-colored building, maybe ruins. I could see them in a clearing, about two miles from the hacienda. I think I'm heading west. Over!"

Voices. They're coming!

He turns off the radio and starts downhill. The jungle thickens. All he can do is put distance between himself and the rebels—and Josh—and hope he doesn't run into anything.

Quicksand! Mines! Rebels! Crocodiles! What's next?!

He pauses and listens for the rebels.

Nothing.

The road to freedom is through there. Go!

He hopes he's running in the right direction—it's impossible to tell in this thick green. Visibility is down to thirty yards. Eyes wide, trying to take in everything, he crosses a stream among huge trees.

Around him is silence. If there were pursuers, he'd hear them.

So why do I have a funny feeling?

271

Wait. That dark patch ahead of you...

Chapter 37

It's on a boulder under a muscular tree branch—right where he was about to sprint through. Behind the leaves. It's moving.

Oh shit!

Yellow eyes peer out from a coat of black. Whiskers. Fur.

Jesus! Don't just stand there. Run!

He can't. It is six yards away. It will run him down. *This is a creature he knows.*

A low growl comes from the branch. The growl of a large, powerful animal. A black panther. Jaguar. Beast. It's here, right in front of him.

Diabo Norte y El Diablo Negro. The creature Enrique was so afraid of.

Do something! It's about to attack!

Slowly, MacLeod steps to the right. The cat stares at him, crouched to strike. This animal is almost twice his weight, ten times as strong—and a hell-of-a-lot faster than any soccer player.

He fingers the club.

What do I do—what do I do—what do I do?

You cannot compete with this animal! Wake up, MacLeod!

He growls. The idea hits him like a sopping, smelly gym sock thrown by his brother. He lets a deep-throated warning become louder, getting a good grip on the club. He bares teeth

273

and drops into a defensive stance. Animals recognize hazard, he's always believed. If he does this, bouncing the club, maybe the cat will understand it's in for a fight.

This is so stupid, Roof!

What else have I got?

The panther's growling back at him. The pitch changes, to his ears. He's unsure what that means, so he keeps up his act. With his right foot—his weaker one—he feels around for obstacles to flight.

His tactic might be working. When he slowly sidesteps right, ready to push off with his left foot, the cat merely watches. He risks a glance toward his desired path of travel. The jungle seems clear. The panther's growling pauses, then continues. It sounds a little less serious than before.

He takes another small step to the right, eyes fixed on the cat. If he was threatening cubs, the panther would've attacked by now, he figures. The animal would have already sunk its canines into his neck.

He lets his own growling die down, keeping his eyes on the cat's yellow-green ones. There's no change. Another small step to the right. Is it going to let him pass without attacking?

This is sheer lunacy.

Another small step. The panther stops growling. Either his imagination is playing tricks, or it doesn't look quite as taut, as ready to strike. Now he can see it a little better—an enormous black cat staring him down from the top of a boulder.

Beautiful! I wish I could have one. Maybe a cub. If this one doesn't eat me.

Noise—from behind him. The panther turns and leaps up into the tree.

Is it Josh or the rebels? Hopefully just Josh, psycho that he is. There's only one of him.

He takes off, confident the Colombian jungle can't throw anything worse at him. He tries to avoid big, eye-level leaves for the sake of his ear. How long had he run before he encountered the black panther—seven or eight minutes? He still has another mile to go, at least. Is it possible he'd miss the ruins in here?

Come on, what did it look like? What did the land around it do? Did it rise or fall? Was there a slope? Were the tops of the trees level, or did they descend one way? God, I'd kill for a photographic memory. Emma has one. Never forgets a movie line, never forgets a recipe.

He pauses to listen. Nothing.

What happens when I get to the ruins? Call for help again. Call for help and stay put.

What happens if they are occupido?

Then I'm fucked. Pray and keep running.

He's flying across a minor gully, his club steadying him against safe-looking tree trunks, when a familiar sound makes him wince.

BOOM!

Chapter 38

He dives for the ground, banging his temple with the radio when he covers. Stuff is unsettled near him, bits falling.

Was that Josh? Where the fuck did he come from?!

He lifts his face off the dirt and decay. After a pause, hearing no approaching danger, he scrambles to his feet and right over a slick, curving thing.

Serpiente? Don't even look back.

If that was Josh, how close was he? Diving and covering his head was quite pointless, he realizes. The sound comes after the shots.

Another shotgun blast, somewhere back there. Not as close. Followed by howling. The cries of a man.

Was that Josh? Can't it be plausible one of these times he'd actually shoot himself?

MacLeod veers right, feeling he must be off course. The ruins looked big enough that he wouldn't miss them. Yet, they are still hidden.

He flies up a little rise and pauses at the top. Sunbeams shine, putting much of the jungle in greenish darkness. Ahead, through the thick trees, a light-colored wall emerges like a beacon.

Yes!

Focusing on that distant color—a hundred yards off—he leaps down the hill, towards a creek that winds around a tangle of vine-choked trees.

"¡Oye, détente," a man's voice says. "¡Détente! Stop!"

What? No!

All the wind is sucked out of him. He freezes by the stream. In the dappled light, a man in a cap and boots stands ready, two strides away, rifle pointed. Fatigues. Bandolier. Equipment belt.

MacLeod raises his hands slowly. The club bounces off his right foot.

A rebel soldier. It can't be. Not now!

The man sizes him up. "American?" he asks.

MacLeod has nothing left to hide. Nothing left at all.

"**Sí**, señor. Yes," he says, nodding his head.

Don't do it don't do it don't do it don't—

"MacLeod," he announces.

The man lowers his AK-47, wearing a puzzled look. "Quíen? Who?"

MacLeod smiles briefly, trying to calm the pounding of his heart behind his tongue.

"Mi llamo MacLeod. Footbol. Yo jugo footbol para los Estados Unidos. Mitch MacLeod."

The rebel's eyes have gone wide. His rifle's pointed down at rocks by the stream. "You lie," he says. "You cannot be him."

"Es verdad. I am MacLeod."

"Here?! Why are you here?"

An explosion pops in the distance, followed by rapid gunfire.

What the hell?

The rebel shifts attention between this event and MacLeod. The glacial comprehension on his face—he has accepted the story. He mutters something that can't be made out and reaches for a whistle around his neck, looking right.

He's about to call his comrades. What now?

He raises the whistle to his lips.

Red—dark blur. Noise. Violent movement.

As MacLeod ducks and covers his head, the rebel falls back.

The noise—my head. It's too much!

Everything is off balance.

Not again. No!

His enemy must be right on top of him, and there's nowhere to run. Skewered by icy fear, he rises to face his fate.

Josh steps into a sunbeam among the tangle of trees. Shotgun forward. Pained grin.

He's going to shoot. What do I do?

MacLeod's feet are in a rocky stream. He has no cover. Just strides away, a few feet above him, a madman points his weapon.

All he has to do is shoot between those tree trunks. Or lean and shoot around, if I move.

Josh's eyes dart to the left for a second. "This looks like the end of the road for both of us." He licks his lips hungrily and blinks. "At least I can tell Old Satan that *I* was the one who got you," he says. His mouth is parted in a Halloween-ready cackle.

278

Here it is!

MacLeod hops right.

BOOM!

Ahh!

His right arm burns.

The curving tree trunk before him is ringed by dust, smoke and flying bits.

You're hit!

Through the haze, he sees Josh's weapon raised briefly, while he pumps it.

Do something. You're dead if you don't.

Grabbing his right arm—windless lightning bolts—MacLeod nearly trips on a rock. A turtle.

Josh steps forward, about to shoot again.

Do something—now!

An idea appears, turns and barrel-rolls in a one-in-a-thousand chance at fruition.

MacLeod slips his left toes under the turtle. Under—dig—loft.

The turtle flies into Josh's path.

BOOM!

Sparks. Blue smoke. A dark blur coming at MacLeod.

Male screaming, from down a deep hole.

Me!?

MacLeod opens his eyes to find he's on his back, knocked over flat. Something struck his chest. Not a shotgun blast—he's still breathing.

What?

The screaming—it isn't his. The world is hazy. He blinks rapidly, looking over his form. No huge holes in his front.

What happened?

The spreading red splotch on his right bicep is all. A single shot got him.

Trying to steady himself in a world of unbalanced, moving parts, he gets to his feet. He coughs, clutching at his struck chest. Before him is a turtle with a smoking, cracked shell.

The world's spinning slows. MacLeod steadies himself and hones in on the shrieking.

Josh is rolling around, clutching his crotch with one hand and his eye with the other. The screams are coming from his open mouth. His quivering hands are both drenched with blood.

How—the turtle?

I lofted that thing like a ball, and all those pellets ricocheted?

He shakes his head against madness, the world starting to come apart again.

Josh's beloved Babushka is lying on the ground nearby, against tree roots.

Do I grab it and finish him?

MacLeod takes a step toward the weapon.

No. Just run! Get out of here while you can!

He's no longer holding the walkie-talkie. It must've gone flying out of his hand when the turtle hit him. After a moment, he draws a bead on the dark brick. His arm burns in protest when he grabs for it.

Don't forget your friend.

Concentrating, wending through Swiss-cheese holes of improbability, he grabs the turtle and runs.

Chapter 39

Carrying the walkie-talkie and cradling the turtle like a football, MacLeod hurries through the green. Sounds are amorphous, air-pressure changes register as degrees and sources of agony. Vomit comes up, chunks of sand or debris sucked back up his nostrils in the attempt to clear it. The sunlight in open ground is coldly blinding, at first.

The ruins. Across a patch of long grass, a tan-colored wall rises three stories in height. Vines have claimed much of its façade.

He heads for stairs on the left. In his periphery, things move across the field.

Fuck. Again?

A crocodile is sunning in the grass, its drab, dark body presenting as a 'C' near the stone wall. He's almost on top of it before he manages to change direction.

Circling back around to what must be the front, he pauses to watch the strange, moving things. These things horrify.

BOOM!

Across the field, a half-mile away, a vehicle is flipping through the air. It's been thrown from a burst of smoke and dirt.

What in the hell?

Something—a person—goes flying out of the jeep, ejected when it crashes down and starts to roll.

RAT-A-TAT! RAT-A-TAT-A-TAT-A-TAT!

He can't see where this latest noise comes from. A helicopter climbs above the trees, near the spot where the jeep was destroyed. More machine-gun fire, sounding as if it's underwater.

Christ, it's war.

MacLeod puts a hand on the stone wall to hold himself upright. His eyes are wet, sweat or tears. A salty, gritty pain spreads from his arm to consume the rest of him. It will merge with the pain from the ear he's afraid to touch.

Move. Get to safety, man.

Trying to crouch, he goes around the front of the ruins. Nobody appears to be up there. Above, up the cracked, vine-covered steps, a wall heads to the right.

Climbing steps in his condition takes effort. He finally gets behind the wall—*no snakes, no monster scorpions!*—and turns on the walkie-talkie. Crouching down to stay hidden seems smartest.

"Mayday—mayday. This is MacLeod. Over."

Static. Click. "MacLeod? You don't sound good. Where are you?"

"I don't feel good. But I'm at the ruins. You gotta get me the fuck out of here! There's a war going on. Over."

When they talk, the static is followed by noise. He concentrates to distinguish competing noises, men yelling at each other in English and Spanish. "Hang on," somebody says.

Machine-gun fire rattles in the distance, sounding very far away. He wonders idly if it's at the hacienda, or closer.

"Does anybody read me? Please get me outta here. There's a-an offensive or something going on. Rebels and Colombian army. Please! Over."

Again, static followed by frantic yelling.

283

What in the hell is going on over there? How hard can this be?

There's an exchange of gunfire. In the distance, puffs of smoke appear on both sides of a helicopter. White streaks into a cluster of trees close to where the jeep was destroyed. Orange sparks flower, parts of trees and jetsam scatter.

Jesus. I gotta get out of here!

His contact comes back on, a voice rising above the white noise. "MacLeod, there's heavy anti-rebel activity in your area. Are you safe? Can you stay put? Over."

Frustration boils over, supplanting fatigue and fear. "I'm *watching* the anti-rebel activity. It's right here. They're using helicopters and rockets. No, I'm not safe. Get your people down here! Over."

"You gotta stay there at the ruins. Don't move! Over."

Where the hell would I go? Back into the jungle? Not a chance.

His grip on the walkie-talkie is slipping from perspiration. Blood is caked on his right arm, but the dime-sized hole isn't gushing. It has a burgundy-colored clot.

"Come get me. Please. Over."

The helicopter lifts up higher. A pale streak flies up at an angle, barely missing the helicopter. More machine-gun fire as the streak turns stark white, lancing the sky.

That was a rocket. The rebels have rockets too. Perfect.

His heavy-lidded eyes search the blue and tree branches for the rocket—that it isn't coming near him—as the helicopter returns fire. There's a flowery burst of yellow and sparks, followed by posterboard-waving thunder. Something goes

arcing. Smoke billows out of a spot where, he imagines,
somebody just died.

*Probably a lot of somebodies. How can this be
happening? Right here, right now.*

*How is it that I've lived through all this shit—Arturo and
Josh and Enrique and Cora and Mister Fucking Olivar—to get
caught in the middle of civil war?*

The bark of an explosion sounds from the forest
somewhere behind him. He has no energy left to cower, or to
wonder about falling rockets.

He sets the walkie-talkie down on the stone and looks
about. He's been so focused on the madness in the field that he
hasn't even noticed the temple has more levels above him.
Freshly determined, he half-hurries up, passing three-foot stone
blocks with snakes and suns carved in them. The next level has
pillars and altars.

*Was this the kind of place where Mister Olivar was
going to cut me open? Was he going to make me bleed all over
one of these altars? And, then, my sacrifice would...cleanse the
land of the abominable curse...the Blue Funk? Azuliqapavor? Is
that how it was supposed to work?*

God, if not for that guy in black...

Men are running this direction. Four of them, crossing
the grass.

Are they Americans? The Navy SEALs?

As they get closer, they appear to be wearing rag-tag
green. Bandoliers and long weapons.

They're rebels. Hide.

The four soldiers may not have seen him. That's all he
can hope for, now. Fifty yards away.

285

Out of nowhere, a helicopter roars by overhead, super low. He feels the closeness of the big metal machine. Wind from the rotor beats down on him. Underneath, between rocket launchers, is a painted red-yellow-blue flag. Colombian.

The noise is intense. MacLeod stays low, afraid he'll be drawn up into the horrible blurred rotor. The helicopter banks right.

They're firing.

His teeth rattle as a machine gun opens fire from the side of the chopper. The men who are running this direction collapse among flying chunks of turf. When he looks again, they are down.

The helicopter moves off. Smoke and steam trail up from the bodies in the grass. One has a detached body part, ending in red scraps. Another form is trying to move. It looks like it's too late for him.

MacLeod's eyes are watering.

This is the real world. This is what it means to be a rebel, to oppose a government—for better or worse.

When he shifts, fresh pain growls from his arm, his ear, his back. He grits his teeth, slows his breathing. He would've urinated again—the gate's been open—if there was anything left.

Will there be anything left of me to rescue?

Come on. Where are you guys?

A new presence makes him look down again, toward the bodies, toward the base of the temple steps.

No, it can't be!

Edging his way up the stairs, looking wildly about.

286

A bloody man.

Chapter 40

Arturo!?

No, I must be hallucinating.

But he looks so real.

He is covered in blood. The spear is still in his side—it's been cut off so a half-foot of it protrudes from his trunk. He comes slowly.

I can't believe this.

He's carrying his handgun with the silencer on it.

Run.

There's nowhere to go, man.

Run anyway. Up the steps. Run or die!

Arturo gets closer in his periphery. MacLeod finds a reserve and lunges up the stairs. Air-gun noises are like someone finger-tapping his jaw. Stone chips go flying past his legs. At the top, he dives away, hoping it will buy him a few more seconds. His elbows and knees bang, the walkie-talkie scoots away.

He must be disoriented as hell. Maybe you can...

What? Brain him with the turtle?

MacLeod risks a look. Arturo's still twenty feet below, looking bewildered and possessed—a retarded demon.

Below him, commotion.

"Você deve morrer," he moans. He fires.

MacLeod gets out of the way. Things ricochet about.

What was behind him? Did you see men running up the stairs? Rebels?

On this level are stone altars with table tops. He can hide behind one, for the moment.

Until he runs out of bullets, shooting at me?

There *are* men at the base of the steps. MacLeod hears them jabbering in Spanish. None of it matters. He can't do anything else. He crouches behind an altar and watches through gaps.

Laboriously climbing the steps, Arturo is oblivious to the men behind him or the madness all around.

A helicopter is coming.

MacLeod glances about. There's no rocks or sticks—nothing he can use for a weapon.

"Você deve morrer, você deve morrer, você deve morrer," Arturo moans, seeking. Blood is spackled across his face and one eye is closed.

Throw the walkie-talkie at him. Wait until he fires. Then do it.

Below him, someone fires a machine gun.

Don't do that, Assholes. It brings the attention here, to me.

Arturo has spotted him. He points the gun. Powder hits MacLeod's nose. The bullet must've bounced off the altar.

Shit that was close.

Arturo squeezes the trigger again, muttering. Nothing happens. Again. Nothing happens. After the fourth time, he looks down at the weapon.

MacLeod realizes he's still holding the turtle. With a pathetic attempt to be tender, he sets it down and grabs the walkie-talkie. A firm, left-handed grip. *It* is now his weapon—a one-pound brick of plastic, wiring and metal.

Feeling dizzy, he steadies himself with a hand on the altar. He winds up to launch and strike, as if for a big clear kick. Arturo's eyes register him, more confusion than anything.

But he deserves to die, so kill him.

No wait—a helicopter.

Behind Arturo, above the battlefield, a helicopter is advancing on the temple. It is an alien menace that shouldn't be coming his way.

Puffs of white show on each side of the craft.

Get behind something!

MacLeod dives left. He balls up, covering his head.

Light.

Noise.

Shaking.

Vortex.

Flames.

Debris flying.

He's knocked back and forth, squashed by the air, crushed by intense heat. Stuff is flying.

My arms are on fire!

He screams out, afraid to open his eyes.

Things stop moving. He's stopped rolling.

Pain vibrates up his left leg toward his groin.

Pressure. Things are on him.

Now he looks, pushed against the wall. Chunks of steaming rock are around him. A slab of stone altar has toppled over, nearly crushing his feet.

He waves his good arm, which is smoking. Arm hairs are curled, blackened and flying off.

My leg is on fire.

The pants leg is puffing blue, partway ripped open.

Get it out.

He smacks at it with an open hand until little orange flames disappear. His leg throbs. He wrings his singed hand, too.

Everything is needles plunging in.

Next to him, where his face was just lying on the stone, is an arm with no body. Shaking, teeth chattering, he looks at his own arms.

Still attached, not on fire.

He recoils with stinging eyes. The arm's severed end is barbecued—stark-white bone against sizzling, dark pink flesh. The loose threads of the ripped sleeve are smoking. There's the odor of something erroneously put on the grill, high heat.

In its hand is a gun with a silencer.

Arturo.

Dead for good.

Bile comes up. A little dribbles onto MacLeod's bare chest. The warm liquid cools his skin. Relief, small relief.

He tries to wave the smell away from his hot face. He feels hollow, sunburned. The acrid stench of burning is everywhere. He coughs for a time, until clearer air comes.

I think you just survived an explosion.

Everything aches separately. Exhaustion takes over. From a couple points nearby, wisps of gray rise into the blue sky. There are two helicopters in the air. One is close, though not close enough to feel.

Now he feels something else. Above, another helicopter hovers into the picture. Stone vibrates below him. This one is different, bigger. It looks like a true war machine, solid black and with no flag painted on the bottom.

No more. Please...no more.

He slowly pulls his leg free of the rubble. It's so sore, he wonders if searing pain is waiting for its place at the head of the table. Burned, broken or crushed—what's the difference? His head's in a vice. His back feels raw, scraped badly. Gingerly, he starts patting himself for injury, though he doesn't really want to touch anything.

His right arm is bleeding again.

Somebody, please make it all stop.

How much more can he physically take? Standing up, movement of any kind—these are fleeting desires.

The big helicopter descends nearby. For a second, he feels too close to a lawnmower blade. With a palm, he smears the tears from his stinging eyes.

Burned popcorn...I don't think I can ever tolerate the smell of burned popcorn again.

There's a lot of things...too much...it's all too much...

Movement nearby, presence coming. He senses it before he sees it, like a change in the air.

Beside him, the disembodied arm with the gun lies still, a fish left out in the sun. There's a little smear of red on the ancient stone.

"Adiós, Amigo," he tells the arm. Trying to sound tough for himself.

He wretches again. Aching. Nothing comes up. Snot from his nose, a desire to rid himself of everything.

Movement—closer to him.

From the debris and clouds, men emerge. Men in black and equipment and helmets. Soldiers.

No! I'm too tired to fight. Who are you?

Four of them are on top of him, crowding around. He recoils, tries to push them away.

More strangers in a wicked land of strangers.

The one closest to him—an Asian man—gives a thumbs-up sign with a quick grin. Then he lifts a patch of some kind on his arm.

Oh my God!

An American flag.

I am going home.

Cooling tears surface and flow.

I can't believe it! Finally.

293

The men have a medical board. One guy is working on MacLeod's right arm and applying a bandage. Another is doing something with his left leg. Before they inject him with medicine, the leader holds up a notecard that says, "pain relief."

Apparently, they know he's deaf right now. He gives them his own, weak thumbs-up and looks around. He points at the turtle—his protector.

He's coming with me.

A pinch in his arm tells him the pain medicine is coming.

What if these guys aren't real? What if they're not Americans? Am I hallucinating?

Do I care anymore?

He rests his eyes for a second. He can't do any more. Movement, he's moving. They're lifting him onto the medical board. The lead soldier holds MacLeod's hand while the sensation of being carried to something is an invitation to sleep.

The man in the tank lets the sledgehammer go slack. Dazed, he peers up at the new sunlight, and accepts a helping hand. Punishment concluded.

Tears flow. MacLeod believes he's crying like a lost child, but he can't care right now. He's incapable of caring, of having any ego left to protect.

Roof MacLeod, Lucky Man.

Roof MacLeod, not the American Hero.

Roof MacLeod, Mollycoddled Bairn.

You have survived.

Chapter 41

The tempest struck in many places.

There were so many storms crashing down that Roof MacLeod couldn't quite keep up with it all from his hospital bed.

As a nation, the United States had stood transfixed while the drama of their favorite hero played out. The number of people who knew the truth—that Mitch MacLeod himself was quite safe—had been restricted to a tight circle out of safety concerns. As a nurse put it, it was as if nobody had cracked a joke or turned off the TV for five solid days.

Among those not in-the-know was Candance DeMeers, who'd never heard of Mitch MacLeod before and was vaguely aware that soccer had become big in America. For most of her professional career, she'd been happily immersed in "shepherding code monkeys and negotiating silo discrepancies" for royal sums. Who needed sports? However, once she saw Mitch's face on multiple TV channels and was alerted by a sharp paralegal, she stayed holed up in her parents' place.

Bruni the paralegal was concerned when she boarded a flight, and then downright suspicious by the time she disembarked in DFW. Roof hadn't returned her calls that morning or the night before. No messages or texts to the office, either. Even for someone she'd just met (a meticulous routine-disciple, by reputation) it was out of character. On her way to Customs, she saw the breaking news flash which seemed to silence the terminal. Afterward, to partners Gupta and Peterson and to federal agents, she'd corroborated O'Malley's dodgy behavior right before his Tahiti trip.

Behind closed doors at the firm, Gupta learned from Bruni and DeMeers what this was all about. He and Gonzalez turned their attention squarely on Quazidyne, intent on removing heads the old-school way.

The truth about Peter O'Malley came to light in his absence. He and Olivar ran an investment firm with two other fat cats. Twenty years of shady deals—however legal—had netted the group almost $3 billion. Housing developments, oil rig construction, a mall in Romania, a marina in Tampa, two stadiums in Brazil. Someone had to pay for the actual cement to be poured.

Once the Navy SEALs flew MacLeod to a ship parked in the Gulf of Mexico, they patched him up and sailed north. The destination was Miami, but a massive international economic summit put the kybosh on that. From Guantanamo Bay, he was flown to San Diego, where he finally came to after sedation. The litany of injuries Emma and his mother and Janice got from a doctor was extensive.

Second-degree burns on his leg and hip, from the Colombian army helicopter's rockets (better off than the rebels who were blown to bits). A fractured left tibia. Two cracked toes in his right foot. A hole in his bicep, which would require physical therapy (could've been worse, considering it was from a shotgun). Four total bullet wounds, where he was grazed here and there. Partial ear removal, involuntary (the excavator encounter). Cuts from shrapnel, scrapes from *everything*. Permanent hearing loss in his right ear (the shotgun or the explosions). A little damage from smoke inhalation (the rockets). More cuts and bruises. Burns. A ligature scar around his neck. A removed fingernail, mirrored by a sprained finger on the other hand (cause uncertain). Bug bites and a scorpion sting (probably from the night in the cave; luckily, it wasn't one of the little red ones, which would've given him a horrid case of hives). Dehydration and malnutrition. Psychological damage.

"Couldn't you have just found a tour bus to run you over instead?" joked the silver-haired Navy physician.

"Next time," replied MacLeod, fully capable of imagining the crushing weight of steel-belted radial tires.

All things considered, he still ended up better than his captors. Cora LeFleur (shot through the heart). Henrique Santos (shotgun, close range). MacLeod didn't know (or much care) that there was an 'H' at the beginning of his name. Fabrício "Mr. Olivar" Olivieri (blood loss, unanticipated leg removal). Jaroušek "Josh" Artim (shotgun and violence, close range). Artur "Arturo" Santos (puncture wound, violence, rocket ordnance via aerial assault). Rib-tickling irony that his chief tormentors bore the last name for "saint." Colombian forces recovered all their bodies, and a bizarre jurisdictional tug of war has ensued. France was not claiming Cora, but not one of them was Colombian.

As for MacLeod's rescuer, everyone was hush. The lead investigator and the man from the State Department have, so far, avoided these questions. Like the guy *was* a phantom. MacLeod can hardly picture him—a British film actor with three days' growth comes to mind—but the man's heroism was clear. Hopefully, his wife or family would get *some* token for it. And it's a bizarre thing to not know whom to credit, whom to thank. Someday, he may be allowed to learn more. Thoughts have turned to a scholarship fund, which he can leave to Emma to fashion.

The chaos at the ruins was due to an "escalation" between the rebels and the Colombian government. "Somebody scratched the itch, and it started up again," the State Department guy had said, as if this Texan-drawl statement was sufficient. MacLeod didn't find that amusing. When the rebels started taking the fight to wealthy landowners (the killing he witnessed at the hacienda) the chief of Colombian Special Forces decided he'd had enough and directed gunships east. Of course, nobody (good guys or bad guys) had *any* idea that MacLeod was lost on the scenic route and fleeing bullets in the middle of an "operation." All that shouting and back-and-forth on the radio— his was the voice of the panicked gringo mouse during a contest of roaring lions. Somehow, to him, the word "operation" doesn't equate to machine guns and aerial rockets. Perhaps that's a benefit of being a first-world citizen.

From what he gathers, the governments of both
Colombia and Brazil are still mortified (while Panama's people
have sat down, stifling smiles). It didn't help that Fabrício
Olivieri—the ringleader—was also a major political contributor.
As a cell-phone king and real-estate czar who (with the
investment firm) owned chunks of São Paolo—as well as being a
rabid *a seleção* fan—it looked bad for a lot of people. Ballsy
reporters were pushing hard on the bit where he was able to set
up all those hideouts in Colombia (true owner yet to be
revealed). Powerful men have powerful, public friends. Brick to
the face, over and over again.

***

"Bright sun, glinting off divots in the surface, gives spots
of rust a vivid look. The orange is a rich color among the dull
steel and puddles of filthy water and oil. The power of that
square of brightness on the floor and wall, on the discarded
sledgehammer. Now the tank has no occupant. "

Eyes closed, MacLeod sees the man standing dazed and
grateful atop a steel tank. He needs a shave, a shower and rest.
Cooling, tropical rain falls in sun-drenched sheets. The man parts
his lips to the sky and drinks in exquisite life.

"May I read it?" Emma asks, taking the legal pad from
Roof's loose grip. After a moment, she says, "Who was in the
tank?"

Roof nods and opens his eyes to the wide view. A
massive cruise ship plies the three million diamonds wrought by
Seattle's March sun. It's a safe sun, single and proud today. The
forecast calls for a rainy week. Today, the sun doesn't care. With
a breeze going and the occasional car on Highland Street, there's

298

little noise. Roof never thought he'd appreciate quiet like this. In a cave in eastern Colombia, it scared the hell out of him. Here, after countless interviews and reporters' questions and phone calls (hospital room, office, home) the gentle stillness is a reward. Pleasure embodied in the absence of threat, need or commotion.

"A man," he finally answers. "Just something that's been on my mind lately."

She sets the pad in his lap and snuggles into him on the park bench. "Keep going," she says.

And he will. He has time. They have another hour before the plainclothes security men (courtesy of U.S. Soccer) come to tell them it's time to go to the restaurant. Mitch MacLeod is flying in via charter (with Lakshmi and security firmly attached). After reuniting with Roof at the hospital, he had to jet back for a Liverpool game. He scored twice—once for Roof and one for the "dandy brilliant bloke" who rescued him. Smiling into the phone, Roof said, "Stop talking Brit, you dork." And, like many times before, Mitch replied, "I know. We're fuckin' Scots."

After a few minutes, Emma asks, "Any new revelations in therapy today?"

"I don't know." A pause. "I was thinking that…Arturo would be plenty mad at his uncle for lying to him. If he hadn't been blown up."

"Uncle? You mean…that Olivar guy?"

"Yeah, he must've known. About me. Or maybe he didn't, if O'Malley lied to him, too." A sigh. "I suppose it doesn't matter anymore. O'Malley's up to his eyebrows in hot water."

The assistant King County prosecutor said, in confidence, they were having a "field day" with *discovery* alone. Roof had simply responded, "Good."

299

Emma makes a noise of assent beside him. In the sunlight, eyes closed, her face reminds him of a content cat.

How different this is from a week ago, terrified in a cave. The rescue. The quicksand. Standing over a wounded Arturo at the excavator, trying to decide whether to mercy-kill him.

Did all that really happen?

"I was in such a dark place down there, you know? I just…"

She grips his arm. "Keep writing them down, those thoughts of yours. We'll tackle them all."

He wishes he had her rock-solid confidence. The questions linger, too numerous to count. Like the sleep issues—with a light on, wrapped in a lightweight sleeping bag, digital things within view. They'll go away, the therapist assures him. Other things will take time. The ligature mark around his neck may never disappear. Two lavender-hued scars from the passage of bullets. He is, simply, too lucky to have regrets.

Did Cora have regrets when her heart was blown open? Or Enrique, meeting a demonic warrior at the door? How did that knife come loose from MacLeod's pants when he flew into the quicksand? How did he survive when it sank out of sight? How is it he avoided being bitten and killed by a Brazilian wandering spider (which honestly wouldn't care which side of the border it was on) all those times sleeping at floor level? Who'd placed the excavator where it was—the one that saved his life? What government or agency or godly faith was responsible for his rescuer coming for him? How did Smokey the red-headed river turtle (*podocnemis erythrocephala*) survive Josh's Babushka? Thick carapaces, apparently. Who would've thought a half-inch of time-melded hair had enough tensile strength to redirect twenty metal shots fired from a weapon? One of many things deemed 'miraculous' during his 'adventure.' The vet says she'll be ready for a new home, soon. The globe's most-famous turtle is about to get a Times Square audience and a line of W.W.F. T-shirts.

And the black panther. He's spent many hours scanning YouTube videos for the cat he encountered—they don't all look the same. So far, a couple possibilities. The clip of one doggedly dragging out and mauling an anaconda—that's his favorite. Emma had worked a little magic, immediately acquiring an art student's painting to hang over their breakfast nook. Yellow eyes will watch him drink his coffee for the rest of his days. That will have to be good enough.

Tomorrow, after his coffee, he plans to place a call to Ms. Belinda Cooke, mother of the deceased Riley Cooke. It will be difficult, and awkward, and embarrassing, he imagines. For an apology, it will likely change nothing and offer no amends. But staying quiet any longer seems dishonorable.

A noise makes him start. After a second, source, confirmed, he relaxes. From the left, beyond a Queen Anne Hill mansion, a news helicopter curls out over the water. Roof watches it. Bright colors on the side, no weapons. The last time he saw an airborne chopper, it was the one that came for him.

"Know what else surprises me?"

She makes a little noise. That's all she needs to do when they're cozy. It might be sexier if she answered, "Yes, Darling." But this little prompt is comfortable, and enough.

After a moment he says, "I'm surprised they came for me. I'm just a guy."

"The rescuer man or the soldiers?"

"Both," he says, noting a distant flare of brightness, sunlight off a metal part. He glances at the nearby security man. Stern, thick and armed. "Definitely the SEALs," he says. "There's no way they didn't know, at that point, that Mitch was safe and I was just...the poor bastard taken by mistake."

"American," she says, putting her head on his lap. "They came for you."

"In a war zone. You should've seen...well, I'm glad you *didn't* see it. They came, anyway. Right into the middle of a firefight. Millions of dollars to do that, political fallout for practically invading a country. It's hard to..." He finds another boat in the water, a speck compared to the cruise ship. "What if I *wasn't* Mitch's brother? Or if I was Pakistani-born, or I was a plumber or a schoolteacher?"

"I know, I know," she soothes. "Maybe you shouldn't ask so many questions."

The remark could be cold—especially with her soft, demure voice. She smiles, though. It is Emma's way. Speculation takes the edge off accusation.

"It's my job," he answers.

Minutes pass in silence before she asks, "What *are* you going to do about work?"

"Oh, that. I don't think it would be healthy for me to stay home for too long. I guess it's really up to Petersen and Raj Gupta. If they think it would be better for me to move on, I will. But Gupta seems to like me."

"You're a likeable guy." A serene smile. "Tomorrow, there's that work party at the park. Come help me pull some weeds? Dig out blackberry?"

Roof MacLeod doesn't know a thing about weeds or blackberry (other than tasty pie). And this is volunteering, helping out. Something he's wanted to do for an achingly long time. Even if it's pissing rain out, the busy day with Emma sounds perfect. Even in a tempest.

"You know, I'll have to take orders from my left. My right-side hearing's gone." Explosions, shotgun blasts. And he looks a little silly in the boot, having his toes re-set with pins. "I'll probably have to wear a disguise, too. What do I say when people ask?"

She rubs his knee. "That's easy, you big baby. Just call yourself Mitch."

THE END

Acknowledgments

I'd like to thank...

My wife, Luanne Schocket, for her enduring patience and support. Time and again, she has exemplified the term 'soldier on.'

My children, Cameron and Erin, for their laughter and sarcasm throughout admittedly tough days. Moon the cat has helped, as well: Undeniably adorable, curious and faithful (if that's how one could define a 5 a.m. squeak-and-paw).

My mother and father, who are happy to help. Also my sister and extended family, and Eve Schocket for support.

My good friend and historian Max Likin, who not only kicked over a domino but continued to provide encouragement and critique.

My friend Mark Watson, who provided thoughtful plot and linguistic analysis (and didn't miss a damned thing). Simply awesome.

Luanne Brown (*always!*), Kathy Brazeau, Amy Rosas and Julianne Bogaty, for being supportive beta readers and pointing out shortcomings and mud. This work is invaluable.

My buddy Brian Walker, for being an early beta reader and devil's advocate (always helpful).

Greg Simanson for his amazing cover art, again.

My friend Erika Klimecky, for her patience, softened whip and marketing savvy.

ᴜne and Clayton Moulynox for suffering through another Edison yarn with a proofreader's pen.

The Lotfis, the Isaksens, the Bertrams, the Parsons and Charlotte Martinez for continuing to believe in me.

Fellow author and community support Bryn Donovan, who allowed me to share pieces of this manuscript with her followers.

The amazing Steffani S., who inspired the fictional shenanigans of the fictional Quazidyne. Many of us look forward to hearing *your* story.

Tony Knox, phenomenal player and Orange Crush coach, who has artfully displayed success on both sides of the field (and allowed me to be part of it).

Fellow assistant coach Norris Smith, for putting up with me.

Band members, past and present, of Alice in Chains, Pink Floyd, Niyaz and Soundgarden, without whose artistic efforts this book simply wouldn't have happened.

The intelligent, open-minded gentlemen of my book group, who are always willing to explore murky waters.

Finally, fellow soccer players Max, Scott, Brian, Mark, Craig, Jay, Ray, Vaughan, Adam "Just stop!" T., and the rest of my Sunday pick-up tribe. There *is* pure joy in sport.

About the Author

Justin A. Edison has been writing fiction and stories for many years. A graduate of the Evansville and Hamline writing programs, he counts soccer (playing and coaching) hiking, travel, cooking and website consulting among his pursuits. He lives in the Seattle area with his wife, two energetic kids and a vocal cat.

Tempest Road is his fourth novel. Previous books include *Watching the World Fall*, *The Churning* and *Endgame* (first in the "Woman at War" series). He can be reached at <u>edisonchurning@gmail.com</u>, jedisonwriting.com, and @jedisonbooks.

Thanks for reading!

My forthcoming novels are *Destruction* ("Woman at War")

and *Frozen at the Wheel* (working title).

www.justinedisonnovels.com